THE JUDGE'S STORY

Joyce T. Strand

McCloughan and Schmeltz Publishing

This book is a work of fiction. Except for historical events and real locations—names, characters, and incidents either are the product of the author's imagination or are used fictitiously, and any resemblance to actual persons, living or dead, business establishments, events, or locales is coincidental.

If you purchased this book without a cover you should be aware that this book is stolen property. It was reported as "unsold and destroyed" to the publisher, and neither the author nor the publisher has received any payment for this "stripped book."

ISBN-10: 0-9961454-0-0
ISBN-13: 978-0-9961454-0-4

Copyright Joyce T. Strand 2015
All rights reserved. No part of this book may be reproduced or transmitted in any form or by any means, electronic or mechanical, including photocopying, recording or by any information storage and retrieval system, without prior written permission of the Publisher.

Printed in the United States of America
McCloughan and Schmeltz Publishing, LLC
2360 Corporate Circle – Suite 400
Henderson, NV 89074-7722

Cover design: Natasha Brown

Author Photograph: Erin Kate Photography
http://www.erinkatephoto.com

For information about the author and her books, and to sign up to receive author's newsletter:
http://joycestrand.com

Other Works by Joyce T. Strand

On Message: A Jillian Hillcrest Mystery
Open Meetings: A Jillian Hillcrest Mystery
Fair Disclosure: A Jillian Hillcrest Mystery

Hilltop Sunset: A Brynn Bancroft Mystery

Author's Note

One day I was having lunch with a friend who, knowing I was an author, mentioned his grandfather's memoir recently discovered in an attic. He said his grandfather had completed it in 1941 about his life leading up to his appointment as a Superior Court Judge of Ventura County—and that he was a law partner with a writer, maybe I knew him, Erle Stanley Gardner?

Given that I was an avid reader of mysteries, I was definitely familiar with the creator of Perry Mason. I'm sure I've read every *"Case of..."* and others written under Gardner's pseudonyms. What I didn't know was that Gardner practiced law in Ventura and lived on a ranch in Temecula, California. And that he was a partner in a law firm with my friend's grandfather.

I wanted to read the memoir immediately, and my friend sent me an online copy. You can read it at the Museum of Ventura County/Library. (Louis C. Drapeau, Senior; *Autobiography of a Country Lawyer*; available at the Museum of Ventura County/Library, 100 E. Main St., Ventura, CA 93001.)

I was enthralled. It tells the story of a boy in the 1890s and early 1900s whose father and then stepfather basically remove him from their lives, how he struggles on his own as a teenager working as cowboy, mule skinner, Borax 20 mule team driver, and dockhand, how he manages to meet and work for a Senator, then earn a law degree from Georgetown Law School, settle in Ventura, practice law, and become a Superior Court Judge by the late 1930s.

I knew immediately that I wanted to write a book about this judge.

I didn't need to re-tell his story, which he does so eloquently in his memoir. What I craved was to create characters and events around the Judge to construct a picture of him for us—like a mosaic—bit by bit. And, mystery writer that I claim to be, I did want to spin an entertaining whodunit around this intriguing character.

I spent a year researching the period during which the Judge lived, and decided to set the story in 1939—a year of turbulence preceding the U.S. entry into World War II, of continued poverty from the Great Depression, and of relief (to some) by the end of Prohibition. It was a year of transition that offered a fast-changing backdrop to produce the characters and the plot.

I hasten to add that, although the story is based on the Judge's memoir, it is fiction. The characters are all fictional, including the Judge himself. There are bits and pieces of some of his cases and his background, but the case on which the book focuses is fiction.

What is real is the network of his values woven into the story. An important reason why I wanted to tell *The Judge's Story* is that he was a hero. I appreciate his actions and values and applied them to the story. Of course, you and I both know that no one is perfect, but overall, the Judge was a positive influence on our judicial system and in the lives of those he encountered. In real life, he went on to become Associate Justice, California Court of Appeal, Second Appellate District, Division 1.

I plan for *The Judge's Story* to be the first of several books about real people who have made a positive difference in our world—all told as mysteries. I hope you enjoy the first in this "Heroes Mystery" series.

Acknowledgements

Thank you, first of all, to my friend Louis Drapeau (who I know as Lou) for sharing Judge Louis C. Drapeau, Senior's *Autobiography of a Country Lawyer*. His grandfather's memoir was both an inspiration and a resource for *The Judge's Story*.

Next, the staff of the Museum of Ventura County/Library located resources enabling me to create the background and feel for the book. This library is a very special place to learn about the history of Ventura County after you've toured the museum itself, and the staff is incredibly helpful. Thanks to all who contributed to providing the resources available at that Library, including, the *Oxnard Daily Courier* newspaper from January to December 1939 (the library stores issues of this daily publication back to the mid-1800s). Other sources from that library that I found useful were: the *Ventura County Peace Officers' Training School Ventura 1939-1940*; *Ventura County – Comprehensive History;* OH Fulkerson, Jonathan, Jr. *Short history on Ventura County Talk given at Moorpark College* 5/24/78. If I have made any mistakes in the historical background of the book, I truly apologize especially to this group of people who enthusiastically located resources for me.

The picture book *Ventura: Then and Now* by Glenda J. Jackson offered insight into the appearance of Ventura in 1939.

Special thanks to Sarah and Barbara Jaeck, librarians *extraordinaire*, who tracked down videos documenting the 1930s that suggested several scenes, including the drive-in theater scene, and helped to assure an accurate backdrop for the novel.

Thank you to my first-draft readers Gail Troutman and Pat Becker who steered the plot for entertainment and credibility, and to my patient editor, Laurie Gibson, who got to polish two versions of this story. Extra thanks to Pat Becker for her final proofing of the manuscript.

I cannot express enough how much I appreciate the continued support of my daughter and son, Laura Strand and David Strand, for their marketing efforts and proofing prowess.

Nonetheless, despite all the incredible assistance from so many, all the errors, typos, historical inaccuracies, and inconsistencies were generated by me.

In memory of my husband, Bob Strand, who would have appreciated the ethics of the Judge

Chapter 01

Judge Akers watched the teenage girl enter his courtroom. She had agreed to testify against a fourteen-year-old schoolmate for theft and murder.

He suspected she was nervous. The room loomed in front of her, with high ceilings, chandelier lights, and seats for at least one hundred people, that day less than one-third occupied.

The Judge sat elevated at the end of her walk. He noticed that she stared at the portrait to his left, perhaps to avoid meeting the eyes of the defendant, a typical ploy of witnesses. She walked slowly, almost as if her legs were too heavy to lift. He saw her look up at the skylight in the ceiling.

The Judge was disappointed that the District Attorney required a sixteen-year-old to convict the defendant. He believed that in the modern California justice system of 1939, children should not have to deliver such testimony. Of course, the defendant himself was just a boy, so perhaps that justified a teenager testifying against a teenager.

As she approached the front of the room, she looked to her right at a middle-aged woman sitting in the third row behind the prosecutor's table, who smiled at her as she walked by. The Judge recognized the woman as the girl's mother. He didn't blame her for sitting on the edge of her seat looking like she wanted to jump up and drag her daughter out of the building.

The girl finally reached the end of her sojourn by pushing through the swinging gate of the divider separating the public area from the actual courtroom. An elderly, rather rotund man, who was sweating due to an unusually high temperature in the courtroom, asked her to hold up her right hand and swear to tell nothing but the truth.

Judge Akers understood that she must be nervous. Before the District Attorney could ask her any questions, he signaled that he wanted to talk with her. He looked down at her from his perch on the dais, and tried hard not to appear too intimidating. However, at six feet five inches he was accustomed to that feeling and the girl was hardly more than five feet tall and quite thin. To the teenager, the Judge probably seemed quite mature with his thick salt-and-pepper hair, which made him appear even more unapproachable.

He was in his late fifties and had been a judge for about five years and a lawyer before that. What the witness probably didn't know that might have made her less nervous was that he was committed to helping juveniles and believed they should be educated and rehabilitated rather than punished—a concept that was becoming popular, including with the Ventura County peace officers.

He tried to smile to convince her that he was not there to make her life miserable, even though he was in charge. He said, "Let's see, young lady. You are Clara Bow Wilson. Is that correct?"

He broadened his smile when he said her name. He was old enough to know who Clara Bow was—a popular 1920s actress known as the 'IT' girl.

"Yes, your Honor, sir," she said softly, biting her lip.

Still smiling, he said, "You'll need to speak up so we can all hear you. Do you understand why it's important that you are here and that you must tell the truth?"

She was beginning to rally some of her fortitude. She responded more firmly, "Yes sir. I know my duty."

The Judge could smell mothballs coming from his black robe. He, too, was sweating. The electric fans didn't seem to help much.

"As you see, there's no jury here to determine the defendant's guilt or innocence. I am the one who will make that decision. So after District Attorney Bilkins and Defense Attorney Alberts question you, I may have some questions as well. Do you understand?"

She nodded again and said, "Yes sir."

Judge Akers turned to the District Attorney, a tall slender man dressed in a dark suit with a vest, whose sideburns extended his red hair down his face causing a two-toned appearance. The Judge said, "You may begin. Just remember she's only sixteen, and I expect your demeanor and questions to take that into account."

Clara now turned to focus on the rest of the courtroom. What she saw first was the boy she had come to testify against—Oscar Roy Briarley—whose head barely rose above the table where he was sitting. While she waited for District Attorney Bilkins to stand up to ask his questions, she studied the defendant, a schoolmate she barely knew. He stared back at her, wide-eyed with lips trembling.

She noticed that he must have had a haircut and a bath. His typically unruly hair was both clean and somewhat controlled. This was a big improvement because at school he usually appeared unkempt and looked more like a dog than a boy, which had led her and her friends to call him "Shaggy."

The District Attorney approached Clara, blocking her view of the defendant. He spoke slowly, perhaps believing that enunciating each syllable would make it easier for a sixteen-year-old to understand him. "Clara, please tell us where you were the evening in question."

She licked her lips, leaned forward, and said slowly and as loudly as she could, "I was at the store—that's the five-and-dime store on Main Street—helping to take inventory. I work there after school sometimes to earn a little extra money."

The District Attorney said, "Go on. What happened?"

She looked at the Judge and asked, "Is that loud enough?"

He nodded. "Yes, thank you, Clara. You're doing fine."

She continued. "Well, I was in the back of the store when I heard a crash. I ran out thinking that Mr. Brant—he was the manager of the store—anyway, I thought he'd dropped something. But instead I saw that the front window was broken and two men were taking stuff out of it."

"What kind of 'stuff?'" asked the District Attorney.

"Oh, radios, tools, clothes, rifles—just stuff that we had on sale that week that Mr. Brant displayed in the window.

They were putting it in a big bag—that looked maybe like it had been some kind of feed bag."

"And you referred to these two as 'men.' What made you think they were men?"

She hesitated and then said, "Well, they had on trousers and at first they just seemed like men."

The District Attorney turned his back to her and stared at the defendant who, at approximately Clara's height, might have been mistaken for a short man instead of a boy.

"A little short for a man, perhaps?" he said gently and then pointed to the defendant.

The District Attorney's carrot-colored hair and reddish brown sideburns diverted Clara. She asked, "I'm sorry. What did you say?"

He repeated even more carefully, "I said, isn't Oscar Briarley a little short for a man?"

"Yes, but at that time I couldn't tell. They both had on pants, so I assumed they were men." She seemed annoyed that the District Attorney would question her assessment.

"All right. So then what happened?"

"Mr. Brant yelled, 'Get out of there, you hooligans!' and then he threw something and ran towards them."

The Judge noticed that she stopped speaking and looked down at her hands, which were clenched. He assumed she had begun to recall that night—a common occurrence with witnesses of a brutal crime. Unfortunately, her hands did not seem to deter her from remembering her boss picking up a bottle of soda pop and throwing it at the intruders as he ran toward the store window. She could still hear the shot that caused Mr. Brant to jerk backward—he looked so surprised—and then he fell. The surprise on his face still caused her to shake and wake up from dreaming about it.

Her inquisitor turned, looked at the Judge, back at Clara, and then said gently—but still enunciating every syllable, "Take your time, Clara. I know this is difficult to have to re-live."

She glanced around the room as if wanting to run out, then looked at the defendant and said, "And then I heard a loud noise—a gun shot—and Mr. Brant screamed. I was afraid they would shoot me next, but one of them ran off right away and the other picked up the bag stuffed with the radios and things and ran away, too, without even looking at me."

"And do you recognize either of those thieves here today?"

"Yes, of course." She pointed to the defendant and said, "Oscar Briarley. He's sitting over there."

"You are absolutely sure that you saw Oscar Briarley that night helping to rob the store when Mr. Brant was shot and killed."

Clara noticed that the District Attorney's face was now a bright red from the heat. She nodded and said, "Yes, sir. I saw Oscar Briarley."

"Thank you, Clara. I know that couldn't have been easy for you. Your witness." He gestured to the Defense Attorney.

The middle-aged, somewhat paunchy and balding man representing Oscar Briarley stood up from behind the table. He was dressed in a dark suit, much like the prosecutor, which must have caused him—and the District Attorney — discomfort on such a hot day. Although the lawyer had spent much of the time looking at papers when Clara was responding to the District Attorney's questions, he appeared now to pay close attention to what she would say. He stared right at her, with sweat dripping down his face, which he wiped repeatedly with a white handkerchief. He had been selected from among a pool of local lawyers required to represent indigent clients. The Judge believed that the boy was fortunate to have drawn a capable lawyer—someone who would be concerned enough to fight for him.

The attorney studied Clara for such a long time that she was beginning to think he'd forgotten what he wanted to say when he asked, "Was it dark in the store?"

She looked confused, and then said, "Well, it wasn't dark outside yet, but the lights were on. Mr. Brant had a really bright light in the window so that the things on display showed up well. So I could see Oscar very well, if that's what you mean."

"Oh, so after you thought there were two men, then you realized one of them was actually a boy?"

She nodded, glared at him, and said, "Yes, the closer I got to the window, the easier it was to see."

"What about the other man? Are you sure he was a man and not a boy?"

She swallowed hard. "No, sir. It could have been a tall boy."

The lawyer smiled. Clara clenched the railing in front of her. "But you said that my client, a boy of just over five feet tall, was in front of the other," he hesitated for effect, "man. Yet you couldn't see him. How could that be?"

She thought about that statement before saying, "Oh, I'm sorry. I should have said 'Oscar was inside the window.' He had jumped up into the window after they broke it. The other person was still standing outside, and he was bent over filling the bag."

The lawyer cocked his head and said, "So Oscar was standing in a place higher than the other person. By how much, do you think?"

She thought about that. She held out her two hands one above the other estimating the distance and said, "Maybe this much—I guess that's about two feet?"

The lawyer nodded. "I see. And was this other person heavier than my client?"

"Sort of. He was wider. I'm not sure if he was heavier."

"What was he wearing?"

She was ready for that question. The Chief had asked it right away that night. "He had on farmer's bib overalls—you know, the kind with the straps over the shoulders—and what looked like an undershirt underneath. It didn't seem any too clean."

"And what about his hair? What color was it?"

She responded with confidence. "I got a better view of the other fellow bent over. His hair was brown and gray and it was long and kind of curly, and very greasy, like it hadn't been washed in a while."

"But you never saw his face."

She repeated, "No, he never stood up. He was leaned over filling the bag the whole time. As soon as the gun was fired, first Oscar ran and then the other fellow grabbed the bag full of stuff, and he ran, too."

"All right. And neither of the two people you saw had on masks?"

"No, sir. I could see Oscar really well, because he was closest to me. I couldn't see the other one because he was behind Oscar."

"So who ran away first?"

Clara shook her head and said with exasperation, "As I just said, Oscar jumped down from the window and ran away first. But I still couldn't see the other fellow. He was stooped over and then he turned away while he was picking up his bag."

"Could you see who fired the gun?"

"Well, I'm sure it wasn't Oscar. I didn't notice one in his hands, and I could make out pretty much all of him. When I heard the shot, I could see Oscar and he wasn't carrying anything. He kind of jerked when the gun fired, and then he ran and almost pushed the other fellow down. But the other fellow was carrying something long besides the bag, and it looked like a rifle."

"How do you know it was a rifle?"

She tried not to sound annoyed when she answered. "Well, it looked like the other fellow was carrying something long in his free arm that was away from me. He was pulling the bag with his left arm, and it looked like he had a rifle in his right hand."

"But you didn't see either of them actually shoot Mr. Brant."

"No, I did not, but I can tell you that it couldn't have been Oscar because I could see him very clearly, and he did not have a gun."

"I see. So was it the other fellow who actually shot and killed Mr. Brant?"

"I have to be honest, sir. When I witnessed the two of them, Oscar did not have a gun. But I did not see a gun for sure so I can't say, but it sure makes sense that it would be the other fellow, especially since it looked like he was carrying something else that resembled a rifle." Clara could not hide the irritation in her voice.

"Could it have been someone else other than either of the two you saw who might have shot Mr. Brant?"

She shook her head. "I don't think so. I didn't notice anyone else. But I didn't catch a glimpse of a gun or who actually pulled the trigger. I just saw poor Mr. Brant."

"And you are absolutely positive that the one person you recognized that night was Oscar Briarley."

She swallowed hard. Before she answered she looked at her mother who smiled back and nodded in support. Clara said, "I understand what this means, but yes, sir. I am sure."

The lawyer again studied her. She looked him straight in the eyes, waiting for his next question, not willing to back down. He seemed to make a decision.

"Tell me, did you know Oscar at school?"

"Yes, sir, I knew who he was, although we were never together in the same classes. He's younger than I am, and I believe he'd been held back a year or so. But we went to the same school, and I saw him around."

"Was he ever accused of being a thief or a trouble-maker?"

"No, I don't think so. But I didn't know him or talk much about him." She paused for a few seconds and then said, "I think his brother was, though, and there was talk about his father. But as far as I know, Oscar never stole anything and nobody ever said he did."

"For right now, I'm not interested in his brother or his father. What do you know about the defendant?"

"Not much." She added, "He didn't dress well. Sometimes he didn't wear shoes. That got him in trouble, and he had to use some old rubbers that belonged to the school custodian." She looked at the defense attorney. "Is that the kind of thing you're interested in?"

"Did you ever see him beat up anyone?"

"No, I don't remember him ever picking on anyone. He kind of kept to himself. Oh, I remember seeing him one time going through the school garbage. But he stopped and ran away when he saw me."

"So did you think of him as dangerous or someone who would rob a store?"

Clara did not hesitate. "No, sir. He always seemed like a normal boy."

He said, "Thank you. That's all."

She stood up to escape, but heard Judge Akers say, "Just a moment. I have some questions."

She sat back down. "Yes, sir."

"What you're telling us is that he didn't have a reputation of being a thief or a bully. Why do you think he stole this time?"

She looked at Judge Akers and then at Oscar. "I'm not sure what you mean," she said. "But maybe he was hungry, your Honor. We know that the Dust Bowl created a lot of hungry people, especially boys and young men. You only have to read Mr. Steinbeck's *Grapes of Wrath* to know that." She punctuated her conclusion with an emphatic nod. Then she glanced at her mother who had closed her eyes and was shaking her head. She looked concerned about what Clara had said.

The Judge looked surprised. "You've read *Grapes of Wrath*, have you?"

She avoided her mother's eyes and looked directly at the Judge. "Yes, sir. I plan to be a writer, like Edith Wharton, so I read a lot."

"I see. You haven't embellished any of your testimony to create a better story, have you?"

She opened her eyes wide, appearing concerned that the Judge would even think such a thing. "Oh, no, your Honor. Everything I said is the honest truth."

The Judge examined her again, looked up at the skylight, then back at her again. "Let's return to Mr. Briarley. Do you think he is capable of killing someone?"

"I wouldn't know." She stopped and thought about the question for a few seconds. "But I don't think so. I remember one time at school seeing his brother beating someone up. Oscar ran away rather than hit him even though his brother held the boy for him to hit and called him a sissy when he refused. It was a good thing that one of our teachers showed up to help out, but I got the feeling that Oscar didn't like to hurt people." She looked at Oscar, who was jiggling in his seat and sort of shaking his whole body. His attorney reached over and patted his arms, which only slowed down the jiggling a little.

The Judge appeared to absorb that piece of information, because he focused on the jiggling Oscar. At this point, he did not feel prepared to reach a final verdict or more important, an appropriate sentence. The boy's attorney was not arguing his guilt over participating in the robbery. He was claiming that he should not be held responsible for the killing of Mr. Brant and that his age should be taken into account.

The Judge believed that the boy had participated in the robbery, but a fourteen-year-old without a prior conviction or proclivity to commit crimes seemed an unlikely murderer. The more he learned about the boy, the less he believed that the youngster was responsible for the shooting and the more surprised he was that the boy had participated in the robbery at all. He still wondered who the other thief—and most likely the murderer and cause of the incident—was. The Chief could not identify him. Clara had not seen him, other than to notice that he was taller and bulkier than Oscar.

The real issue boiled down to the situation that Oscar Briarley was unwilling to identify his partner, even though it was most likely he who fired the fatal shot.

The Judge knew about Oscar's home life because of his brother, whose trial he had presided over more than a year earlier. He lived in squalor, and it was possible that Oscar was looking forward to prison as a much better place to exist than his own home, so that's why he was keeping quiet. He had refused bail, although the Judge doubted that his family had the bail money. Anyway, he chose to stay in one of the four bunks in his juvenile cell at the next-door Ventura County Jail. The bunk was probably the best bed he ever had. So it was not outrageous to think that he might welcome going to prison, where he would be fed regularly and have his own bunk to sleep on—which could explain why he refused to identify his partner.

The Judge looked at the defense attorney and said, "Are his parents here?"

The attorney shook his head. "No, your Honor."

The Judge responded quickly, "I assume they were informed."

The lawyer nodded. "Yes, sir. They were informed. I sent someone out to their place to personally let them know."

Judge Akers then turned to Clara, his face showing disgust. He could not abide derelict parents. "Just one more question, young lady. I assume the Chief probably asked you this. But do you know any of Oscar's friends?"

She responded, "Not really. He seemed to be pretty much a loner, except when his brother was with him, and he hasn't been around in a while. Quite frankly, I didn't see Oscar at school all that often. I think maybe he might have only been there when the truant officer made him come."

The Judge noticed that the defendant was smiling. He probably enjoyed evading the truant officer.

"And did he ever come into the store to buy anything while you were working there? Or did you ever see him anywhere else around town?"

"No, I never saw either him or his brother in the store." She hesitated but looked at the Judge as if she wanted to say more.

He said, "Did you have something else you wanted to add?"

"Your Honor, I'm not sure if this matters, but you seem to want my opinion, so I'm going to tell it." She swallowed hard again, avoided looking at her mother, and then decided to just say what was on her mind. "I don't believe that Oscar can read. I believe he was held back at school because of that. And if he could, well, I think he'd be different. He's just never known anything other than his family life."

"Did you learn that from *Grapes of Wrath*?"

She looked embarrassed and said nothing. Her mother rolled her eyes.

The Judge smiled and said, "Thank you for your testimony. For the moment, you are dismissed."

Clara stood up and started to make the long walk to escape from the courtroom. She looked at her mother, who smiled as she went by. She glanced at the people seated in the gallery and saw Mrs. Brant and her children in the row next to her mother and the Sheriff and the Chief next to them. She didn't know the well-groomed, attractive young man in the row behind the defendant. There were a few dozen more people in the rows behind Mrs. Brant. There was no one else in any of the rows behind Oscar. It seemed that people had lined up to support the widow and her family.

She was part way out of the courtroom when District Attorney Bilkins said, "Your Honor, I know that this boy is only fourteen. But I do need to remind you that Mr. Brant was the father of four children, and he left a wife alone to care for them. This was murder, pure and simple, and even if the boy didn't actually pull the trigger, he was there and shared in the culpability under the California felony-murder rule."

The defense attorney stood up and shouted, "Your Honor, we know how heinous a crime this was, but really, this boy was not responsible for killing anyone! What is most likely is that he was influenced into participating by whoever pulled the trigger. He's just a boy. He does not deserve to be punished for a murder committed by someone else."

The Judge looked down at both of them. He asked the Defense Attorney, "I didn't see anyone else on the list of witnesses. Do you have someone to testify on behalf of Mr. Briarley?"

Attorney Alberts looked like the Judge had punched the wind out of him. He said quietly, "No, your Honor, but you heard what Miss Wilson said—he did not have the reputation of being a thief or a bully."

"District Attorney Bilkins, do you have any additional witnesses?"

"No, sir, but I believe it's clear from Clara Wilson's testimony that Oscar Briarley is the one who helped rob the store and kill Mr. Brant. The defendant himself doesn't even deny it. Your Honor should deliver a verdict of 'guilty' and send him to jail—"

The Judge interrupted, "Yes, I know, Mr. Bilkins. However, I am not prepared to make a decision today. I want to study the defendant and the case and see if we can track down the partner who pulled the trigger to learn more about Mr. Briarley's role. I am postponing a decision for one month pending additional information. If we cannot collect more information, I will deliver my verdict and sentence at that time. The defendant will be remanded in the county jail until then unless he can post bail."

The last thing Clara heard before exiting the courtroom was the bailiff saying, "All rise for the Honorable Judge Grover Roswell Akers" as the Judge departed.

Chapter 02

The Judge walked swiftly into his chambers and greeted his secretary and all-around organizer of his life, Irene Alvarez, a handsome blonde woman in her late twenties dressed in a woman's gray suit.

Irene asked, "How was the Oscar Briarley trial?"

"I didn't render a decision. The Court will be scheduling a hearing in a month for me to make up my mind."

"Oh? What happened?"

"The boy is only fourteen. He didn't pull the trigger. The only real witness is a sixteen-year-old girl, who admittedly is credible, but I just think we need to try to find the real culprit. Otherwise, based on the felony-murder rule, I'll have to sentence him to more time than I believe he deserves."

"I take it the boy still refuses to tell who his partner was?"

"Right."

Irene sighed. "Well, maybe the Chief will find out who did it. Do you want me to ask Jim to see what he can find?" Jim was her husband, who did investigative work for the Ventura County Sheriff, the town of Ventura Chief of Police, and occasionally the Judge.

The Judge shook his head. "No, he'd just run into the Chief or the Sheriff. They're working different angles of the case. I do believe they're looking hard. I just wish there was some way to convince the boy to identify his partner. No one even seems to know any of his friends, so we don't have a starting point. I doubt that his family would be much help either."

He retreated into his inner office and grimaced at the stack of paperwork on his desk. He started to go through it to assess priority, even though he knew that Irene would have placed most important and most urgent items on top. He gave up procrastinating and read the one on top while Irene returned to her typing.

Irene had just finished pulling a document from her machine when she looked up to see a woman and two young children enter the room. She might have been pretty once, but time had not been kind. Her face showed lines and her eyes betrayed exhaustion. Her dress was clean but faded pale blue with darning threads in the shoulder where she had patched the thinning material. When she walked, she remained bent over as if carrying something heavy. Her black hair was pulled up and displayed streaks of gray.

Irene, who did not recognize the woman, asked, "May I help you?"

The visitor spoke softly, but precisely and with a slight accent. "Hello, yes, I am Mrs. Martinez. I would like to speak to his honor Judge Akers, please."

The Judge walked out to the woman and greeted her, "Hello, Mrs. Martinez. It's nice to see you again. How can I help you?"

"Thank you, your Honor, sir, for seeing me. You helped my husband once, and we need you again. May I speak to you, please?"

"Please come in." He led the way into his inner chamber and motioned for them to be seated. The woman first arranged her two listless children, who obeyed her direction with little complaint. The older boy of the two, barely four feet tall, stared at the Judge through long black hair that fell over his eyes. He held onto his little sister's hand and said to her, "It's all right. The Judge will help Pa-Pa."

The Judge noticed that the children's clothes also had signs of darning, but both they and the clothes were clean. He smiled at the children and then said to Mrs. Martinez, "Now, what can I do for you?"

She swallowed hard, took a breath, and then said, "My husband has been put in jail, and I need to help him. He didn't mean to do it. He killed a cow, but he meant to kill a deer."

The Judge feared that she wanted such a favor. He had heard about the case, and he knew her husband. He had defended him years ago—unsuccessfully—when he was an attorney. He said, "Mrs. Martinez, I personally cannot help you. I am a judge now. But I can refer you to one of my former partners. Since the firm handled your husband's case before, it is logical that they could handle this one."

"But, your Honor, sir, it was you who helped Antonio before, and you were so kind. He hardly paid you anything." She lowered her head when she mumbled this as though she were ashamed that they couldn't pay him, although they had managed to bring some amounts toward the bill over the years, which was when he had first met her.

The Judge looked at her and shook his head, his eyes concerned for her. "Well, first, I didn't help him very much. He was convicted of theft and served a year's sentence, even though the District Attorney never proved that it was he and not one of the other two living with him who stole the jewelry. Second, I'm sure the firm I'll refer you to will work out a reasonable payment program."

"But, won't you at least listen to why he's in jail? Maybe you could think of some other way to help him."

The Judge continued to look at the woman, his eyes still reflecting distress for her. "All right. I won't be able to hear the case anyway, given my history with your husband. What happened?"

The woman said, "We needed food. The children—" she pointed to them—"hadn't eaten much of anything for a couple of days. So he went hunting. He was looking for deer, but he accidentally killed one of the neighbor's cattle."

Judge Akers shook his head. "The law is very clear about that here in Ventura County. I don't necessarily agree with it, but the cattleman's association is very strong. Killing cattle is serious."

The woman looked up and the Judge noticed tears in her eyes. She said, "But he didn't mean to shoot the cow. He thought it was a deer. We were so hungry."

The Judge nodded and said, "I understand. Wait just a minute." He got up and went out to Irene. "Could you call John and see if he has a minute to talk with me?"

She picked up the phone and asked for a number. After speaking to someone on the other end, she gave the phone handset to the Judge. "Hi, John. Listen. I have a case I'd like you to handle." He cupped his hand over the mouthpiece and said quietly, "I'll pay the fee." Then he continued in a normal voice and said, "A Mexican fellow accidentally killed a steer by mistake, thinking it was a deer. Can you defend him? I know the issues—he's a Mexican—and we know how our race doesn't understand them, which will make a jury trial risky—and the law is pretty straightforward on killing cattle, but maybe you can do something for him. You may remember him, he's the same one I defended early on who got sent to San Quentin for theft."

He listened for a minute or two and said, "Thanks, John. I'll send his wife to you right now. I appreciate it."

He re-entered his inner office and walked over to the pleading woman and patted her hand. He pulled a card from his desk and a five-dollar bill from his pocket, which he carefully folded and hid under the card, and handed them to her and said, "It's all arranged. My colleague will help you. His address is on the card. He's waiting for you now. The office isn't far. You and the children should be able to walk there in about ten minutes."

She looked at the card and then the money and stuttered, but eventually managed to say, "Thank you, your Honor. I cannot tell you what this means. We feel so helpless."

The Judge helped her to stand. "I haven't done much, but at least you'll have adequate legal representation. Good luck."

The woman held a hand of each of her children, and the trio walked out of the Judge's office slowly. The boy turned and looked at the Judge. He started to say something but his mother pulled him along so he turned to follow. She didn't look back at the Judge or Irene, whose expression reflected the hopeless concern exhibited by the Judge. She stared at the floor as she walked. Neither the Judge nor Irene said anything as they watched them leave.

The Judge shook his head. "I hope John can help, but precedence is not in their favor."

Irene sat down and started writing in a notebook. "I'll see what I can do to help. Mrs. Martinez is a seamstress. I might be able to find some customers for her. Will she have a place to live?"

The Judge looked doubtful. "I'm not sure. I don't know if they own their place or rent it. Can you ask your husband to check out what her resources are? Make sure she's got food at least to get through the trial."

Irene looked up. "I'm not sure Jim's back yet from the library, but as soon as he returns I'll ask him."

In addition to serving as an investigator, Jim also was attending college to become a lawyer. He and Irene lived on a farm and had two children, ages five and eight. When he wasn't farming or doing investigative work for the Judge or local law enforcement, he was at the library studying or at the community college taking classes.

"When do you expect him?"

"Probably not until later tonight. He's got an exam coming up. Will tomorrow be soon enough?"

"Yes, I think so. I slipped her a five-dollar bill as she was leaving. That should hold them until tomorrow."

The Judge started to go back to his desk and then turned to Irene. "Is there anything else I need to do today, or can I go home now and attack that stack of papers tomorrow?"

Irene smiled. "No, you're clear. And it is after five, so you can go home." She smiled.

The Judge picked up his Fedora, perched it at its usual cockeyed angle, and headed out the door, relishing the walk home. Citizens throughout Ventura recognized him. He appeared often in his three-piece suit and brown Fedora walking the streets at a rapid pace with his long stride. Tonight was unusually warm for Ventura, but he nonetheless started out moving vigorously. Normally he would stop for dinner at a local café, but this evening he had leftovers waiting for him at home.

He passed by and greeted other walkers, including many with their dogs. He enjoyed the *camaraderie* of walking and talking with his neighbors. He knew almost everyone he greeted that night, some better than others. He appreciated the experience as an opportunity to throw off his immersion in the seedier side of life he experienced as a superior court judge. Here on the streets of Ventura were normal, everyday, law-abiding people, not murderers and thieves.

Therefore he was delighted when, as he approached the block where his house sat, he saw a young girl, who couldn't have been more than seven or eight, walking what appeared to be a fox on a leash. He went over to get a better look.

"Is that a fox?" he asked.

The girl sighed and responded, "Yes. My dad was hunting with some of his friends and they brought it back as a baby. I've raised him, and he's my pet now."

She told the story as if she had repeated it many times. The Judge asked, "What kind of fox is it?"

The girl rolled her eyes and said, "Obviously it's a gray fox."

The Judge nodded. "Of course it is. And you've raised it since it was a baby."

"Yes, and he's my pet now. I have to go." She and her fox on a leash left the Judge smiling and wondering what would become of a wild creature tamed to walk the streets of Ventura.

The Judge shook his head and turned toward a wood-framed house with a large porch and painted blue shutters. He opened the door into a parlor room on the left and steps and a wood banister on the right, and a hallway straight ahead. Despite the hot summer day, the room was dark and a few degrees cooler due to the closed shutters.

He entered his house with mixed emotions, as he always did since his wife's death. For more than twenty years, she had welcomed him home when he arrived, but not for the last decade, and he still missed that greeting. He went into the parlor and sat down on a leather divan set on a multi-patterned carpet between two dark-wood tables holding electric lamps with tiffany lampshades. Although this room was a parlor, it truly was the Judge's room. Bookshelves full of books lined one entire wall, a radio dominated one corner, and a dozen *Life* magazines were piled on the floor next to a leather chair.

The Judge picked up one of the framed pictures on the end table. It showed a younger version of him with a pretty woman whose hair was pulled up on top of her head. She was smiling at the Judge like he really was someone special. As he studied the photo of his wife and him caught in a happy moment, he remembered her death from tuberculosis as if it were yesterday—all the details of her final days haunted him. He willed himself to stop thinking about that last miserable week. He put down her photo and picked up one with the couple and his children when they were teenagers. This one made him smile.

He was proud of his children: his daughter was a teacher, his one son worked for the railroad, and his other son was studying to be a doctor. But he doubted he'd been a particularly outstanding parent. His own parents had divorced when he was quite young, and he never knew why. Neither his stepfather nor his biological father ever really liked him, so he was on his own as a teenager but had managed to overcome much to attend law school, set up his own law practice, and then become a judge. He had assumed that his own children could succeed without much help as well, which resulted in a parental approach devoid of much empathy or assistance.

"Enough of this self-pity," he mumbled. He got up and turned on the Benny Goodman show on the radio. There was supposed to be a special speaker from the L.A. Philharmonic that evening.

Chapter 03

A few days later the Judge was at the corner of Main and California Streets getting ready to walk up the hill to the Ventura County Courthouse when he responded to a couple coming out of the Ventura Hotel who asked for directions to the San Buenaventura Mission. He had just finished explaining its location down Main Street, when he saw the witness from the Oscar Briarley trial. He tipped his hat and said, "Hello, Miss Clara Bow Wilson. And where are you going today? No school?"

She said, "Oh, school doesn't start for another week. I'm going to a meeting of the County Scribblers—you know, they're a group of writers and their fans. I'm going to read my story there. I won a writing contest."

He said, "That's fine. Good for you. That's right, I remember you talked about *Grapes of Wrath,* didn't you?"

She responded, "Yes, I think it's a very important novel. I love reading Mr. Steinbeck's books."

"I agree. If I ever want to learn about something, I have gone to a book to find out about it. But I'd forgotten that you wanted to become a writer, like Edith Wharton, right?"

She opened her eyes wide, impressed that he remembered. "Yes. She writes about how life really is. She was the first woman to win a Pulitzer Prize, you know."

"Given your name, I'd have thought that perhaps you might want to become an actress."

"Oh, no. That's my mother. She named me Clara Bow after the famous actress because she liked her. But I'm going to be a writer. I plan to write about Shaggy Briarley next."

The Judge frowned. "Shaggy?"

"Oh, I'm sorry. That's what we call Oscar. You know, the boy I testified against the other day. We didn't mean anything by it. He just always looked like he needed a haircut."

"Oh, I see. What kind of topics does a sixteen-year-old girl like to write about?"

Clara said proudly, "Well, the story that was selected by the County Scribblers was about a teenager who runs over a little child with his car and doesn't stop and the child dies."

When the Judge looked surprised and frowned, she explained. "You see, I keep reading about all the accidents here in Ventura and how there are a growing number of drivers—I read that there were 12,000 licensed drivers in Ventura County last year. Can you believe it? Anyway, I was reading this article about this teenager and I wondered what he was feeling. He got caught, you know, even though he drove away. It wasn't his fault. The child ran into his car, but he didn't stop to help. So I wrote a story about how it feels to be a teenager and do something you really regret but can't make better."

The Judge said, "That's interesting that you would write about that. I would have thought you might write about growing up, finding your mate, and getting married."

Clara looked disappointed. "I'm sorry you think that way."

The Judge noticed that he had upset her. "Oh, I didn't mean to imply that—" He interrupted himself. "How do you decide what to write about?"

"Well, I keep a secret diary that nobody knows about—except my parents, and they never read it—and now you know. In it I make notes about various things that interest me, like the teenage driver. I couldn't possibly write about everything in it. The world is in such a mess right now. I mean, just look at poor Oscar. He can't even read. In today's world, mind you! And what's he got to look forward to? And look what's going on in Europe."

The Judge's eyes got wide. "You know about Hitler?"

Apparently sixteen-year-old girls weren't supposed to be aware of world events.

Clara responded, "Of course. I read the newspaper, you know. And it's full of Hitler invading Poland and our friends from Great Britain having to fight them. They had to do something. I just hope we have enough sense to keep out of it."

The Judge shook his head. "Maybe we can't keep out of it. I think it's wise of President Roosevelt to build the Navy. I'm worried that we could face an invasion from Mexico."

Clara frowned, apparently not wanting to further discuss the potential of war. "So anyway, I keep this diary and write down whatever I'm thinking. Besides the newspaper, I read lots of books."

"What are you reading now?" the Judge asked.

"Right now—*Brave New World* by Aldous Huxley. And I just finished *Little House in the Big Woods* by Laura Ingalls Wilder. I liked it a lot. I think *my* books will be about how we grow up in today's world coming out of a depression and living in a time of a major war, if the newspaper stories about Europe and Hitler are to be believed."

"Well, young lady, I find that impressive. I don't read much fiction. It takes all I can manage to keep up with the court documents. But I can see how it might help young Oscar to see different worlds through books."

The teenager looked eager. "Anyway, how's Oscar doing? Will he go to jail for a long time?"

The Judge said, "I can't discuss the case. I haven't made my decision yet. We've set the date for it for next month."

"Oh, of course." She looked at the Judge closely before saying, "Do you know if I could visit Oscar in jail? I mean, I'd like to see him, and if I write his story it would be good if I could talk to him there."

He stepped back and stared at her, considering her statement as a possible solution to his own problem of comprehending Oscar Briarley and solving his dilemma of sending a fourteen-year-old to adult prison. Could one teenager get another teenager to talk and identify his partner? "I think that's possible. Let me check into it." He started to leave and then stopped and turned back. He said, "Do you really believe that if Oscar knew how to read, that it would change his life?"

Without hesitation she said, "Oh, you probably know the answer to that question, but, yes, your Honor. I think it would open a world he's never understood or seen. He only has his family as an example—and certainly there's a lot more to living than what we see here in Ventura. Imagine what he might do if he could jump into the world of *The Count of Monte Cristo* or *The Three Musketeers.*"

The Judge nodded. "Thank you, Clara Bow Wilson. I think you've given me an idea. I'll get in touch with you about speaking to Oscar." To himself, he thought that maybe she could extract some information from the boy that could help him make a just verdict and sentence.

The two parted. Clara headed down Main Street. The Judge continued up the hill past the statue of Father Junípero Serra, which the Judge stopped to study for just a moment. The statue had been a project of the federal Works Projects Administration in 1937, sculpted by John Palo-Kangas, and he thought that it was a fine accent to the neo-classical County Courthouse Building which stood behind it with its terra cotta façade, Doric columns, arched windows, and twenty-four Franciscan padres' faces on the building. He was a history buff and knew that the Franciscans had founded Ventura, or Buenaventura, in the late 1700s. He loved coming to work there, and no matter how difficult a case he might be facing, entering this magnificent edifice always managed to instill a sense of fulfillment and pride in him.

He continued through the doors, across the foyer, and up the marble staircase to the courtroom and his chambers, tipping his hat and saying, "Good morning," to everyone he passed.

Irene and Jim greeted the Judge as he entered his chambers. Irene looked relieved to see him and pointed to his calendar and said, "You've got maybe ten minutes with Jim before you need to go to court. Why are you so late?"

"Oh, I met up with Clara Wilson, you know, the witness against the Briarley boy. She might be a possible solution to help convince Oscar Briarley to identify his partner."

When both of them said nothing and simply stared at him, he said, "Do you know she told me that there are 12,000 licensed drivers in Ventura County? Whew. No wonder traffic is so heavy."

Irene smiled. She knew the Judge reveled in facts and figures. The girl probably impressed him by knowing that number.

Jim, a good-looking, muscular man with dark hair and just less than six feet, ignored the new statistic and looked skeptical. "How can she help with the Briarley boy? That doesn't make sense. It's her testimony that will convict him."

The Judge held up his hand. "I know, I know. But she wants to be a writer and write about him. She's quite precocious, that one, and quite the talker. Anyway she has asked to visit him in jail so she can learn something about him as a writer. Maybe a teenager talking to another teenager might make him more likely to say something."

Jim looked at Irene. "What do you think?"

Irene hesitated before saying, "Maybe. But we should definitely check with Attorney Alberts first. He could ask the boy if he wants to speak with the person who's putting him in jail." She rolled her eyes. "But, who knows? Also, you should check with the girl's parents for permission, and I would at least mention it to the District Attorney and maybe even the Sheriff. If the boy and her parents respond affirmatively and no one else sees a problem, it certainly can't hurt."

The Judge stared at her for several seconds and asked, "Anything else?"

She smiled, then shook her head. "No, but if I think of anything more, I'll let you know."

"Good. That's decided. Can you make it happen, please? But now, Jim, what do you have to tell me about that school where I've been invited to speak? Should I go?"

Irene said, "You've now got five minutes before you need to leave for court, and that's only allowing you three minutes to get there."

"It won't take me long," Jim said. "The school is a workable alternative place for unhardened juveniles, but I'm not so sure how successful it will be at rehabilitating hardened ones. Also, they haven't been around long enough for me to assess their effectiveness."

"That's good to know. It will determine what I say. And I guess it's good that we have someplace to consider besides the Preston School of Industry and Whittier Boy's School. I'll mention it to the District Attorney."

He grabbed his robe and headed for the courtroom and entered promptly at the court start time, triggering the bailiff to say, "All rise. Judge Grover Roswell Akers presiding."

He sat in his dais overlooking the courtroom and was met with three pairs of frightened eyes from teenage boys sitting next to Attorney Alberts. He waited for the bailiff to begin the proceedings and listened to the District Attorney outline the crime of the three boys breaking into a store and stealing a dozen radios. The boys were pleading guilty and the Judge needed to decide their fate.

The District Attorney said, "This is an easy case, your Honor. These three boys, without any regard for the storeowner, broke into his store causing an estimated $500 worth of damage in order to steal a dozen radios, which they then attempted to sell to someone who contacted the Chief. They should be punished to the fullest extent possible and serve time at Whittier. I'm asking for one year without probation."

The Judge nodded. "Thank you, District Attorney Bilkins."

Defense Attorney Alberts stood. "Your Honor, the boys fully admit they stole the radios—"

The Judge interrupted. "Mr. Alberts, I read your petition and plea, so am familiar with your request. However, I'd like to hear from the boys now." He pointed to one of them and said, "You, take the stand."

The boy's eyes grew wide. He looked at his attorney, then at the other boys, then back at the audience and to his parents. He swallowed and said, "Me, sir?"

"Yes, you. Bailiff, swear him in."

The boy stood and reached more than 5 feet 5 inches tall. His dark hair was trimmed as if a bowl had been used to guide the scissors. He was dressed in a white shirt, suspenders, and slacks, which were not quite long enough to reach his ankles.

Attorney Alberts waited for him to be sworn in and then said, "Your Honor, may I ask him some questions first to put him at ease? He's barely fourteen, and I'm sure he's nervous."

The Judge nodded. "Go ahead. Ask your questions."

Attorney Alberts said, "Can you tell us why you decided to participate in taking the radios?"

The eyes of the youngster suggested that he was more than scared. He tried to say something, but only a hoarse sound came from his mouth. Judge Akers looked at him and said, "Son, take your time. First, look at me. Now tell me your name again."

"Wayne, my name is Wayne Tolance."

"All right, Wayne Tolance. How old are you?"

"I'm fourteen."

"And these two fellows here are your friends?"

Wayne looked at the two other boys seated at the defense table. He nodded.

The Judge said, "You need to speak up so we can write down what you're saying."

The boy responded, "Yes, sir. They are my friends."

"I want you to tell me in your own words what happened that day. Is that all right with the District Attorney and with you, Attorney Alberts?"

They responded simultaneously, "Yes, your Honor." Attorney Alberts sat down, having decided that the Judge's questions were not to the detriment of his client, but ready to object to protect his rights if necessary.

"Go ahead, Wayne. What happened that day?"

The teenager swallowed, looked back at the Judge, and said, "Well, we needed some money to go to the movies. We wanted to see *Stagecoach*. You know, the Western. It's supposed to be a terrific movie—lots of shootin' and stuff. None of us had none, but Billy said we could pick up some radios easy and sell 'em fast."

The Judge nodded. "So you decided to steal radios so you'd have money to go to the movies?"

"Yes, sir."

Attorney Alberts tried to interrupt. "Your Honor—"

"My turn, Mr. Alberts. Go on, Wayne Tolance."

"Well, sir, your Honor, sir. There ain't much more. We broke in and took them radios, but when we tried to sell 'em, the Chief come along and took us off to jail. And then we had to stay in jail 'cuz none of our folks could afford the $500 bail."

"I see. Did it occur to you that maybe you should work for the money to go to the movies?"

"It's hard to find a job, sir. And if'n I earned any money, I'd give it to my pa to help pay for food. He's been off work for a long time, and we're just getting by."

The Judge absorbed that statement, and then looked at the District Attorney. "Is this his first offense?"

"Yes, sir. The other two were caught breaking a store window a month ago, but as far as we know, this is Wayne's first attempt at any kind of crime or misdemeanor."

"All right, did either of you have any questions for Wayne?"

Both the District Attorney and the Defense Attorney responded, "No, sir."

"I'm finished with you, Wayne. You can return to your friends. Attorney Alberts, did you have something else you want to add?"

"Your Honor, all three boys come from respectable families. Their parents are here in court today." The lawyer pointed to the first three rows of the seats, which were indeed full of couples, with grandparents as well as parents. "They are willing to take responsibility for their sons and recognize that what they've done was wrong. They will pay for the damages to the store caused by the robbery, although it may take a while to make the payments. They ask for leniency so that they can help their sons become responsible family and community members."

The Judge sat quietly for a moment. "Have all of the radios been returned to their rightful owner?"

The District Attorney nodded. "Yes, sir. And they were recovered without damage."

"Let me review the situation. All three boys have confessed to stealing the radios, which have been returned. However, there is damage to the store they broke into, in the amount of $500. They have served three weeks in the County Jail awaiting this hearing. None of them has a job. Their families are willing to accept responsibility for them." He looked at the District Attorney and Attorney Alberts. "Have I forgotten anything?"

Attorney Alberts said, "Two of the three are good students at school."

The Judge said, "And the third boy?"

"He has been absent off and on for the past six months because he's been helping his father take care of his mother while she recuperates from a serious illness. However, her recovery is complete now, so the boy can return to school full time."

"Thank you, Attorney Alberts. I appreciate that you've done your research and know your clients." The Judge hesitated and then looked at the defendants. "I'm prepared to give my decision now."

Attorney Alberts jumped up. "Your Honor, I've not had the opportunity to present a case for leniency."

"Go ahead. I thought you were finished since you told me about their backgrounds."

"I recommend that the Court grant them probation and that they be placed in the custody of their parents. They've already served time. Thank you, your Honor."

The Judge did not even wait for the attorney to sit down. He said, "First, I want to say that thievery is never an option. You boys were wrong to rob the store for any reason, much less for something so trivial as cash to see the latest movie. You need to understand that the store owner, Mr. Miller," the Judge pointed to a bald man in a suit sitting in the front row, "had to work hard to pay for those radios and to purchase his store. By taking them from him, you deprived him and his family of their livelihood. You need to acknowledge that." The Judge glared at them.

"Second, you are very, very fortunate to have parents who are willing to stand up for you. Believe me, I have seen boys in this court who have no one. Think about that for a minute. What would you do if you were here alone with no lawyer and no parents?" He paused.

"It is my belief, however, given your history, that with strong parental involvement, a job, and an education you can all become contributing members of the community. Therefore, here is my ruling: You are sentenced to three weeks' jail time, which you have already served, along with two years' probation and a fine of $500 to compensate the store owner for the damage you caused. That fee is to be paid within the next month. If that's a hardship on your families, please present a reasonable payment plan to the storeowner. I'll accept his signed agreement in lieu of a payment in one month.

"During your two years' probation, you will attend school daily except for weekends unless you are excused by the principal. I expect a weekly attendance report to be given to the Court. And I expect you to receive at least passing grades. Next, you will each get a job. If you do not have a job within two months, you will report to the city or county jail for two hours every weekday after school for the Chief and/or the Sheriff to use you however they see fit. I expect written notification from your employer when you are hired. You might check with Mr. Miller to see if he would employ you in exchange for payment toward repairs. However, he must agree to such an arrangement.

"Next, your parents will enforce a curfew for you. You are not to be out after 7:00 at night without an adult accompanying you, or as required by your job, unless you have written permission from your parents.

"And before you leave today, I expect each of you to tell me in your own words why what you did was wrong. I'll start with Wayne."

Wayne stiffened. He undoubtedly assumed he was finished and had escaped. Attorney Alberts had to prod him to get him to stand up. He looked at the Judge who stared at him without blinking. After a few seconds he managed to say, "It was wrong to steal because we took something from the store owner's family that coulda cost him money so's his family didn't have no food. I'm very sorry. I'll never do it again." He sat back down quickly.

The Judge nodded and looked out to the gallery when he heard the sobs of a woman, most likely Wayne's mother. But he did not relent. "Next," he said.

The middle boy stood up and said, "It was wrong to take something that didn't belong to me. I'm sorry. It won't happen again."

The Judge nodded. "Next."

The final boy stood up and said, "I won't do it again." Then he sat down.

The Judge held up his hand. "That's not good enough. Do you have something you want to add?"

The boy stood up and said, "It was wrong to steal. I'm sorry. And I'll do whatever I can to help my parents pay back the store owner." This time, however, he didn't sit down.

The Judge said, "Was there something else?"

"Yes, sir. It will be very hard for my folks to come up with the money to pay the store owner, so when I get my job I'd like to make sure that whatever I earn goes toward that payment."

"That's an excellent idea," the Judge said. "The bailiff and Sheriff will implement the decision. The boys will return to the jail so that they can be released appropriately. Their parents can pick them up there."

The Judge stood, and the bailiff called the session closed.

Chapter 04

Two days later, the Judge was sitting in his Chambers with Irene, who informed him that she had talked with Attorney Alberts and the District Attorney about Clara Wilson meeting with Oscar Briarley.

"Alberts claimed he talked to Oscar, who not only said it was all right but seemed outright excited that someone would visit him. Apparently he doesn't get any visitors."

"What about the District Attorney? Is he all right with it?"

"Yes. He didn't seem to care. I'm sure he thinks nothing will come of it and that he's got a tight case against Briarley, so he's not worried." She added, "Oh, and the Sheriff says it's fine with him. He hopes you can get the boy to tell us who actually did the shooting. He and his deputies and the Chief have all tried to talk him into identifying the gunman with no success. They're still looking for him, of course. No one seems to know Oscar and no one saw anything that evening except Clara."

The Judge looked pensive. "We'll have to move carefully. My hope is that Clara can earn his trust and then eventually he'll tell her what we need to know, but I'm not sure how committed she is, especially once she delves into his life, which is not the type of life she's accustomed to. It will take more than one visit." He thought about what was next and asked, "What about her parents?"

Irene shook her head. "I haven't contacted them yet."

The Judge said, "I'll call them this evening and see what they think. She seems intelligent and capable, but she is still a teenager, and I can tell that she has been sheltered."

Irene looked at him. "I'm wondering if it wouldn't be better for you to go see her parents and her at their home. Let them know what you have in mind, or at least get an idea of who they are. I think it's always better to do things like this

The Judge's Story

face-to-face. Sometimes the telephone can get in the way when you can't see how the person at the other end is reacting."

"You're right. I'll call and ask to visit. Good idea. What's next?"

"The Sheriff and the District Attorney want to speak with you about the Rodriguez case."

The Judge looked startled. He recalled that the Rodriguez case concerned a man who had been stabbed to death ten years earlier. Deputies had found his body on the beach, but the Sheriff's office had not been successful in identifying the killers. The Judge assumed by now they'd given up on it. "What? Has something happened?"

"Yes. They think they've caught the killers, which is all they told me. Do you want me to call the Sheriff now?"

"Yes, get the Sheriff on the phone. That's a highly publicized case. The newspapers will be reporting on it."

Irene asked for the Sheriff, waited for a moment, and gave the handset to the Judge. "Sheriff," he said, "what's this I hear about you capturing Joe Rodriguez's killers? Only took you ten years," he joked.

He listened as the Sheriff informed him that they had picked up and jailed two suspects. Apparently one of them had stepped out on his wife, who got jealous and turned them in. The suspects claimed they were innocent.

"So I'll see them tomorrow in court. Who's their attorney?"

The Sheriff didn't know. The Judge said, "Well, they should have legal representation before they plead. It's murder so I'll have to consider not releasing them on bail, but I'd like someone there to make the case for it. I'll check with Bilkins."

He hung up and asked for the District Attorney. "Will you be in court tomorrow with these two suspects in the Rodriguez killing? And do you know who's representing them?" He listened to the response. "Oh, that's good. I wouldn't want to have a plea if they weren't represented."

The Judge replaced the handset to its cradle and then asked Irene, "Is Jim around?"

"He's studying at the library again."

"Maybe when you see him tonight you could ask him to gather as much information as he can on the Rodriguez case—it's been a while since it happened—"

Irene handed him a folder with some notes and some clippings. "I got this from our own files, but I'll ask Jim to see what else he can find."

The Judge smiled. "I don't deserve you, Irene. Thanks. This will help refresh my memory."

"Will they be in court tomorrow?"

"Yes, and Bilkins says they have an attorney. A jealous wife could just be trying to get them in trouble. Although if the Sheriff arrested them, there must be something there."

He glanced at the article. "It says he was stabbed to death fifteen times and that the money from his wallet was gone. His wife at the time claimed he was carrying a significant amount of cash, seemed he didn't have much faith in banks—probably wise in 1929."

Irene asked, "Are the suspects Mexican?"

The Judge looked at Irene and understood her concern. Although she herself was not of Mexican descent, her husband, Jim, was, and they frequently encountered problems with the local citizens, who remained prejudiced against them. So Irene was asking whether the Judge would face that issue when presiding over the suspects' trial. The Judge said, "I don't know. I didn't ask. Mr. Rodriguez was."

He continued to read while Irene cleared her desk.

Irene said, "That's all I have for today. I just wish this heat would break. It's so unusual for Ventura."

The Judge nodded. "Yes, it is. You know, I wonder if I can catch anyone at the Wilson home now? I think I'll try. Does Mrs. Wilson still teach?"

"Yes, at Ventura Community College. Do you want me to try to reach her? I have their number."

"Yes, could you?"

She asked the operator for the number of the Wilson home and was rewarded with the answer of a woman. "Mrs. Wilson? Hello, it's Irene Alvarez."

She responded to the greeting at the other end, "Yes, it has been a while. We're all fine, and you'll be pleased to know that Jim is taking classes and plans to become a lawyer. But I'm calling today for Judge Akers. Do you have a minute to speak with him?"

The Judge looked at her, questioning her conversation with Mrs. Wilson. She put her hand over the mouthpiece. "Jim took classes from her. She's an excellent teacher, by the way." She gave the handset to the Judge.

"Hello, Mrs. Wilson. Thank you so much for taking my call. I'd like to meet with you to discuss your daughter's request to visit Oscar Briarley, the boy she testified against in court."

He laughed. "I agree. It does sound contradictory, and yes it was her idea, but we've checked with the boy and he would like her to visit. Apparently no one else has come to see him, including his parents. Would this evening be convenient for me to stop by? It shouldn't take long."

He nodded. "Great. When is a convenient time?" He listened. "All right, I'll see you at 7:00."

The Judge hung up, said goodbye to Irene, and grabbed his hat. He was hungry so headed to his most-frequented café where he decided to splurge and have a T-bone steak. He greeted his favorite waitress, Molly, and enjoyed her attention as she brought him his food.

While pouring his third cup of coffee, she said, "If I drank that much coffee, I'd have the jitters so bad I wouldn't be able to sit still."

The Judge smiled. "I don't believe I've ever seen you sit down much less sit still. How long have we known each other?"

Molly looked out the window as she calculated. "Well, maybe six or seven years, now. And you're the most regular customer I've got."

The Judge enjoyed talking to Molly. She was always cheerful and waited on him with no complaints. He typically gave her a large tip. It seemed small enough reward for the energy she brought into his life.

"Well, I can't stay and chat tonight, Molly. I've got to go see some people about a case." He noticed that she looked disappointed. He said, "Don't be too sad. I'll see you again—probably tomorrow."

"Of course."

He paid his bill, said goodbye, put on his hat, and walked to the Wilson home, where he knocked on the door at exactly 7:00 p.m. A man about six feet tall wearing a white shirt with the sleeves rolled up, tan slacks, and suspenders, opened the door. He said, "Judge Akers?"

"Yes. And you are Mr. Wilson?"

"Come in. Clara is very excited that you're here and that she might get to talk with that boy in jail. She is anxious to write about him. She'll be right in."

The Judge removed his hat when he entered and extended his hand to Mr. Wilson, who shook it. He nodded to Mrs. Wilson, an attractive woman in her thirties with curly dark hair bobbed in the style of the day. She greeted him and invited him to be seated. The Judge sat on a divan upholstered with large maroon flowers set in a beige background. He noticed that the two beige easy chairs matched and the dark maroon carpet pulled the room together. He appreciated the Tiffany-style lamps, similar to his own.

The Judge said, "I'm so pleased to meet you both. You have an exceptional daughter. I see a lot of criminal juveniles, so it's been a pleasure to meet Clara." He smiled at the teenager as she entered the room.

Mr. Wilson said, "Thank you. We are proud of her—most of the time."

Clara glared at her father.

Then Mrs. Wilson said, "We expect that she'll be successful with her writing, but we're also encouraging her to learn a trade where she might earn some money, just in case."

The Judge smiled. "That's quite practical."

Clara asked, without hesitation and exhibiting her typical sense of curiosity, "What made you decide to become a judge?"

"Well, I chose to study the law due to a Senator I met and worked for. But I did quite a few jobs before then. I was always getting into trouble and getting fired, you see—not that I want any of my juvenile boys to know about that, however." He smiled.

Clara looked puzzled and asked, "Why did you get fired so much?"

The Judge smiled. Given that he was there to ask a favor, he decided to be more forthcoming with his background than he normally would be. "I'm not sure, exactly. I recall a lot of arguments and fisticuffs with my bosses and fellow workers. I guess I was a little hotheaded. My mother, who was a teacher, by the way, and father were divorced—I never knew why—and my stepdad didn't take to me much nor did my real dad, for that matter. Eventually, though, to answer your original question, I ended up scribing for a U.S. Senator and went to Washington with him, where I eventually went to law school. Then I set up a law practice here in Ventura, got married, and had three children. But a lot happened in between. By the way, Mrs. Wilson, I understand that you're a teacher. So is my daughter."

Clara's mother responded, "Oh, where does your daughter teach?"

"She is in San Francisco. I'm planning to go visit her soon. I want to see that new Golden Gate Bridge. It's supposed to be really something. I haven't been there since they built it."

Mr. Wilson, an engineer, nodded enthusiastically. "It's incredible. We took the train up to San Francisco for our vacation last month. I couldn't believe it."

The Judge said, "Oh, how long does it take on the train now? That's how I was thinking of traveling. It's just a little too far for me to drive, I think."

Mr. Wilson, always eager to talk about whatever route he'd taken in a car trip or the latest in transportation, responded, "It was nine hours on Southern Pacific. But what a trip! Beautiful scenery."

Mrs. Wilson offered to get him something to drink, but he refused admitting that he had just eaten. He said, "Thank you so much for seeing me. I don't know if Clara told you but we met on the street a few days ago, which is when we discussed the possibility of her speaking with Oscar Briarley, the boy who robbed the store. She thought it would be a good opportunity to learn about him and make him the subject of one of her writings."

Mrs. Wilson said, "I do hope she didn't bother you. We are proud of her ambitions and she does seem to have a flair for writing, but if she intruded—"

The Judge hastened to interrupt. "No, no, not at all. Actually, just the opposite. We are having difficulty getting the boy to reveal his partner. If he doesn't tell us, I might have to sentence him to long jail time. I could be more lenient if he co-operates. I'm not saying that I will—there's much more involved in my decision—but it would certainly weigh positively on his case if he helped us catch the real killer. He is just a boy, and none of us believes that he was responsible for the death of Mr. Brant."

Mr. Wilson said, "But I understand that he was there; he did help rob the store."

"Yes, the boy doesn't deny being there, and we have Clara's testimony to that. But I'm interested in catching the person who put him up to it. We think that it might be more likely that Oscar would tell Clara who it is than he would tell the Sheriff or even his own lawyer."

Mr. Wilson concluded, "So what you're asking is that in exchange for Clara getting to interview this boy, she should try to get the name of his partner from him."

"That's correct, although it's not a requirement. We're just asking if she would."

"And how would this come about? Would she be in any danger?" He looked at his wife, fully aware that would be her question.

"Oh, no. It would be in the visitor's area of the jail. I can take her there and introduce her to the deputies and the prisoner. Oscar is very excited about having her visit. No one else has, including his own parents. And the Sheriff is on board. We're all hoping she can be successful. But if she isn't, well, I don't see that there's any harm to anyone. And it would certainly please the boy, and maybe Clara would get some material for a story."

Mrs. Wilson said, "I find it difficult to believe that Clara can get this boy to talk with just one visit. He doesn't even know her. Why would he tell her when he has been unwilling to divulge the name to anyone else?"

The Judge nodded. "You could be right. What I'm asking is—could she try one visit, see where it takes her, and then we'll figure out what to do next? It might require more than one visit, certainly."

"Oh, please, can I?" Clara looked eager. "What could happen to me? I mean, it's just going to be a visit and I'll talk to him and then it'll be over and I'll have a story."

Mrs. Wilson looked at her daughter and said, "But this is not a story, Clara. This is real life. This boy is living through this. You will probably encounter more than you anticipate."

The Judge started to say something but Clara interrupted. "Mother, I'm sixteen now and both you and Dad have said I need to learn more about the real world if I'm to become a great writer."

The Judge said, "Why don't I let you folks discuss it? Call Irene Alvarez and let her know your decision. She can arrange the visit, and I'll be on hand to escort Clara to the jail. But, Clara, your mother is right. This is real life, and you may not like what you learn." He picked up his hat. "Thank you so much for seeing me this evening. You have a lovely home."

The Judge left the small family to discuss a decision which the Judge realized could have an impact on the life of a young sixteen-year-old—one who had been reared by loving, well-off, and educated parents, and who had limited exposure to a world outside those boundaries.

Chapter 05

The Judge started the next day in court greeting District Attorney Bilkins and a young defense attorney he did not know, along with two middle-aged unkempt men who looked haggard and angry.

The District Attorney spoke first. "Your Honor, these men are accused of ruthlessly murdering Joe Rodriguez ten years ago by stabbing him fifteen times and robbing him of $200 in cash. We have spoken to several of their acquaintances as well as friends of the deceased and they all say that these two men had knowledge of the victim's cash and that they both came into sudden money shortly after his death. We believe that is enough evidence to hold them without bail until we can prepare the case against them."

Their attorney responded, "Your Honor. My clients are both respectable working members of our community. It's been ten years since this crime was committed. We hardly think that a jealous wife's comments are enough to justify holding them in jail. We ask for bail in the amount of $200."

The Judge said, "How are they pleading?"

The attorney looked embarrassed and said, "Sorry, your Honor. They are pleading 'Not guilty.'"

The Judge looked at the District Attorney. "Mr. District Attorney. Please state in more detail why you think these men should be remanded without bail."

"Yes, sir. First, we have testimony from three of their friends and two of the victim's friends that they knew the victim and his habits of walking from his home to work with sums of cash to pay his employees. The Sheriff is right now searching for more evidence on the basis of information received from one of the suspect's wives. Second, they have enough resources that they might flee. And third, they do represent a risk to the community given there is a possibility they have killed brutally before."

The Judge nodded and looked at the defendants. "I hereby remand you both to be held in the Ventura County Jail without bail until your trial."

The two men glared at their attorney. One of them shouted, "You said we wouldn't have to go to jail today! You said we—"

The Judge interrupted, "Will the bailiff please see that the accused are escorted back to jail."

A slovenly woman, in a soiled flowered dress with stockings rolled around her ankles, yelled, "That will teach you to step out on me! After all I done for you. I lied for you and raised your brats. Well, I guess I got you."

The Judge banged his gavel and said, "Please be quiet or you will have to leave the courtroom."

But she was already gone.

Chapter 06

Later, after a long day in Court, the Judge waited for Clara to meet him in his chambers so that he could escort her to the county jail next door to meet with Oscar Briarley. Her parents had agreed to a one-time meeting, although they also said they would consider a second meeting depending on the result of the first and their daughter's reaction to it. The Judge sat at his desk reviewing a proposal by a defense attorney regarding a couple of bookies who'd recently been arrested.

Irene interrupted him. "Clara is here. Are you ready?"

"Yes. Hello, Clara. Thank you for agreeing to do this." He added, "By the way, how was the first day of school?"

Clara smiled, "Oh, it's been all right so far. I like all my teachers."

"Who do you have for history?"

"Mr. Baker."

"Good. He knows a lot about local Ventura history, and we have a rich heritage, you know. It isn't every county that has a mission." He was referring to the San Buenaventura Mission founded in 1782 and still standing in Ventura.

She nodded, although perhaps not quite so enthusiastically as the Judge had hoped. She preferred more modern sites, like a new movie theater in downtown Ventura.

The Judge stood up. "Are you prepared to talk to Oscar Briarley?"

"Yes, I think so."

He said, "Do you know what you're going to ask him?"

"I have some questions." She pulled out her notebook. "Mostly I want to know about his life. I mean, his parents, his brother, his home. Do you think it's all right to ask him those questions?"

The judge nodded. "Yes, I do. I hope he'll answer. I believe that a boy is formed—or not—into a man by his family. Most of the juveniles we see in the courts are boys from broken homes."

"Really? That's very interesting. I must add that piece of information to my journal."

The Judge took long strides, and Clara had trouble keeping up with him. "We need to get to the jail. They like to shut down to visitors at 5:00. You won't have much time."

Clara looked puzzled. She had assumed that judges make the law and therefore he could arrange for her to spend however long she wanted with Oscar, but it occurred to her that day that judges simply assure that the law is carried out in a fair and just way.

He greeted just about everyone on their short walk between his chambers and the jail. She asked, "How come you know everyone?"

He laughed. "Well, I don't know everyone, but I've been involved with the justice system here in Ventura for a long time—first as a lawyer and now as a judge. I like living here. In a small town like this, you can meet and become acquainted with most of the people residing here. Not like in the big city, where you only see and greet a few people in your surrounding area."

Clara wasn't so sure about the benefits offered by a small town. She found Ventura constraining and not helpful to adding the experiences she needed to write new and interesting stories. She said, "Have you ever lived in a big city?"

"Yes, I lived in San Francisco and in Washington, D.C.—of course that was a while ago—but it was long enough for me to experience big-city living."

"Really, what was it like?"

"Well, I can tell you that I didn't know many of the people in either city. In fact, I knew very few. And not many people knew me. Especially in San Francisco. I really had to fend for myself."

"Will you tell me about some of your other cases sometime?"

He again turned to face her, shook his head, but then stopped. "Maybe, but only those where people are not still around. Confidentiality plays an important part in a lawyer's practice and in a judge's surroundings. I'm not so sure my former clients would appreciate reading about their cases in one of your stories."

He smiled and held open the door to the Sheriff's office. It smelled of disinfectant and tobacco. It was larger than the town police building. The main room housed half a dozen desks, a wall lined with rifles, and three deputies busy typing or filing. That afternoon, it was hot despite the fans.

The Judge said to Clara, "This is quite a significant jail. It can accommodate 122 prisoners, and the custody tank has sixteen beds." Clara noted that the Judge seemed to know all kinds of facts, something she appreciated.

Just after they entered, a thin, stooped man with a gray beard walked through a second door carrying a cage holding what appeared to be an opossum. He said to a uniformed officer sitting at a desk, "Well, tell the Sheriff that I think Rusty here got most of the rats." He pointed to the opossum. "I've got two more jails to cover. Let me know if you have any more trouble and I'll bring him back."

The Judge and Clara moved out of the man's way. Clara wanted to write some notes on the opossum, but the deputy sitting at a desk interrupted and said, "Hi, Judge. Is this the young lady to see Oscar Briarley?"

"Yes, this is Clara Wilson."

"I'll bring him to the visitor's area. Pete will let you in."

A tall, thin man with a moustache and dressed in a suit entered the room. "Why, hello, Judge. To what do we owe a visit by you today?"

"Hello, Sheriff. I'm just escorting this young lady to your fine jail. She wants to visit Oscar Briarley."

"That's right. Irene called. I'm glad someone's coming to see him. Poor boy. I sure wished he didn't do what he did. Not sure he's ever had a chance, though." He put his hat on the rack, and his wet hair and sweat-covered upper lip indicated he, too, was suffering in the heat. "By the way, I got the dental report back from L.A. on those teeth we sent there. No identification."

He was talking about a body that had been found on the railroad tracks—a victim who had been beaten to death. They had been trying to identify it for weeks without success. The story had been in the newspaper, and Clara was curious to know the latest information.

The Judge grunted. "So what now?"

"Well, we were able to get his fingerprints, and I've sent them off to Washington to see if there's a match. I think that this poor fellow is a Chinese who refused to contribute to the Sino-Japanese war in Asia, and they killed him for it. Of course, that's just my speculation."

The Judge nodded. "It's as good a guess as any, I guess. Here's hoping they can identify him with his fingerprints. It's a long shot, however."

Clara recalled that the Sheriff's speculation had appeared in the newspaper stories as well. It was an interesting case. She was hoping to learn more. However, just then the deputy came back into the room, looked at Clara, and said, "You'll have to leave your bag here. I can't let you take anything in."

"Could I just take paper and pen?"

"Not the pen. The paper's all right. But nothing else."

She pulled out her paper with her questions and placed her bag on the shelf the officer had indicated. The Judge took her arm and steered her to the door where the man with the opossum had come through. Another uniformed officer on the other side pushed a button that made a loud "bzzzz," and they were admitted to a room that was about the size of one of Clara's classrooms. The door closed muffling the sounds of typing and chatter. There were several tables with uncomfortable-looking straight-back chairs around them. Clara sat on one of them, and the Judge stood next to her. There was no one else in the room.

"Is this where we'll meet Oscar? I won't get to see his cell?"

The Judge shook his head. "No. But you can ask him about it. As a juvenile here in the county jail, he's separated from direct contact with the older prisoners. He stays in a cell with three others, although I believe he only has one cellmate at the moment. I'm going to leave you now. As the adjudicating judge, it's not appropriate that I be present with you. The officers will take care of you."

Clara didn't realize that he wouldn't remain with her and felt a flash of concern, but to show confidence she nodded at the Judge, then watched him knock on the door, heard it buzz, and saw him walk out the door—leaving her to stare at the questions on her single sheet of paper. The room seemed ominously quiet.

In a few minutes, the door across from her opened and Oscar bounded out followed by the officer. His hair was clean, although it still seemed to have a mind of its own. Also, he looked heavier than at school. He actually smiled when he saw her.

"Hi, Clara." He seemed pleased to see her. He kept nodding and walked in a fast jerk-like manner that appeared to be his typical gait.

"Hi, Oscar," she said.

He sat down at the table across from her as he said, "It's sure swell of you to come see me. I'm not sure how long I'm gonna be here. My lawyer says I gotta go to another jail soon's the Judge makes up his mind."

"Oh, I see. It was the Judge who got me in to see you. How are you doing? You look great."

"Yes, I never 'et so well as here. There's a farm. Just the men folk work it. They don't let us boys do much. Then the women folk do the preparin' so there's always something to 'et. I like it here. 'Cept there's not much to do. Sometimes I wish there was more to do."

"Oh, I could bring you some books."

"That'd be nice if n' there's pictures in them. I cain't read much, ya know."

"Oh, that's right." Clara studied Oscar, watching him as he started to jiggle. Then she said, "Listen, Oscar. I have an idea. Just tell me if you don't want to do it, but I was thinking maybe I could help you with your reading. I love to read. I don't know what I'd do if I couldn't. If you agree, I'll see if they'll let me come back and—"

"Mebbe. You could ask the sir." He looked around at the deputy, who was reading in a nearby chair. He looked up and nodded.

Oscar smiled, continued to jiggle, and said, "But I don't know how long I might be here. Do you got some questions? They said you might."

"Yes, I do, but you don't have to answer them if you don't want to. I'm a writer, you see, and I like to understand experiences—you know, what people go through—so I can write about them. And I thought maybe you'd fill me in about what it's like to be in jail."

For some reason he continued to jiggle. When she had seen him jiggling in the courtroom, Clara had assumed he did that when he was nervous, but he didn't seem nervous now. Maybe it was just a habit.

He said, "Sure. What ken I tell 'ye?"

"Well, first. Who has come to see you and how difficult is it to have visitors?"

"You're my only visitor, so you ken answer that one yerself."

She looked at him. "What do you mean? What about your parents? Or your brothers?"

"Let's see, now, my older brother Tommy, he's in jail, too, and my younger one cain't travel on his own. Pa wouldn't let Ma come see me 'cuz she's probably liquored up."

It didn't seem to bother Oscar that none of his family cared enough to come see him. He seemed to accept that as the way things were. Clara wasn't sure what to ask him next. She said, "Well, tell me about your brother. I remember him from school, but mostly I stayed away from him."

"You mean my older brother, Tommy?" Oscar frowned. "I'm s'prised you remember him from school. He didn't go much, and the truant sir was always after him. He's in prison now. He's Pa's favorite-like. They used to do lots of things together, like ketch squirrels, rabbits, and even cats and pull them apart. They liked to bet on which one would scream the loudest. I didn't like that, so Pa didn't take much to me. He called me girly-like. They'd cook and 'et 'em. Not me though. No matter how hungry I got. At first, Tommy didn't like it neither, but Pa talked him into it. They did other stuff together but they never asked me to go with them no more. Is them the kind of things you want to write about?"

Clara stared at Oscar, not knowing how to respond. "I'm not sure. Why is your brother in prison?"

He shook his head and said, "Lawdy knows. All he did was shoot one of them Mexican boys. I mean, they's not like you 'n me, Pa says, so why did they go and put Tommy in jail for it?"

"Did he die?" Clara was appalled.

He looked confused, but stopped jiggling. "Did who die?"

"The boy your brother shot. Did he kill him?"

"Oh, yes, ma'am. If'n Tommy shoots at somethum', he don't often miss. That Mexican was sure daid."

She stared at the boy. He had no sense that what his brother had done was wrong. She wondered if he understood that what he had done—robbing the store and being there when Mr. Brant was killed—was wrong.

"Oscar, do you know why you're here?"

"Sure. It's wrong to steal. Attorney Alberts told me. I don't mind, though. It's nice here."

Not sure what else to say, she decided to see if she could do what the Sheriff and his attorney had failed to accomplish, and what the Judge was hoping she might discover. She said, "Oscar, I couldn't see who was with you that night in the store. Who was it? Can you tell me?"

He squinted and grinned. Then he said, "Now, I ain't gonna tell you."

Clara tried to smile back and said, "All right."

Oscar laughed.

She then asked one of her prepared questions. "Tell me about your mother."

"Ma, well she likes to drink. And when she drinks, well, watch out. She gets really mad at everything. So's if I was in her way—or Tommy or even Pa—she'd wallop us with whatever was handy—a belt, a pot or pan, or a stick. Don't matter what. She threw hot coffee on me one day. That's this scar here." He rolled up his sleeve to reveal red, crinkled skin. He said proudly, "She's quite a gal."

Again, Clara wasn't sure what to say. But she was beginning to realize that she had no idea about Oscar's life. The Judge must have known that. Suddenly she was angry with him for making her realize how stupid she was.

Then she looked at Oscar. He was smiling. He was proud to talk about his family. He was pleased that she was interested in learning about him. He wasn't ashamed or embarrassed.

He said, "Oh, Pa sometimes works in the oil fields when they need cleaning up. Or, he'll help some old lady move stuff around—although sometimes he moves her stuff into *another* barn." He laughed.

"Is that how he earns a living?"

He started to say something, then looked down at his hands. "Mostly. What does your pa do, Clara?"

She said, "He's an engineer in the oil fields. My mother is a teacher at the community college. What about your mother? Does she do any work?"

He looked up and laughed. "No, she's just a piece of worthless drunk—that's what Pa says, anyway."

The deputy interrupted. "Time's up. Maybe you can come back another day. If you want, I'll check to see about reading lessons. Since he's a juvenile, it might be possible."

Clara wasn't sure if he'd been listening to their conversation. She said, "Sure. That'd be nice." But after hearing about Oscar's home life, her heart wasn't in it.

She was surprised at how fast the time had passed. She didn't even have a chance to ask him about life in jail. If she were to return, she'd have to try to get more time with him or be more efficient.

Oscar also stood up. "If you need to know anything else, you jest ask. I liked talkin' to you." He waved to her with a face full of his grin as the deputy led him back through the door to his cell—a place he seemed to prefer over his own home. Clara turned and walked to the opposite door to go home—a place she now longed for over any new experiences that might take her to places she did not want to go. She had not enjoyed learning about Shaggy's life.

Judge Akers had not waited for her. She feared he would be disappointed when she told him she could not get Oscar to tell her who his partner was. She didn't know if she ever wanted to speak with the boy again.

Chapter 07

The Judge had left Clara at the jail and returned to his chambers to check in with Irene, but she had gone home early to pick up her children. She had left him some more information from Jim on the Rodriguez case, as well as a note to let him know that the defendants had hired a new attorney from Los Angeles. In the meantime the Judge knew that the Sheriff continued to interview the defendants' friends and acquaintances. He saw on his calendar that he needed to be in the courtroom the next morning again to give his verdict on the bookies, a fairly straightforward case that shouldn't take long to complete. By 5:30 he was hungry and headed for his favorite café to see Molly and eat his dinner.

The waitress greeted the Judge. "Sit anywhere you'd like. Not too many people here tonight."

"Thanks, Molly." He chose a table out of the way, against a wall with a picture of some people standing in front of the restaurant that he knew to be the owner and his family.

He ordered lemonade and chicken potpie. While Molly was getting his dinner, the Judge wondered whether Clara had had any luck with Oscar Briarley. It was a long shot, at best. But he believed in using whatever means available to solve a problem. And to him, Oscar Briarley's situation was a problem. Although the fourteen-year-old did not pull the trigger, under the law he was just as guilty as the person who had done the deed. And unless he offered information about the real killer, the Judge would have to sentence him to as many years as a murderer—twenty-five to life. But the boy still refused to tell what he knew.

The Judge had been pleased when he heard that Attorney Alberts was representing Oscar. He had known him for years and watched him fight for his clients above and beyond what most lawyers did. Not only that, he didn't seem to do it for the money. Most of his clients were indigent, and he did not give the impression of profiting from their defense given his dilapidated automobile and rundown house. And he was a bachelor, so his money wasn't spent on family. The Judge wondered if Alberts might be working on anything else to help Oscar. He wouldn't like it that a fourteen-year-old with no prior criminal history might be facing such a long sentence.

Oscar certainly wasn't like his brother, Tommy, who had killed a young Mexican man with no remorse. The Judge shook his head remembering Tommy's statement in Court despite his attorney's attempt to stop him from testifying. "That Mexican walked in front of me instead of behind me like a Mexican should do with a white man." Tommy had said. There were other charges, including rape and robbery, that were pending against him, and he probably would spend most of the rest of his life in jail.

But Oscar wasn't like that. Even in court he appeared to be a boy who just didn't know which way to go. He'd laugh when others would laugh. He'd look angry if his attorney appeared angry. And he'd look sad if the person testifying looked sad. He was a boy caught in something he didn't understand.

But that didn't explain why he would not divulge the name of his partner.

About then, Molly came to place his dinner on the table.

"Thank you, Molly."

However, she hesitated before she went back to the kitchen and said, "Judge, could I talk to you before you leave tonight?"

He looked surprised. "Of course you can. Is everything all right?"

"Well, no, but we can talk after you eat."

The Judge was concerned. Molly never seemed to have any problems. She was always cheerful and helpful. She'd been waiting on him for years and had never asked him for anything. But then he realized that he didn't really know much about her personal life. She had never spoken about it, and he was not one to pry.

He ate as quickly as he could, anxious to finish so he could help Molly. He refused her offer of pie for dessert and paid for his meal. She said, "Wait by the door. I'll be there in a minute."

As instructed, he got up and walked to the door. Molly joined him a few minutes later, carrying her purse. She said, "Please, Judge, I really need help. You probably don't know, but my husband is very ill."

The Judge took her hand. "I didn't even know you had a husband. You've never talked about him. How can I help?"

"Please come with me. I'll show you." She led the way down the street and beckoned him to go after her, not talking and shaking her head when he tried to ask her anything. The more they walked in silence the more the Judge was worried. After two blocks, she pulled keys from her purse and headed toward some steps on the side of a building. She started to go up the stairs. "Please, come with me. I wouldn't ask you but I just don't know what else to do."

The Judge followed her up the narrow stairs. When she opened the door, a foul odor confronted him.

"Earl?" Molly called. "Where are you?"

The Judge tried to ignore the stench but quickly forgot about it when Molly turned on a light and he saw a man so emaciated that he could see his veins. He sat on a stuffed chair, drool coming from his mouth, which twitched incessantly, and his arms dangled loosely by the sides of the chair. Molly touched his face gently. "Oh, Earl, you soiled your pants again. I'm so sorry."

The Judge said, "Is this your husband?"

She nodded. "Yes, we've been married for fifteen years and most of that time I've cared for him. He's got some sort of head problems. I don't know what, but the doctors say there's no cure. I'm scared for him now, though. I can't get him to eat, and he doesn't know me at all any more."

The Judge looked at her. "Why did you never ask for help?"

"He's my husband. It's my duty to take care of him."

The Judge looked around. "Do you have a phone?"

"No, sir. Who are you going to call?"

"I'm going to call the hospital. We'll take him there."

"No, Judge. I can't afford a hospital. I'm barely making ends meet as it is."

"Don't worry about that," he told her.

"I don't take charity."

The Judge went to her and put his arm around her. She was trembling, and he could smell the perspiration from her day's labor at the restaurant. "It's just one friend helping another. It's not charity."

She looked up at him and nodded.

He said, "I'll be back as soon as I can."

The Judge helped Molly sit down next to Earl, who didn't move. He was still drooling. What were left of his teeth were yellow. His eyes watered. His stringy hair stuck to his scalp, the only indication that his body was aware of the heat. He just stared straight ahead. Once in a while, he'd move his fingers, which were now in his lap. His fingernails were long and yellow.

Molly just stroked his face and said, "I'm so sorry, Earl. It will all be fine. We'll take care of you." She sat like that, waiting for the Judge, repeating over and over, "I'm here, Earl, I'm here."

In less than ten minutes, the Judge returned. "The ambulance will be here soon, Molly. It won't take them long. I'll wait until they get here, and I'll go with you to the hospital."

She attempted to smile at the Judge and then looked at her husband. She didn't see the debilitated man in front of her. She only saw her husband. "He's been like that for days. He used to talk to me once in a while, and he'd even tell a joke now and then about how he married a good little waitress who waited on him. He'd even talk about when we met. He was so handsome. I was a waitress at a little restaurant, and he came in and said he wanted the best piece of pie in the place. I gave him a piece of our apple pie. He stayed for another hour and pretended to be eating that apple pie, but he just kept watching me. That was the first time I saw him, but he came back every night for two weeks before I agreed to go out with him. I don't know what I would have done if he hadn't kept coming back."

The Judge was at a loss for what to say. He managed, "That sounds nice. You're lucky to have found someone to love and who loved you."

She didn't seem to hear him. "But lately he hasn't said anything. It's been so hard to get him into bed; keep him clean; dress him." She looked at the Judge. "I didn't know who else to turn to. You have always been so kind to me. I thought you'd know what to do."

The Judge held Molly's one hand, while she patted her husband's shoulder with the other. Tears were dropping from her eyes and she made no attempt to stop them.

"You are a great person for taking care of him," the Judge said.

They sat there together, the Judge holding her hand while she cried and patted Earl's shoulder.

When there was a knock at the door, the Judge disengaged himself from Molly and escorted two men to Earl. He cried when they helped him stand. Molly wanted to clean him up but the Judge shook his head. The two men easily picked him up and carried him seated in their clenched arms.

The Judge reassured her. "They'll take care of him at the hospital." So Molly followed and spoke to him—telling him it was all right, she was there. She stroked his face, and then patted his shoulder—always keeping physical contact with him. They carried him down the stairs to a waiting ambulance. Molly accompanied him, always keeping physical contact with him.

The Judge stayed with Molly until Earl was settled at the hospital, and offered to remain longer, but Molly said, "No. I want to sit with him alone." She gave the Judge a kiss on the cheek and walked slowly back toward Earl's room, then turned and said, "Thank you. I didn't know what else to do."

He responded, "It seems too little. Is there someone I can call to come stay with you?"

"No, I'll be all right. Right now I just want to be with Earl."

The Judge watched her as she disappeared into her husband's darkened room. He marveled at her courage and pondered the amount of love she had for her husband—a man who had obviously disappeared within himself.

Chapter 08

A few days later the Judge arrived at his chambers just in time to get to the courtroom, so he didn't get to speak with Irene other than to say, "Good morning." The case of the four Ventura bookies had been postponed until then, and they had decided to plead "guilty." He fined them each $200 and put them on two years' probation. Then he heard a case about a twenty-one-year old woman from San Diego who was arrested for reckless driving. It turned out she had taken a friend's car without permission. The Judge sentenced her to two days in the Ventura County Jail.

He finished by lunchtime and returned to his chambers, planning for Irene and Jim to join him for lunch.

He found Irene busy at her desk and Jim reading. "Hello, you two. That was a quick morning of hearings." He took off his robe and hung it up.

Irene said, "I have some bad news. Molly called from the hospital and asked me to tell you that Earl died. She wanted you to know."

The Judge took a deep breath and shook his head. "I'm not surprised. We need to do something for her. I suspect she needs cash, but she's not going to take it willingly. Any ideas?"

Irene nodded. "I'll arrange for some to be donated from friends 'In sympathy.' I'll have it delivered in a card. That way, it will appear like a gift."

"Thanks, Irene. That's a good idea. She'll accept it as a gesture of sympathy, not of charity."

Irene nodded. "How sad for her. To have been alone with him in that condition for all those years."

The Judge agreed. "Yes. But, you know, she said that she had moments with him when he was coherent. It sounded like she lived for those moments."

Irene and Jim were both aware of how much the Judge missed his wife. Irene decided it was time to change the subject. She said, "Where are we going to lunch?"

Jim said, "I thought we'd just walk down the hill to the café. It's close by."

The trio started the walk to their lunch destination down the marble staircase, across the foyer, out through the doors, by the statue of Father Junípero Serra, and down the hill to Main Street.

The Judge looked back at the courthouse and said, "I really like that building."

Irene nodded. "So you've said, many times." She laughed.

"Well, I like it. So how's the farm coming?"

Jim responded, "There's one thing the war in Europe is good for—it caused an increase in the price and demand for our lima beans."

The Judge frowned. "I'm concerned about this latest escalation. With Hitler invading Poland and Britain preparing for war, well, I'm not sure we can stay out of it, you know."

Jim nodded. "I fear you're correct."

Irene interrupted, "Enough about war. Judge, are you still planning to go to L.A. this weekend?"

"Yes, I am. I'm speaking with those boys at that school Jim researched."

Jim looked puzzled. "How did you get involved in that school, Judge? Did someone invite you to speak there?"

The Judge nodded. "Do you remember Carl Warren?"

Irene jumped in. "I do. He was one of the men you defended years ago who was accused of robbing a bank. As I recall, you managed to get him off on probation by promising to monitor his behavior. His parents had died, right?"

"Yes. He'd been on his own for a year or so and had just turned 18. He got drawn into helping a friend hide some money from a bank robbery, but he himself didn't participate, and he claimed he didn't realize the money was stolen. He thought his friend just needed a place to hide some cash. Anyway, I did get him off with probation and he lived with me for a few months, then found a job, got married, and has been quite successful at a new company he started. And he also has made it part of his life's work to help juveniles. He helped create this new school and he's the one who asked me to speak to the boys."

Jim said, "Good for him. I hope I can do something that noteworthy."

Irene smiled and patted Jim on the arm, applauding his good intentions. Then she turned to the Judge and said, "Are you still going to go to the drive-in movie theater afterward?" Irene asked.

"Yes, I'm really looking forward to it. They're showing *Mr. Smith Goes to Washington* with Jimmy Stewart. I hear it's quite good—criticizes Congress where it should, but ends up hopeful."

Jim asked, "Are you driving yourself?"

"Yes, it should take about four hours. You want to come along and bring the family? I bet a drive-in is the perfect way for children to see a movie. They could just sleep in the car if they don't like it or get bored."

Irene responded quickly. "No, not this time. Maybe when they're showing a movie the children might enjoy. I'm not too sure about the whole drive-in movie idea. How many theaters are there now?" She was sure the judge would know. It was his nature to gather facts and figures about many things.

"Well, there are only two in California, and they are both in Los Angeles. And the last I read, there were fewer than twenty throughout the whole country. They've only been around since the early 1930s."

Jim said, "By the way, Judge, didn't you just get a new car?"

"You bet—a dark blue four-door Chevrolet Master DeLuxe sport sedan. This will be its first long trip."

Jim smiled. He knew that the Judge loved cars. He imagined him dusting it frequently and cleaning its garage regularly.

They arrived at the restaurant and spotted the District Attorney and the Chief of Police. They joined them at a table, interrupting their conversation about the latest events in

Europe and how Hitler was on the march. They also complained about the weather, which continued to be unusually hot for Ventura.

The Chief, however, was pre-occupied with a series of burglaries that remained unsolved. "I just can't figure it out. They're all over Ventura, and I hear from the Sheriff that other towns in the area are seeing them, also."

Jim said, "I know about the one with Oscar Briarley at the five-and-dime store, but that resulted in Mr. Brant's death. What about these others?"

The Chief responded, "The five-and-dime store was different. There were people in the store. Also, the boys that stole the radios from the storeowner—that one was different, also—no skill involved whatsoever. The ones that seem to have a pattern occur at night after stores or businesses are closed. The robbers get in and out very quickly. They take all kinds of goods, like guns, automobile parts, even farm equipment, and where there's a cash register, you can be assured that the money gets taken. And they're not too careful about destroying property while they're making off with the goods. But we've yet to see any of the goods show up anywhere, so they must be selling them off somewhere beyond Ventura County."

"I was aware that there had been a few burglaries, but didn't realize there was a pattern," said Jim. "That indicates that the same people are participating. Any other clues? Do you want me to see what I can find out? I have to admit, I haven't heard anything from my contacts."

"Your snitches, you mean." The Chief laughed. "No, nothing. And they seem to know exactly what to do so that we can't track them down. They're in and out very fast," he repeated. "We got a call that a robbery was in progress at Clarkson's gun store but by the time we arrived, they were gone."

"And it's the same pattern in the other towns?" Jim asked.

The Chief nodded, "Yep. That's what the Sheriff said."

"I'll see what I can find out," said Jim. "By the way, how's your boys' club doing? I heard you had almost twenty attending your Saturday meetings.

The Chief smiled. "Yes, I'm pleased. I believe if we can reach them before they commit a serious crime we can steer them away from a criminal life."

"What kind of things are you doing?"

The Judge smiled. He knew that the Chief loved talking about his boys' club, which he had created just six month ago without much funding and only volunteers to support it. He teased, "They play games."

The Chief nodded. "Well, we do have marbles and an erector set so they can build things, but we also ask them to write down what they did during the week that they're proud of. And we have guest speakers who talk about how they make a living, their vacations, their work, music, or art—because we want to impress on the boys that there's more to life than what they see in Ventura. We even have instructors to teach skills like carpentry."

Jim looked interested. "I wish I'd had a place like that to go to when I was young. If it hadn't been for the Judge, I'm not sure where I'd be today."

"Do you ever have young speakers?" the Judge asked. "Do you remember Clara Wilson? She testified against Oscar Briarley at his trial. Well, she wants to be an author and she won a prize for one of her stories. It might be interesting to see how the boys react to hearing from her. She's quite bright and even visited Oscar in jail."

The Chief looked doubtful. "I don't know how the boys would react to a girl telling them anything. But if you think so, Judge, let me know when and I'll make sure there's time for her."

Irene interrupted with a tone in her voice that suggested the Chief would do well to consider the opportunity. "It would certainly do the boys good in this community to learn that women can do more than wash clothes and have babies!"

The Judge smiled. He knew the Chief had hit a nerve. "If Clara's willing, I think it would be good for the boys to see a smart girl who has ambitions beyond getting married and raising children. I'll ask her and let you know."

The Chief shrugged, decided it was wise to say nothing, and then nodded.

Irene looked at her watch. "Gentlemen, I hate to be the bearer of bad news, but I believe it's time for us all to return to work."

They groaned, got up from the table, and walked back up the hill to the courthouse, except for the Chief who returned to the city jail, which housed his office.

Chapter 09

The Judge had not heard from Clara since she had met with Oscar a week earlier. He decided to follow up on his suggestion that she speak at the boys' club meeting, with the hope that he could also convince her to visit Oscar again.

Her father answered the phone, and when the Judge explained his request, he responded, "Just a moment, Judge. Let me check with her."

The Judge could hear Mr. Wilson as he asked Clara, "It's Judge Akers. He wants to know if you would accompany him to the boys' club meeting tomorrow—the one started by our chief of police. I guess you've been talking to him about your writing. He'd like to present you as someone these boys should respect. Given your age, he thinks you'll make a credible source. Apparently, many of them don't have well-read female examples in their lives."

Before she could respond, he turned back to the phone and said to the Judge in a concerned, serious tone, "I'm not sure, Judge. What kind of boys are these? Are they criminals?"

The Judge responded, "These boys are not criminals. That's why they're attending the meeting. They are boys who may have done some foolish things, like calling in a false fire alarm, and the Chief has them meet to discourage them from doing anything worse. We help them get jobs, for example, in the belief that employment keeps them from getting into mischief. And you can tell Mrs. Wilson that both the Chief and I will be there, so nothing bad can happen to Clara. I think it would be a good experience for her as a writer. And it would help to give the boys an example of a well-read girl."

Her father relayed what the Judge said, and Clara, still uneasy after her meeting with Oscar, nonetheless saw this as a chance to learn more about people she typically would not encounter. As her mother told her repeatedly, it was not befitting for a well-brought up girl to meet and talk with boys.

The practice of the day was that boys associated with boys, and girls associated only with other girls. This meant that Clara seldom had the opportunity to gain the perspective of the male gender, which could impede her development of male characters. If she agreed to speak at the boys' club, she would have the chance to speak directly to them and hear what they had to say. It could definitely help her with her writing by gaining insight into how boys think. She said, "Of course. That sounds great. What time?"

Her father gave her the handset. "Here, why don't you talk directly to the Judge?"

"Hello, Judge Akers. Yes, I'd like to go with you. What time and where should we meet?"

The Judge said, "I'll pick you up at 9:30 in the morning. The boys arrive at 10:00, but I promised the Chief I'd come early to help him set up. I'm sorry about the short notice, by the way. Is that a convenient time for you?"

"Yes, that should be fine. Oh, I need to be at work at two o'clock to make deliveries for the store. Will we be back by then?"

"Yes. We'll be back by lunch."

Chapter 10

The following morning, the Judge knocked on the Wilson's door promptly at 9:30. Clara answered the door and followed him to his car. As he started the engine, he said, "Your parents are interesting, and they are certainly proud of you."

"Yes, most of the time I like them. Once in a while they keep me from doing what I want to do."

The Judge laughed. "Be thankful that they care enough to do that. Would it surprise you to learn that the parents of most of the boys you'll meet today seldom prohibit them from doing anything? Since most of them come from broken homes, where the mother and father live apart, they don't have consistent rules."

"I can't imagine not having both a mother and father, but I guess it's not so unusual. Do you ever see cases where there *are* two parents?" She wanted to test his theory that most of the boys who committed crimes were from broken homes.

"Yes, a few, but most of the juvenile criminals come from broken homes." They arrived at the local service-club meeting hall, which had a room in the back where the boys met. The Judge opened her car door and then the back door where he had piles of papers and boxes of pencils and a stack of books.

She asked, "How come Oscar isn't at the City Jail? Why's he at the County Jail?"

"Oscar's being tried in the Superior Court of Ventura County because of the murder. It's to his benefit to be in the County Jail. It's newer and has more space."

"Oh."

He said, "I decided to take your advice and loan some books to these boys to see if that could influence them."

She picked up several piles of papers to carry into the building, but was more interested in the books the Judge was carrying. She said, "I have a few books I could loan, too. They're all fiction, though."

The Judge nodded. "Good. Let's see if they're interested in these. They're all nonfiction, so I suspect they'd prefer your titles."

They entered the large room, which was organized into several different areas. There were mats in one corner; tables and chairs in another; chairs in a circle; and the fourth corner had a table with toys, including an erector set, log cabin blocks, and bags of marbles. She followed the Judge to the empty tables and placed the papers on it. They were mostly blank. "Are these for the boys to write on?" she asked.

The Judge nodded. "Yes, we ask them to write down what they've done during the past week that made them proud." He put the books on a different table.

The Chief and one of his deputies arrived. The Chief said, "We're going to have a social event here next week, Judge. One of the boys asked if he could have one. He wants to show the place off to his mom and stepdad."

The Judge smiled. "That's great, Chief. You've certainly made this place a success. You remember our young author, Clara Wilson."

The Chief nodded. "Of course. She helped us track down Oscar Briarley."

The Judge said, "Today she's going to talk to the boys about what it's like being a writer."

The Chief nodded and said, "Welcome. And thank you for taking the time."

They continued to get the room ready. A few minutes before 10:00, the boys started to arrive. Several went immediately to the table with the marbles and started a game to see who could win the most. Two others were building something with the erector set. Then more boys arrived. Soon the room was filled with approximately twenty of them—some doing exercises on the mats; others writing their week's "What-I'm-most-proud-of" story; and some sitting down in the chairs that were in a circle.

The Judge went to the group in the circle of chairs and motioned to Clara. She joined them, feeling uncomfortable and out of place. She had recognized a few of them and was sure they would make fun of her in school, so wasn't pleased to be in her current position. But it was too late to back out.

The Judge said, "This is Clara Wilson. Some of you may know her. What you might not know is that she is a writer. She's already won prizes for her writing. She's going to tell you about it, in case you might want to be one, too."

Clara looked concerned. She didn't realize that she would have to do a speech. The Judge noticed that the boys did not appear at all interested. But he still believed that it would be valuable for them to hear what she had to say. They needed to be exposed to a person near their own age who was an achiever.

He said, "Clara, what can you tell us about writing a story?"

She looked at the Judge, her eyes expressing doubt, and said, "Well, I'm not sure what they'd like to know. Maybe someone could ask a question." She seemed momentarily pleased that she had thought of a way out of her predicament—but not for long.

The Judge countered by saying, "Why don't you tell them about the story that won a prize from the Scribbler's Club—about the teenager who ran over the child."

Clara stared at the faces and wished she had said "no" when the Judge asked her to participate. But instead she started to talk, telling about her story of the teenager who drove over and left a child to die.

When she finished less than three minutes later, the Judge looked at the boys and said, "Does anyone have any questions?"

One of them put up his hand and asked, "Yeah. Are you the one who ratted on Oscar Briarley?"

She managed to sputter, "What do you mean?"

Another boy stood up and shook his fist at her. "You're a squealer, huh?"

The Judge stood between the boys and Clara. "Just a minute. Why do you believe that Clara is a 'squealer'? And what does that mean?"

The first boy said, "She told the cops what he done at the store."

The Judge faced him. "And you think it's wrong for her to do that? Let me ask you, do you believe it's right for Oscar Briarley to rob the store and for his partner to shoot and kill Mr. Brant?"

The second boy who'd spoken up said, "Maybe not. But it ain't right for her to rat on him."

"So he should just get away with it?" He looked at the first boy who had accused Clara of "ratting" on Oscar. The teenager sat with his long legs stretched out, leaning back in the chair with his hands locked behind his long, blond hair. The Judge said, "Harry, what if someone stole your bicycle and I knew who it was so that you could get it back. Are you telling me that you believe I should not tell the law on him?"

"No, if you know who it was, you should tell me and I'd beat the hell out of him." Harry sneered and then glanced around and laughed, inviting the others to join him.

"But what if he's twice as big as you and has a gun? Wouldn't you want some help from the law to catch him to get your bicycle back?" The Judge scanned the group. "All right, I think we need to discuss this. Does everyone believe, like Harry, that what Clara did was wrong?"

A short boy in the second row stood up and said in a shaking voice, "No. They killed my dad. That was wrong. I want them to go to jail and rot in hell forever!" The Judge recognized him as one of Mr. Brant's sons. He wondered why the boy was at the meeting.

The Judge held up his hand and asked, "So what about it, boys? Billy here has lost a father because the thieves—against whom Clara testified—killed him. If she doesn't testify, the killer or his partner could go free. Is that the kind of world you want to live in? What will happen if crimes go unpunished because people like Clara refuse to tell what they saw?"

A boy in the far end of the first row said, "Criminals would think they can get away with their crimes and they'd do more and more stealing."

The Judge nodded. "Of course. We need the law and the police to apprehend those who break it so that we can deter or stop crime. That's one part of the law. We want to reduce the temptation of someone to do wrong. The other part though is that we want to increase our determination to do right—and that's what this club is all about."

The Judge looked at Mr. Brant's son and said, "Billy, you know how sorry I am that you lost your father. I hope that you and your family are doing better." He studied the rest of the boys in the circle. "Does anyone else have anything to say about why testifying to punish a wrong-doer is the right thing?"

Clara had remained quiet during the discussion, although she had lowered her head to stare at the floor and tried to make herself as small as possible. But now the Judge turned to her. "Clara, maybe you can tell us why you testified against Mr. Briarley."

Clara expression said that she wished the Judge would pick on someone else. However, she stared at Billy, who was blinking back tears and pointed to him. In a quiet, shaky voice she said, "I saw his father get shot and killed for no reason other than he was trying to stop two men from robbing a store. It was wrong. We don't often have a chance to make things right, and we can't bring Mr. Brant back." Some of the boys sniggered, which caused Clara to become angry. She stood up, faced the group, and, face flushed, hands moving, continued in a much firmer and louder voice. "But we can do our best to see that it doesn't happen to someone else. I know that Oscar Briarley didn't kill him, but he was part of the robbery, and he knows who did. That person must be locked up, because if he killed someone once, he might do it again. And I couldn't sleep nights if I found out he did it again because I hadn't told what I know."

She looked at the Judge, who was watching the boys closely.

He appeared satisfied. "Are there any other questions about why it's important to speak up in our current justice system? Harry?"

Harry shrugged. He didn't look convinced, but he also didn't look like he really cared. He had managed to disrupt the meeting, which seemed to satisfy him. He said nothing.

The Judge turned back to Clara and said, "Why don't we get back to talking about writing. Harry, do you have any questions about that?"

Harry smirked. "Sure. How do you know what that teenager was going through? What gives you the right to decide what he's thinking?"

The Judge turned to her and asked, "Well, Clara, can you tell us how you figured out how he felt?"

Clara, whose confidence had partially returned, now looked less sure of herself again. Nonetheless, she responded firmly, "Yes, maybe. To write this story, I tried to put myself in his place. If I had run over someone and driven away and then been caught, I would have been mortified. I don't know if I would have stopped, either. I'm not sure if I could have continued to do my regular things, like go to school and even read. I don't know if that was how he felt, but it would be how I would feel."

Another boy called out, "So you don't write the truth?"

Clara appeared confused, but answered, "I write fiction, which is different from the truth. It's a story to help readers understand the truth, or to understand life."

Harry said, "So you write lies and pretend they're the truth."

Clara stuttered. "No, er, I'm not a reporter who reports news. I'm a writer of fiction, er—"

The Judge interrupted. "Fiction is not lies. Lying is telling something you know that's not true, usually for some kind of gain. Fiction is telling a story either to entertain us or to help us see things more clearly. You've all heard fairy tales or seen movies. They're not lies; they're stories. What Clara was trying to show in her story is that there's more to an event than what you read in the newspaper. And she *imagined* what that would be."

He looked around the group. "Do any of you have the desire to make your viewpoint understood by others? Is there something you want people to understand about you? If so, you might want to think about writing."

The boys started to talk to each other. The Judge wasn't sure if they were talking about writing or if they were figuring out what they would do after the meeting. He looked at Clara and hoped he hadn't scared her away for good. He wanted them to challenge her and question her fundamental beliefs so that she could expand her approach in her writing but also so that she would be more inclined to continue to interrogate Oscar. However, the boys might have challenged her too much. Instead of persuading her to proceed, they might have dissuaded her and shut down her investigative nature.

One of the boys in the back put up his hand. The Judge said, "Boys, be quiet. We have a question. What is it, son?"

"What's a good book for me to read, if I want to be a writer?"

The Judge smiled, relieved. He hoped that would reassure her. "Clara, what would you recommend?"

She stared at the boy and then smiled. "Well, what kind of stories do you like—mystery or adventure or romance—"

Several of the boys giggled at the mention of romance. But the boy who had asked for a recommendation said, "I like adventure stories that are fantasy. I want to go to a different world than this one."

"Then I recommend Mr. Tolkien's *The Hobbit*. It's quite an adventure, and I'd be pleased to loan it to you."

The Judge nodded.

Chapter 11

The following Monday, the Judge knew his plan had worked when Clara walked into his chambers in the late afternoon. He was sitting at his desk, reading some papers. He welcomed her, but cautioned, "I only have a few minutes. I need to meet someone by 5:00 and have some work to finish before then. How can I help you?"

"I would like to give reading lessons to Oscar Briarley and was wondering if you could help arrange it. The deputy at the jail said he would, but I haven't heard from him."

"That's a good idea. It will help you to gain his trust. I'll check into it and let you know. Do you think there's still a chance that you could get him to identity his partner?"

Clara looked uneasy, but said, "I think so. Do you know how long he'll be in jail here?"

"I can't discuss the case, Clara. You know that. But I need to make a decision in a few weeks so you have at least that much time. It might help me to make a decision to know who actually pulled the trigger. So you're on a bit of a timetable to get him to talk."

Clara started to get up, but then said, "You know my mother's a teacher and she can help me to teach Oscar."

The Judge nodded. "That's good. I just hope you're not disappointed. Not everyone understands how important reading is. I'm sure your parents will warn you, also. Just be ready for that." He hesitated for a second as if thinking and then said, "Why do you want to help this boy? He participated in the death of Mr. Brant—even if he didn't actually shoot the gun."

"Well, sir, first, I don't believe he is truly a criminal. I believe he's just never known anything else. He's never had a chance. Besides, what could it hurt? I'll be inside a locked room with a deputy. If I fail, it's just a failure that no one will care about."

"What about you? Won't you care?"

"Of course. But at least I'll have tried to do something that makes a difference, which my parents are always telling me I should consider. Besides those boys at the club really made me think. I need to follow through on what I believe, which is that reading is important and can make a difference."

"All right. Please check with your parents. They should know that you're continuing to meet with him. Actually, I'll ask Irene to phone them. And I'll also have her see about arranging for you to visit him with the idea of teaching him to read. You'll probably know after the first lesson if it's worth continuing. We need to move quickly, as I said."

The next morning, Irene contacted the Sheriff's office first thing and was rewarded with a quick "yes" to her inquiry about whether Clara could give reading lessons to Oscar. The Sheriff himself told her, "I doubt much will come of it, but she still might get him to tell us about his partner. She can come any time in the afternoon before 5:00. Ask for Deputy Brown."

Irene called the Wilson house. She first talked with Mrs. Wilson, who agreed to the lessons, and then spoke to Clara. She asked, "How about tomorrow after school?"

When Clara agreed, Irene gave her the Sheriff's instructions and then asked, "How often do you want to come?"

"At first, if possible, I'd like to come every day after school for just an hour. We'll take off weekends. He shouldn't have to go to school on weekends."

Irene laughed. "All right. That sounds good. Let us know if he tells you anything about his partner."

The next day Clara managed to find the jail without bothering the Judge, and Deputy Brown took her into the same room where she had last spoken with Oscar. Again, she left her bag outside and took only the primer her mother had provided into the room. Oscar smiled broadly when he saw her. He continued to look physically well—he seemed to have filled out and his hair was clean. He still appeared more like a boy than a man. His voice hadn't changed yet, and his face was round and soft. But most important to her was that he sat down immediately and said eagerly, "You come to learn me to read, Clara."

She nodded and handed him the primer and asked him to read the first word. He put his finger on the first word, but failed to say it. "What's the first letter?" she asked.

"B," he responded.

"What sound is a 'B'?"

He sounded a "BA." Then they went to the second letter, which was an "A." She asked him about that letter, until he finally had all the letters of the word "baby" and was able to sound out the word. They continued with each word in the same manner. He was eager and never slowed down trying out each new sound to have it combine with other sounds to create a word.

The hour passed quickly, and Clara was pleased with his progress. They stuck to the lesson most of the time. He did interrupt once by asking, "What's happening at school? I wish I could go to school. Pa thought it was a waste of time. I liked seein' everybody. Most of them didn't want to talk to me, though. Pa said it was cuz I was strange-like."

Clara shook her head. "You're not strange, and going to school is not a waste of time. Learning to read will help you learn other things and will give you a chance to have a better life than your pa and see a whole different way to live."

"Well, I'm not sure I'll ever have a chance to live outside of jail, but that's better than livin' with Ma and Pa. It was hard gettin' food and even water sometimes. Here it's all free and I get it every day. And with me here, why, Pa only has three mouths to feed instead of four."

Clara didn't respond. She had always relied on her parents for meals, and they had never struggled as far as she knew. And she believed in the value of reading. "But even if you're behind bars, you can go to all kind of worlds with books."

That seemed to appeal to him. He returned to the primer eagerly. It gave him purpose.

Chapter 12

Early the following Saturday morning, the Judge started the drive to Los Angeles. The narrow road from Ventura to L.A. curved through the mountains over multiple hills and bumpy pavement. The Judge didn't mind. He was looking forward to taking his new car for a longer distance that just around town.

During the drive, he reflected on that week's events. It had been a week since Clara had spoken to the boys at the Chief's meeting. She had started to give reading lessons to Oscar the following Tuesday and gone to the jail every day through Friday, but so far, Oscar had not divulged his partner's name to her. Irene guessed it would take a while, but the Judge was concerned that they wouldn't learn it in time to factor into Oscar's sentencing.

The Judge smiled when he thought of Irene and Jim and their children. They had become good friends. He wondered about how Jim was doing with helping the Chief out with the burglaries. He had been checking with his various sources to see what he could discover. Most of the Chief's deputies were not detectives, and Jim had become quite adept at research. But Jim, too, had not been successful at learning anything about the robberies, although he was following up on a lead this weekend, which he wanted to discuss with the Judge on Monday. He was convinced that there was an organized group involved given the widespread nature of the crimes. It seemed unlikely that one person—or even two—could manage the number of robberies and the distribution of the stolen goods without some kind of connections.

The Judge shifted his focus to his goal of traveling to L.A. He planned to meet his friend, Carl Warren, at his L.A. school for boys and spend the afternoon talking with the inmates. His friend had arranged a room where he could speak to a group of almost thirty youths. He encouraged the Judge to tell his story of how he managed to overcome a difficult time as a teenager to become a lawyer and then a judge. The Judge had also asked to speak separately to two boys he had sentenced there from Ventura.

The drive proved fun but uneventful and he arrived at the school on time. Carl met him and led him into the room where he was to deliver his talk. He had arranged for a sandwich for the Judge. He asked, "How was the drive in the new car?"

The Judge finished his bite and said, "It's a great car, Carl. I'm really liking it. How's your wife? You said she wasn't feeling well."

"I think it's just a cold, but she's staying home just in case. She got through that bout of pneumonia, and we just don't want to take any chances. By the way, who are these two boys you want to talk to? Do I know them?"

"Last name of one of them is Chissum; the other is Jones. Sound familiar?"

Carl shook his head.

"Well, I sentenced them for assault a few months ago, but I always believed they might make it."

"Do you want me to keep an eye on them?"

"Yes, if you can. I was pleased that they agreed to see me. I'll let you know what they say."

Carl looked at the clock and said, "It's time to get started." A buzzer sounded and a group of thirty teenagers between the ages of thirteen and sixteen entered the room talking with one another. They didn't look at the Judge or his friend sitting at the front of the room, and continued talking even after being seated—until two deputies started to walk toward them. Then they stopped talking and looked to the front of the room. The deputies stood on either side of the room. Carl sat down next to the Judge and introduced him.

When speaking to incarcerated youth, the Judge typically focused on their ability to make choices, even when in jail. He repeated, "It might not be easy, but you are in charge of making choices." When he didn't get much of a response he asked, "Who here believes he controls what happens in his own life?"

At first no one said anything. Then one boy raised his hand and said, "I sure don't."

The rest of the boys laughed, as did the Judge, but then he asked, "Why not?"

"Look around. This is *jail*. Them officers controls my life."

"I see. And what do you do while you're here?"

"Ye'r crazy. I cain't do but what they sez I do. I go to the classes they sez, and I do the chores they sez."

"You're at a school where you can learn, can you not? Do you read any books?"

"What?"

"Can you read?"

"Of course, I ken read. You think I'm stupid?"

"No, but I believe that even in here you could help yourself by reading. Maybe even learn a way to make a living, like a trade. That's a choice you get to make—even here."

The Judge wasn't sure if he had made an impression, but he was there to try. However, as the boys left the room he heard one of them say, "Oh, you got choices—sure you do. Like mebbe you can choose which foot to put first as they shoves us around." Loud laughter followed.

Carl patted him on the back and said, "You never know. You might have gotten through to one of them. I know you did with me. One of the boys here is learning to be an automobile mechanic. I've brought him several books and have lined up an apprenticeship at a local auto shop. We won't know for a few months whether you reached anyone else. They have to act tough in front of each other."

The Judge nodded. He was eager to speak with Eddie Jones and Hiram Chissum, the two boys from Ventura he had sentenced for beating up the theater usher. He had sentenced them to one year at this school and wanted to follow up to see how they were doing. He had insisted that they tell him why beating someone up was not a solution. The usher had told them they couldn't sit in certain seats because he was saving them for his friends. He said if they didn't move, he would move them. They decided they didn't want to move, especially since there were no other good seats left. Instead, when he tried to remove them, they beat him up. They managed to bruise the usher's ribs and almost broke his arm. The Judge challenged them to think of alternative ways to have handled the situation. When they laughed at him, he sentenced them to a year in a reformatory school, and, because the Preston and Whittier schools were full, they had ended up here.

During his presentation to the group, the Judge noticed that they chose to sit together in the back of the room, and they said nothing. He was surprised, because Carl had told him that they appeared eager to speak with him, yet they seemed distant when he arrived, and non-participatory.

Carl said, "I'll leave you to talk with your two friends." They were sitting at a table in the back of the room waiting for the Judge.

The Judge said to Carl, "I hope it's all right for me to come to your home after the movie tonight? Are you sure you and your wife won't join me?"

"No, I'd better stay home with her just in case she needs something. You go and enjoy."

"Thanks. After I speak with the boys, I'm going to do some shopping, and then I'll head over to the movie. I'm really looking forward to it and the experience of the drive-in theater."

He sat down at the table with the two Ventura boys. He wasn't sure how they'd greet him and was pleased when they smiled, nodded, and held out their hands for a handshake.

Eddie Jones, the older one at sixteen, said, "Thank you for seeing us, your Honor."

Hiram Chissum, at fifteen, echoed, "Yes, sir. It's swell of you."

After shaking each of their hands—the Judge wondered if his friend Carl had instructed them to do so—the Judge sat down. "How are you boys doing?"

Again Eddie took the lead. "We're doing all right, sir. You are so right about learning something here. We go to classes, and we both read and work hard to learn. And we learned the tough way about beating people up and how that doesn't solve much, does it, sir?"

The Judge sighed, recalling his own history as a teenager who tried to solve many of his problems with fisticuffs. He said, "Not usually."

Hiram pushed Eddie's arm. "Ask him, Eddie. Hurry, before we have to go."

The Judge realized then that the boys had something on their minds. He said, "How can I help you? Is there a problem?"

Eddie looked at Hiram. He acted like his protective older brother. Both boys were hefty, so it didn't occur to the Judge that they were being bullied at the school. He waited patiently for the older boy to speak. Finally he said, "Judge, it's about Hiram's younger brother. He's thirteen, sir."

Hiram interrupted. "He's a good boy. Not like me. He gets good grades in school. He's never been in any trouble until now."

The Judge said, "What kind of trouble is he in? I haven't heard of anyone with the last name of Chissum mentioned by the Chief."

Hiram looked at Eddie. "You explain, Eddie."

The older boy nodded. "Sir, Hiram's brother—his name is Eugene—well, we think he's gotten in with a bad group. Hiram's ma was here a couple weeks ago and she said that Eugene had met this older boy and his father who invited him to a party. When he came back, Hiram's ma said he was shaking, but wouldn't tell her anything. He just grabbed our dog Spike and went to bed. Then a few days later, she found he'd snuck out of bed at night. She doesn't know what time he left but he got back just when the sun was coming up."

The Judge was both concerned and curious. "What else can you tell me?" he asked.

Hiram said, "My ma said when she asked Eugene about it, he started to cry and then he screamed that she mustn't tell anyone, that they'll kill our dog and her and him if he does."

The Judge said, "But—"

Hiram looked at the Judge. "You can't tell the Chief. Somehow you gotta help Eugene without getting the Chief involved."

The Judge put his hand on Hiram. "Son, I can't promise that. What I will promise is that we'll do everything we can to make sure no one sees the Chief or his men getting involved. But if Eugene's and your mother's lives are being threatened, and if Eugene is being extorted to do something he doesn't want to do, we need to involve the Chief. He's reasonable. He'll move to do anything with care."

Hiram slammed his fist on the table. "You can't let the Chief know. You can't. See, Eddie? I said it was a mistake to tell the Judge."

Eddie looked with pleading eyes at the Judge. "Sir, you've got to make sure the Chief doesn't talk to Eugene or his mother. We don't know who these people are, and we don't know how many there are. We only know what we hear in here, and it sounds like there's someone rounding up boys to steal things."

The Judge's mind was working fast. Could there be a connection between this boy and the Chief's thefts?

"Do you hear anything about who these people are? Are they adults? Other teenagers?"

Eddie looked at Hiram. "I gotta tell him what I know. I trust him to do what's right, Hiram." He turned to the Judge. "We think it's parents of some of the other boys, but we don't know any names. There are rumors here. But none of them says any names."

The Judge sensed that what Eddie and Hiram just told him was significant, and that the Chief would want to act on it as soon as he heard the information. But looking into the boys' pleading eyes, the Judge knew it could be disastrous to go blundering into the situation without some finesse. These boys were frightened, and given their experiences, they probably had reason.

He said, "I might have an idea. A friend of mine does investigations for me and for the Chief, but he's not a deputy. I'll ask the Chief to send him to speak with your mother,

Hiram, and he'll be careful when and how he does it. Then he can go back to the Chief, and between them they can work out a plan to catch whoever is responsible. Does that sound all right?"

Eddie looked relieved, but Hiram still wasn't sure. His mother and brother were those involved. He said, "Promise me that you'll do whatever you can to protect them. Promise."

"I promise," the Judge said, with every intention of keeping his word.

An officer entered the room and said, "I'm afraid we'll have to end this now. They need to get ready for dinner."

"Of course," the Judge said. "I'll keep in touch with you boys as best I can. My friend, Carl Warren—he's the one who was here today with me—will contact you if I can't. In the meantime, please try to learn as much as you can in here so that you'll be qualified for some kind of work when you leave. There are jobs popping up all over, and if you have the right skills you'll find one."

They stood up, and again Eddie offered his hand to the Judge. "Thank you, sir. You'll never know how much we appreciate what you're doing. We just didn't know who else to turn to, and you set us straight once so I figured you would help us again."

"Of course," the Judge said.

The Judge watched the guard lead the two away. He wanted to call Jim immediately, but they didn't have a phone at the farm, a situation that the Judge had badgered them frequently to change. His information would have to keep until Monday when he returned. He would consult with Jim first before filling in the Chief. He knew it was best to approach the Chief with a plan so that he could make a decision, rather than give him an open-ended situation, which could invite him to visit Hiram's mother and brother immediately without considering the consequences.

Meanwhile, he looked forward to a relaxing evening seeing a movie at the drive-in theater. After doing some shopping, he arrived while it was still light. He lined up behind other cars to pay to get in. Once he drove into what appeared to be a large parking lot, he saw rows and rows of parking places, each spot with its own steel pole holding a detachable speaker. He quickly deduced that he should park facing a huge elevated screen at one end of the area. The concept of the drive-in theater was you got to sit in the privacy of your own car, eat popcorn or whatever, and talk without bothering anyone. Why, some families even took their children dressed in their nightclothes.

It wasn't quite dark enough to start showing the movie when the Judge pulled into a spot next to the speaker resting on its pole. He succeeded in finding a parking place that was slightly elevated so he would see the movie without a car in front of him blocking the view. Carl, a regular drive-in attendee, had advised him to do so. His spot was also near the concession stand—which was where the projection cameras were—and he could smell the cooking popcorn.

He looked around and saw how others were hanging the speaker on their half-opened window, and he did the same. He noticed the radio-like dial on the speaker that regulated the volume. Then he sat waiting for the movie to begin. It was still light enough to check out the different makes of the surrounding cars, a favorite past time of his.

Since the movie would not start until it was dark, the Judge decided to go to the concession area to get some popcorn. He hadn't been to a lot of movies but he always associated popcorn with them; a movie and popcorn went together, whether at a drive-in theater or a regular one.

Just as he approached the door of the concession area, he noticed several boys who turned away from entering when they saw him. One of them, a lanky, familiar-looking youth wearing a hat over his blond hair, and dressed in a long, untucked shirt over dark slacks, deliberately hid his face. The Judge was curious, because he was not acquainted with many people in Los Angeles, and started to greet the boy, but his nose caught the alluring smell of popcorn popping, so he continued inside and made his purchase.

Walking back to the car, the Judge was thinking how much he'd been looking forward to this film ever since he first heard about it. The drive-in theater was a new experience, and he welcomed it on top of seeing the movie itself. When it finally became dark enough to show the film, the projectionist started the newsreel and they were treated to that night's version of Hitler's actions in Europe and what Britain and France were doing to stop him.

The feature movie, *Mr. Smith Goes to Washington*, which the Judge found inspiring, was almost over when he heard someone shouting. At first, he thought it was part of the movie. But if it was, the talking was definitely not synchronized with Jimmy Stewart's speech as he chastised Congress for its lack of caring about the people.

The Judge heard someone shouting, "Stop him. He's robbed us!" He jumped out of the car and headed for the commotion and walked rapidly toward the concession stand, where most of the noise originated. Just as he got close to the entrance, someone ran out the door, knocking him over. A young man in a theater uniform followed and slowed when he saw the Judge on the ground, but the Judge motioned to him to continue.

The encounter with the Judge slowed the pace of the runner enough for his pursuer to close the space between them, but the runner started to weave in and out of the cars, causing people to blare their horns when he obstructed their view of the movie, which continued to run uninterrupted. He apparently realized that he would be trapped at the end of a row hemmed in by a tall fence, so he turned and headed back toward the concession stand. His pursuer took a shortcut through the cars and managed to get close enough so that he could tackle him.

The runner, however, still had some fight left. Screaming "Let go!" loudly, he pulled loose and headed to where the Judge was now standing, perhaps assuming he could knock his way through him again. The Judge tried to obstruct his path, but the boy again yelled, saying, "Get out of my way." He pushed the Judge and continued to run. This time, the Judge grabbed a nearby pole and was able to remain standing. The uniformed man chasing the culprit ran past the Judge and tried to catch up, but the boy had managed to increase the distance between himself and his pursuer, who was now breathing heavily.

The thief ran through the cars and out the exit. The theater attendant gave up and returned to the concession area. He went over to the Judge, panting and bending over with his arms on his knees, and said, "Are you all right?"

The Judge responded, "Yes, I'm fine. Listen, I know that boy. I'm a Superior Court judge from Ventura, and that boy is from Ventura."

The man was still breathing heavily from running. He asked, "Are you sure? We called the police. They should be here soon. I sure wish I could have caught him. I work here. He got a bunch of cash from the register—like almost fifty dollars. It's the third time this month we've been robbed." He tried to catch his breath. "If you know his name, that would really help. You can tell the police when they get here."

The Judge said, "Has it always been the same boy who robs you?"

"I'm not sure. I wasn't here the other two times. But I'll check with my co-workers to see if the description matches. Or the police can check with them." A second young man in a uniform similar to the panting pursuer walked over. "I called the police and the manger. They're both on their way."

The Judge nodded. "It's curious that the boy would come here for a robbery. It isn't easy to get from Ventura to here. Why come all this way?"

"Well, it's not too hard if you really want to do it and have the time. I have a friend who hitchhikes back and forth all the time. And maybe the thief figured no one would know him here, so it would be easier to get away with robbing us."

"Could be. Did you see if he was with someone?"

The panting worker said, "No, I just saw him with his hand in the cash register. I started to chase him."

The Judge was scanning the area. The movie had ended, people were starting to leave, and cars were lining up at the exit. "There wasn't anyone else nearby?"

The young man shook his head. "I don't think so."

The Judge murmured, "It seems unlikely he could get here on his own. Someone must have dropped him off." He turned back to the two theater attendants and said, "Neither of you noticed him coming from any of these cars?"

They both shook their heads.

A police car managed to get into the area against the outgoing traffic and drove up to the concession area. Two uniformed officers got out and walked to the group.

The young man who had chased the robber met the officers. "I'm afraid he got away. I chased him but he ran too fast."

The officer asked, "Was he on foot or did he get into a car?"

"He ran out, although he may have had a car on the other side of the gate. Or, we'll see if there are any left after everyone is gone, although that's not likely. He probably would have taken it."

"Which way did he go? We didn't see anyone on the way in here."

"He went out the way you came in. Maybe someone picked him up. It doesn't matter. This man—he's a judge from Ventura—he says he knows him."

The officer didn't seem impressed that he was talking to a judge. Maybe it was the Ventura part he didn't respect. "Yeah? How do you know him?"

"He attends a boys' club that I mentor. His name is Harry Winter. He lives in Ventura. You can call the Chief of Police there and he'll contact his parents and watch for him. He's only sixteen years old. Oh, he lives with his stepfather, and I'm not sure of the man's last name, but it's different than Harry's. The Chief will know. Just tell the Chief that Judge Akers said to look for him."

"All right. Let's hope he goes home. Do we know how he got here?"

"No."

The young man who had chased Harry said with great importance, "And I'm sure there was no one else near the cash register when I saw the boy and chased him. He was alone."

The officer turned to the Judge and asked, "Can you describe him?"

"Certainly. He's about five feet nine inches tall and I'd say he weighs maybe 150 or thereabouts. His hair is kind of sandy blond, and he was wearing dark brown slacks and a long shirt. Please be careful with him. He's still in school; he's only a boy."

The policeman glared at the Judge and mimicked a girl-like tone, "Yes, I know he's a poor, misguided child who needs love." He lowered his voice, "Believe me, we run into them all the time."

The Judge's face remained passive. "He doesn't have a criminal history. Remember that he is a juvenile and you need to treat him as such."

The policeman said, "He's sixteen. And that's plenty old enough to know better."

His partner stepped between him and the Judge, and he turned away. The partner looked at the Judge and said, "Thanks for your help. We'll get in touch with the Chief. I know him. And any additional assistance you could provide we'd appreciate."

The Judge said, "I did see several boys at the door of the concession area when I was entering. One of them could have been Harry, which would mean that there was more than just him involved."

"Can you describe them?"

"One was tall, maybe six feet, and was wearing some kind of uniform shirt like maybe he'd wear at work, but I didn't recognize the emblem." He shook his head. "I think it was some kind of chair, if that makes sense. And the other one was more Harry's size. They definitely changed their direction when they saw me. And the one I think was Harry hid his face from me. I didn't see his face until later when he ran into me."

The policeman grunted. "Well, we've got the one boy's name, so we'll go get him. Then he can tell us who the others are. Judge, can I get hold of you through the Chief in Ventura?"

The Judge nodded and watched the police car retreat with its large light beaming on the road and empty space around the theater. He went back to his car wishing that the day had turned out more positive. He had even missed the end of the movie.

Chapter 13

That Monday, the Judge met with Jim in his chambers. He explained what he had learned from Eddie and Hiram, the two Ventura teenagers he'd spoken to in L.A. following his presentation at the school for boys. He asked Jim what he deduced from the information about a possible group of hoodlums who might have threatened Hiram's younger brother into committing crimes. He also asked him what he recommended as a next step, given the need to involve the Chief without anyone knowing he was taking part.

Jim pondered. "Well, first, although we need to give the Chief a plan, we can't keep this information from him for too long. It's too pertinent to the crimes he's trying to solve. What I'd recommend is that I visit Hiram's mother—that would be Mrs. Chissum?" he asked. "The father is long gone, right?"

"Yes, Mrs. Chissum takes care of the family on her own, although she only has her son Eugene right now while Hiram is at the school. I forget where she works. That might be a place to begin. How long do you think we can keep it from the Chief before he feels betrayed and does something?"

"I'd tell him right now. Why don't I go visit him with the suggestion that we use me to follow up with Mrs. Chissum? After I talk with her, we can ask her to find out from Eugene when he's going on another junket at night, and we can hide a deputy or me near her place and follow the boy who will, we hope, lead us to the ringleader."

The Judge nodded. "That sounds like it would work. Just impress on him the situation—that the boys are terrified the mother and younger son will be harmed if the perpetrators believe they have talked to the Chief."

"I understand. I think if we propose a plan as a way to catch the ringleader or the rest of the group that he will agree to it." Jim stopped talking. He looked at the ceiling and then at the Judge. "You know, this could be a link to the other burglaries. It could be part of a group of thieves. You may have accidentally encountered the link we've been searching for."

That same afternoon, the Judge had just returned to his chambers from the courtroom when Clara walked up to Irene's desk and asked to see him. Irene stood and stuck her head in his inner office. "Do you have time to talk with Clara? Your schedule is open because you finished early, but I didn't know if you had anything else you needed to do."

The Judge finished hanging up his robe and said, "Well, do I have anything else on my calendar?" He smiled when she shook her head, and then said, "I can see her. Is there something wrong?"

Clara overheard him and said, "Oh, no, sir. Oscar had to finish some kind of chore before our lesson, so I thought it would be a good time to catch up. I was just stopping by to let you know that Oscar is really interested in learning to read. He's doing quite well."

"Good for you, Clara. Glad to hear it. Has he told you anything about his partner yet?"

Clara shook her head. "No, sir. Not yet, but I'm hoping he will. He seems to like me."

"Well, I hope you can get him to tell, but if not, at least he'll have learned to read."

"Yes, sir. I was just wondering, and you don't have to tell me if you don't want to, but at school some of my friends were talking about Harry Winter and how you tried to stop him at the drive-in theater in L.A. And he wasn't at school today. I don't mean to pry and if it's a secret, never mind, but if you want me to help find him, maybe I could. Some of my friends think that this wasn't his first robbery."

"What do you mean? He's stolen before?"

"Yes, and apparently he has some friends that do, too. They smoke cigarettes, too, and drink beer." She looked embarrassed. "I inquired about him after he asked me all those questions at the boys' club."

The Judge pondered her statement. Recalling that Jim suspected a gang might be responsible for the robberies, combined with what he had just learned from Eddie and Hiram, all added to their theory that Harry could be part of a gang, or know some gang members. "Thank you for telling me, but I'd really prefer that you focus on Oscar and getting him to tell you about his robbery. Did he know Harry?"

"I don't know, but I can ask him."

"That would be useful. But, please, don't say anything else at school about any of this, all right?"

"Sure. Everyone knows the Chief is looking for him. The principal called us together at an assembly and told everyone to watch for him, that he's a criminal."

"That's unfortunate," the Judge said. "I wish he hadn't done that. We still have a judicial system that assumes innocence until a suspect is proven guilty."

The ringing telephone interrupted their conversation. Irene answered. "Oh, hello, Deputy. Yes, she's here. All right, I'll tell her."

Irene hung up and said to Clara, "That was the deputy from the jail. He said to tell you that Oscar can't make it to his lesson today."

Clara was alarmed and asked, "Nothing's happened to him, has it?"

She smiled. "No, he's fine. Apparently he was helping to plant a garden outside the jail, and he wanted to finish. He told the deputy that you'd understand."

Clara smiled. One of the first stories they read was about a boy who couldn't go out and play until he finished planting a garden. Oscar must have taken that lesson seriously.

She looked at Irene and then at the Judge, very pleased with herself. "I do understand. That's so exciting. I believe that Oscar's wanting to finish his chore is directly related to what we read in one of the books—and it was just a primer. Imagine what might happen when he reads more complex stories!"

The Judge looked puzzled, then said, "So you think that reading the book influenced his behavior?"

"Yes! Isn't that amazing? I was right. Reading *does* make a difference."

The Judge actually chuckled. "I believe you may be right, Clara Bow Wilson!" When he saw that she was confused by his laughter, he said, "Good for you! I'm really proud of you. It's a small success that you earned through your perseverance."

Clara was beaming. The Judge was proud of her.

Chapter 14

The next afternoon Clara went to see Oscar with a definite goal. The Judge had implied that if the teenager were to tell who his partner was, then maybe that would help reduce his time in jail. Clara was determined to get him to tell who had killed Mr. Brant so that she could write a happy ending to the story she envisioned.

She arrived at the jail, greeted the deputy, and placed her bag where indicated. She had a new book for Oscar, who was waiting for her at the table. He looked up and smiled when she entered.

"Hi, Clara. You brung me a new book?"

"Yes, Oscar. I 'brought' you a new book. The word is 'brought,' not 'brung.'"

"Oh. You brought me a new book?"

He appeared ready to read and learn. His eyes were different than when she had seen him at the trial. Then they were blank, darting from place to place in confusion. Now they wanted to say something, concentrating interest and enthusiasm.

Clara was pleased. "Oh, and tell me about the garden you were planting. I missed you at our last lesson."

"Right. I told everybody I'd finish it. And that boy in the book said he should do what he said. So I finished it. That's good, ain't it?"

"Yes, that's good, but what did I tell you about 'ain't'?"

"Oh, yeah. That's good, isn't it?" He looked at the book in her hand. "Can we start now?"

"Sure." She put the book on the table and opened it so they could both see it. He read the title and then eagerly turned the pages, using his finger to follow along. Clara helped him sound out various words. He wanted to finish it, and became impatient when she slowed him down. "You need to learn the new words so you can read more books," she said.

He complied and slowed down and practiced. Then right in the middle of the reading, he said, "Pa came by yesterday."

Clara wasn't sure if that was a good thing. "Oh. Were you glad to see him?"

"Well, he's my pa and all. But he said I should stop this book-learning. That it would just make me unhappy."

Clara was upset that his father tried to influence him in such a way. How could he? "You don't agree with him, do you?"

"He's my pa. But he said he heard Tommy is really sad on account of he's been doing book-learning."

Clara was perplexed. "Why would learning to read make your brother sad? Did he go visit your brother, too?"

Oscar shook his head. "Dunno. Book-learning makes me feel good. I like it."

She smiled. "Me, too." But she was still upset that his father had visited him and told him to stop learning to read. What if he came back and continued to tell Oscar that "book-learning" was bad for him? That was against everything she believed.

She asked, "Is he planning to visit you again?"

Oscar laughed. "Naw. He just wanted to be sure that I—" He stopped, wagged a finger, and said, "Oh, no, you don't."

"Why did he come to see you, Oscar?"

"He just wanted to see how I'm doing." He smiled and nodded. "Yes, that's all. He just wanted to make sure I got what I need."

But Clara sensed he wasn't telling her everything about his father's visit. Although he didn't know a lot, she had figured out that he was smart. Before dealing with Oscar, she always thought educated meant smart. She didn't understand that people could be smart but not educated. Or that they could be educated but not smart.

But Oscar refused to say anything more about his father, although he seemed to want to talk about something else. He would start to look at the book and then stop and look around. Normally once he started to read, he would focus on it.

"Oscar, is there something else you want to talk about?" Clara asked.

He bit his lip and nodded, but said nothing.

"You can tell me. Did your father say something else that upset you?"

"No, not Pa."

Clara waited patiently. "Did something happen here at your cell?"

He licked his lips and said, "I jest don't get it. I'm afraid mebbe it will happen to me."

"What will happen to you, Oscar?"

"They said one of the growed-up men, he was helping to wash floors, and he went crazy. Started yellin' and then he ran and throwed hisself out the window and it was high up and he killed hisself—squished, like a bug, they said. That won't happen to me, will it?"

Clara didn't know what to say. She looked over at the deputy and he nodded, so she assumed the event had really occurred. She asked him, "What happened?"

The deputy replied, "Pretty much like Oscar said. We don't know why. He and three other inmates were cleaning the floors and he just went crazy. It was three stories up, so there wasn't much chance of him making it."

She asked, "Was he trying to escape?"

"We don't think so. He wasn't someone who caused trouble, and he was only serving a two-day sentence. It just didn't make sense."

Clara looked at Oscar, who was staring at her as if she had the answers to all his problems. She said, "Oscar, didn't you tell me that you like it here?"

He nodded. "Yes, ma'am."

"Then why would you try to run away? If you like it here, don't you want to stay so you can learn to read? And have a bed to sleep in? And get food every day?"

He looked at Clara, then he pursed his lips, looked to the right, and then to the left—almost like a typewriter moving from page to page as words were typed out. Then his eyes got wide, he nodded, and said, "Yeah." He pulled the book closer to him, placed his finger on the page, and started to read, finger following along. The officer looked at Clara and shrugged.

Clara had searched for something to read that might push him toward revealing his partner in crime, but had not found anything. So today he was reading a third-grade primer. But she knew she would have to step up the level next time. Despite his initial concern about the poor man who jumped out of the third-story window, he finished reading the book in less than half an hour, and they still had another twenty minutes left.

Fortunately she had written out some new words ahead of time and helped him learn them. She usually did this at the end of each lesson, but only two or three words for a few minutes. Today they had more time, and she was relieved that she had prepared a longer list of words that might help lead him to reveal his partner. "Crime, life, murder, blood, partner, window, steal, judge, care, home, family, gratitude."

He sounded out each one and he learned them all by the end of the lesson.

He concluded, "So crime, murder, and steal are bad things. And judge, care, home, family, and gratitude are good things." Clara hadn't realized that she had composed the list that way, but when he pointed it out, she nodded.

When the officer arrived to take him back to his cell, he seemed more disappointed to return than usual.

"Clara," he said. "The word 'gratitude,' that's how I feel to you."

"You're welcome, Oscar. But we've got lots more to do so don't think you're finished with your lessons yet."

He laughed a boy's laugh, and she watched him leave the room feeling again a sense of satisfaction and pride. She picked up the book and notebook and waited for the door to open. Oscar's attorney had asked to speak with her for an update, and they had agreed to meet at the jail after she'd finished with Oscar. True to his word, he was waiting for her.

"I appreciate your meeting with me, Clara. I've been meaning to thank you for what you're doing for Oscar. It's having a significant impact on him."

She thought about that for a moment. "Yes, and on me, too."

"I understand you want to be a writer."

"Well, yes, and this will help me be a better one. I'm learning things from Oscar, too, about life, I guess."

The lawyer hesitated before saying, "What I wanted to talk to you about is this partner of his. He's being very stubborn about revealing who it is. I don't think he understands how important it is to his future that he reveal him."

"Have you explained it to him?" Clara asked.

The lawyer passed his hand over his forehead. "Well, I've tried, but I think he's too young and too slow to understand. We tried to get his father or mother to help, but they are not at all interested in him, and I believe Oscar would be better off without them around, quite frankly. The Chief and I have told him that he needs to tell us for his own good."

"Oh, Mr. Alberts. He's not slow. And I think if you explain it—that he might not have to go to jail for as long a time if he tells you—I think he'll understand. But it's more than that. He believes that the rest of his life will be like what the first fourteen years have been. He still doesn't understand that his life could be different."

The attorney studied Clara—a short, skinny girl who probably knew little about the real world and lived among characters in books in a household of educated parents who doted on her. She sensed his assessment and said, "Please. I know I'm just a teenager myself. But you must believe that Oscar is smart. And he's learning new things every day."

He said, "I'll tell you what, Clara. You seem able to reach him. Why don't you describe this situation to him—your way? Then I'll talk to him and tell him in the legal way. Let's see if that works."

Eager to help, Clara nodded. "I will."

As she started to leave, the attorney said, "Oh, and you should probably do it sooner rather than later, so that the Judge can factor it into his ruling. We have a little more than two weeks. The boy could be sent to a much harsher prison for a significantly longer time, if the Judge doesn't have a good reason to rule for the boy to reduce that sentence."

"Oh, but he can't."

The attorney shook his head. "I don't think he has an alternative. This is murder, and the law demands that the responsible killer has to pay. And Oscar is responsible under the law because he participated. Judge Akers always tries to do what is right and just, but he may not have much of a choice here. And, again, we only have a few weeks until he has to announce his verdict. He's delayed it as long as possible."

She nodded understanding. "I'll think about it some more and talk to Oscar tomorrow."

The next day Clara carried two books to read with Oscar. The guard now allowed her to bring one pencil into the room, with the promise that she would not allow Oscar to use it or take it back to his cell and with the stipulation that Deputy Brown would be there, which he always was anyway. That day she planned for Oscar to read the first book, with the promise of a second, and in between broach the topic of telling who his partner was. She wasn't going to ask him to tell her who it was; just lay out what he could look forward to if he did or did not provide the name. She had to get him to tell someone, for his own good.

Her plan was proceeding well. He attacked the first book and finished reading it quickly. She couldn't believe how many words he'd learned and remembered. But she kept to her plan.

She said, "Oscar, we need to talk. Or, rather I need you to listen."

"I don't wanna be mean, Clara, but I'd rather read that other book you brung, er, brought."

She smiled. "That's good, Oscar. You remembered 'brought.' But please, just listen to me for a few minutes. You don't have to say anything."

He sat back in his chair, folded his arms, and nodded. "All right."

Clara studied his posture. She was pleased that he was not jiggling. He was trying to appear like a grown man barely tolerating Clara's interruption of his reading. She ignored his impatience and said, "I've been talking to your lawyer and to Judge Akers. You know that you could go to jail for a long time—and not this jail but one where you have to do hard work and don't get to have visitors or maybe even reading lessons."

She wasn't sure what the difference would actually be; she needed to ask the Judge about life in different prisons. She continued, "Anyway, no one wants to send you away for a long time because you're just fourteen years old. And you should go to school; live in a nice place; and grow up and maybe even have a family."

Oscar stared at her in a way that suggested he wasn't listening. It occurred to Clara that he couldn't imagine such a life because he'd never seen anything but whatever his home life had been up until then.

She plunged on. "But the law's the law. It says that if you help someone commit a crime, especially murder, then you are just as guilty as they are."

He seemed to understand that concept. "That's a stupid law. I didn't kill nobody. I jest helped—take some things so's we could have something to 'et."

"It may be stupid, but it's the law. And the Sheriff has to enforce it and the Judge has to decide your fate—that means what you'll do for the rest of your life—based on it."

She studied him to make sure he was following. His eyes showed no confusion, only stubbornness. She said, "The only thing that might help is if you tell your attorney and the Judge who it was that actually did the killing. Then, they'd—"

He stood up suddenly, ignoring the movement of the deputy toward him. He said, "I thought you was different. I thought you understood. It goes against me to rat out somebody."

She stayed seated and reacted with calm but mixed emotions. On the one hand, Oscar had just refused to tell her what she wanted to know. On the other hand, he had just explained that he understood why he wouldn't tell. She was pleased to notice that she remained calm largely because she had anticipated some kind of negative reaction. She had thought about what to say for several hours. And she had discussed it with Attorney Alberts, so she was prepared. "Oscar, I know. I do understand. And I respect you. But I just want you to understand what that means. Your attorney wasn't sure if you did."

He said nothing and just glared at her, still standing, clenching his teeth—the deputy hovering close by.

Clara looked at the deputy and held up her hand to keep him from doing anything. She said, "You are very smart, Oscar Briarley." Oscar cocked his head in surprise, his eyes wide and his mouth open. "Yes, you are. Book-learning and being smart are two different things. You use your smarts to learn things. Do you understand?"

Oscar took a step toward Clara and then nodded. The deputy put his hand on him, and he returned to his seat. She was delighted that he understood, and also fascinated that this was something that she herself had just learned, that is, that being smart and being educated are two different things.

She continued. "But you may not understand that you don't always have to live with your mother and father—your ma and pa. If you continue to learn to read, you can do all kinds of things. You could work for the oil company, or even be a teacher. And you could fall in love, get married, and have your own children." She was surprised that Oscar blushed and looked down at his feet when she mentioned having children. "All I'm asking is that you think about what you're giving up. If you tell your attorney who your partner was, you have the chance to do all those things. If you don't, you'll go to jail for a long time." He glared at her again and shook his head, arms again folded in front of him.

She said, "And maybe you should think about the person who made you help him steal. Was he doing the right thing? Is killing a person right? Why do you owe him your loyalty?"

Oscar couldn't help himself. He so wanted to learn. "What's loyalty?" he asked.

"Here, I'll write it." And she printed out the words "loyal" and "loyalty" and showed them to him. She said, "Being loyal means being faithful to someone or something no matter what and doing or saying things that support a person or thought or idea."

He studied the paper. "So I'm 'loyal' to my, er, partner by not telling you his name."

"Yes. That's a correct use of the word."

"How else would you use it?"

"Well, as U.S. citizens we're loyal to our government. If we do something to threaten it, we're guilty of 'treason.'" She wrote that word out and showed it to him. "Oh, and dogs are loyal to their masters."

"Really?"

She smiled. "Yes, really. Pets like dogs are known to be loyal, even if they are mistreated."

"So it's not a bad thing—to be loyal."

"No, not necessarily. Although there's something called 'blind loyalty.' That's when someone is faithful to another person or cause that's wrong and harmful. I think of the Nazis in Germany that way. They are loyal to Hitler, and he's harmful."

Oscar laughed. "Pa likes Hitler. He thinks he's got things figgered out pretty good."

"Do you?"

He stopped laughing, probably sensing her distaste. "I don't know. But I ain't gonna tell you who my partner was, so it don't matter."

"Oscar, I just want you to give me your word that you'll think about what I've said. I swore to Attorney Alberts that I would make sure you understand it's your entire life that's at stake. Promise that you'll think about it."

"I promise. Now can we read the other book?"

She had reached the end of the discussion. It would take more time to help Oscar open his mind to other ideas. As fast as he was progressing, she sensed that he couldn't digest much more at that point, and she feared that his current understanding of himself would prohibit him from revealing his partner's name. How ironic! What little sense of right and wrong he had adapted could land him in prison for a long time. But she also sensed that to betray that sense would strip Oscar of whoever he was. She didn't understand why, but she believed he needed to have a reason to betray his loyalty to his partner—some other something to put in its place. But she wasn't sure what that would be.

When she finished with Oscar that day, she wanted to talk to the Judge, so she walked over to his chambers on the chance that he might be there. Irene was just getting ready to leave—her desk was clear, and she was walking to the door. She smiled when she saw Clara, but pulled her aside and said, "He's here. But he's not very happy. An inmate killed himself, and the Judge is upset."

Clara nodded. "Do you think I should come back rather than talk to him now?"

"No, I think it will do him good to speak with you. Just a minute, let me tell him you're here." She walked to the door to the Judge's chambers and said, "Judge, Clara is here. Do you have time to speak with her now?"

Clara heard a mumble, and saw Irene turn and nod at her, so she went in. The Judge managed to smile, but she could tell he was not happy. His shoulders were hunched, he kept fiddling aimlessly with papers on his desk, and he took a breath before looking up. "Hi, Clara. Were you just visiting Oscar?"

"Yes. And I wanted to talk to you about him. He's learning so much, but I need more time. How much longer will I have with him? I'm trying to get him to tell us who his partner was, but he thinks that it's wrong to rat him out."

"That's fairly common. But usually we can convince criminals of the problem with logic—if not by any other means, we can tell them they'll go to jail for life if they don't confide."

She looked at the Judge to see if he was sincere. He wasn't like his usual reasonable self. "I don't think that would work with Oscar, sir. He hasn't had a chance to develop many beliefs, but what he's got he's holding onto tight. It will take time to loosen that one so that he'll tell us."

The Judge again sighed and looked at her. "I'm sorry, Clara. I need to tell you something. You remember that Oscar's brother was in prison, up in San Quentin?"

She said, "Yes. I believe his name is Tommy?"

"Well, he killed himself. The guards aren't sure how, but he managed to hang himself in his cell with a bed sheet."

"Oh, no! Why? I can't imagine what it would take to make me want to kill myself." Then another thought occurred to her. "When will you tell Oscar? This could cause him to not want to learn to read anymore."

"I don't know. I'd heard it was rough up there. Some of the guards are being charged with beating prisoners following a food fight. I just don't know." He looked around the room. It was as if he was trying to see why it was the way it was.

She didn't understand. "Well, did they beat him? Is that what caused him to be so sad that he would kill himself? How old was he? Did he have a long term to serve? Was that why he did it?"

The Judge looked down at his desk, shook his head, and then stood up. "He was twenty-one. And, yes, he was in for a long time. Remember, I told you. He killed someone in cold blood—a Mexican—for which he was convicted for twenty-five years. And he also was waiting for trials for theft and rape."

"So maybe he just couldn't take the idea that he'd be in jail for the rest of his life?"

"Well, do you remember what you said in court that day we first met? You said that Oscar didn't know how to read and that the only world he knew was the one his parents gave him. That's why you're teaching Oscar to read now, isn't it?

To give him a chance to live a more fulfilling life. You agree, right?"

She was uneasy with the Judge's conversation and wasn't sure where it was going, but she nodded. "Yes. I believe that reading can take you to interesting places and show you different ways to live."

He nodded and looked out the window. He was quiet for a few minutes, and she was just getting ready to escape when he said, "Tommy learned to read. Apparently he was smart enough, and I'm told he read dozens of books. He couldn't get enough of them."

She took advantage of a pause in his conversation to say, "Yes. I think Oscar is smart, too. It's a shame they weren't raised by other parents. I don't think much of the dad. He told Oscar that book-learning was wrong and would harm him."

"What? When?"

"He just visited him the other day, but just once. I hope he never visits him again. He told him that Tommy was sad because of his book-learning. "

"I wonder how he knew that. He never visited Tommy, apparently, but I assumed that was because he couldn't afford the trip."

"And I understand the mother drinks liquor and can sometimes be violent."

The Judge turned and stared at Clara. "That explains a lot." He looked pensive and then his face turned to a frown. "I thought Tommy was doing so well. I was pleased to see his progress."

She asked, "What happened?"

"He managed to write a note, which was surprising given his level of education. He said he couldn't live with what he'd done in his life. He read about how other people live and he was so disgusted with himself that he had to take his own life."

Clara looked at the Judge with wide-open eyes and an open mouth. "How could that be? I don't understand." Then she thought about it. "Oscar said his brother and father did awful things to animals and would bet on which one could scream the loudest. You said he killed a man simply because he thought he was better than him. I wonder what else he might have done that we don't know about?"

The Judge smiled. "*We* know about?" Then he squinted and said, "Well, maybe you might be aware of what's happening with that family given your relationship with his brother. I don't know what else Tommy might have done, but the idea of rehabilitation is to help inmates become contributing citizens—not to regret their crimes so much that they take their own lives."

She wasn't sure what to say, except that Oscar and Tommy were different. "Maybe Tommy was just too far gone. He felt, maybe, he could never make up for what he'd done. But Oscar's different. He only went along with someone to help steal something, and he's never killed anyone or—"

"Tortured animals or hurt anyone," the Judge interrupted. "I understand that, Clara. But what I had hoped was that even in prison Tommy could have contributed something. But apparently he so loathed himself that he could not even do that. And reading books only reminded him more of what kind of person he was. Rehabilitation through education is an important concept that many of us have embraced, but we need to investigate the consequences more thoroughly. We cannot have twenty-one-year-olds killing themselves when they comprehend the nature of their crimes. There needs to be some kind of emotional bridge from crime to contribution."

Although again concerned about the depth of the Judge's emotion, Clara said, "I understand. So many things are so much more complicated than they seem to be at first. But that doesn't mean we should stop doing them. What I've learned is to go ahead and do them and then later think about whether they worked."

The Judge didn't seem to listen. Instead, he listlessly said, "We'll need to inform his parents. They don't have a phone, so someone will have to go out to their place."

The Judge looked at Clara and again squinted, like he was trying to remember something. "What was it you wanted to know? When you first came in here, you asked me something."

"I'm not sure this is the right time. I think Oscar is learning very fast and is appreciating other things, but it's taking longer than I thought. So I was just hoping you might be able to keep him here longer. I think I can get him to tell us who his partner is, but it will take a while. There's so much he has to understand. And now with his brother's death, well— I don't know what that will do to him."

The Judge sighed and shook his head. "I'll talk to his attorney, but his hearing is set for two weeks from today. And there's not much I can do. Why don't you go home and be with your family now?"

She stood up and looked at the Judge, not knowing what else to say. "Sir, I want to thank you for all you've done for me. I feel like you've taught me about the real world. You have helped me a lot."

The Judge looked at her and cocked his head, studying her before he said, "You know, Miss Clara Bow Wilson, I believe I have."

Chapter 15

Clara arrived at the jail the next afternoon, uneasy about how Oscar would react to the death of his brother. On the advice of her mother, she had the foresight to write out a lesson in case he didn't want to see her. It seemed important to give him something to do even if they didn't have a lesson. So she wrote out ten reasons to learn to read, ending the list with the question, "Why else should you learn to read?"

As she waited for the door to the visitor's room to open, Deputy Brown approached her and said, "He can't make it today. He said to tell you he doesn't want to learn to read anymore." The deputy added, "His attorney told him about his brother. I think he just needs some time."

Despite Deputy Brown's reassurance, she was concerned that she needed to get to Oscar quickly. She had learned how stubborn he could be when he got fixed on an idea. So she held up her sheet of paper and said to the deputy, "Can you give him this? It's our lesson for today. Maybe he could just look at it and then I'll come back tomorrow for our next lesson."

He nodded and took the paper, reading it as he walked away. He turned to Clara and smiled. "This might help. He really seems to want to learn."

"Thanks."

She decided to see if the Judge was available. Irene was typing and looked up when Clara entered. "Hi, Clara. No lesson today?"

She shook her head. "He says he doesn't want to learn to read now."

"I'm sorry. But he could change his mind."

"Maybe. I have a plan, but I'm a little discouraged."

Irene said, "Let me see if he has time to talk to you. He was trying to leave early." She walked in and said something quietly to the Judge that Clara couldn't hear.

Then she heard the Judge's voice. "Of course I'll see her," he said, followed by his appearance at the doorway. "Hello, Clara. I understand Oscar doesn't want a lesson today."

"Not just today. He says he doesn't want to learn to read anymore at all. I left him a list of the most important reasons to learn to read. Deputy Brown and I both think he wants to learn, so maybe he'll read it. My mother suggested that I write a story about Oscar for him to read. And I'm going to do that. But I don't know, sir. I may have lost him."

Her mother's suggestion had buoyed her for the moment. But facing the situation head-on was bringing her back down. She looked at the Judge and said, "Do you have any ideas? I mean, I know you have always succeeded, and maybe you—"

The Judge interrupted, laughing, "Do you really believe that I've never failed at anything?"

When she said nothing, he continued, "I failed to win my very first case as a lawyer and have never forgotten it."

"Really?" Clara assumed that the Judge always won. "What happened?"

"An insurance company convinced the presiding judge that my client's automobile accident was caused by his diabetes rather than by another car running into him. He got no compensation, even though he was crippled. His wife had to go to work to support him and his family."

Clara thought about what it would mean to lose your first case. "Was it hard to take a new client after that?"

"Yes, but my circumstances changed. I went on to win some cases and lose others. What I'm trying to say is that you will grow older and your life around you will change. Oscar's situation isn't your only endeavor. You'll take on more. But how you handle this situation will contribute to who you become, what you decide to do with your life. Will you go to college to learn to be a great writer? Or, will you travel to gain new experiences? Just as you are trying to help Oscar clarify his options, so you, too, have options. And your choices are much more numerous today than fifty years ago—even with the potential of war looming before us."

While listening to what the Judge said, Clara changed her position from slouching at the back of her chair to moving forward to sitting upright on its edge trying hard to absorb his words so she could act on them—or at least write about them. For the past few weeks, she had struggled with a growing concern about the world at large and its impact on her future. Although she hadn't vocalized it to anyone, she was worried about whether the European war would change their lives in Ventura. The news she read every day seemed to bring them closer to it, and people were talking about the situation more and more. It was no longer some event "over there." It was becoming something that could be very real at home, although she still hoped the U.S. would not get involved.

But for the moment she tried to set aside that worry and consider what the Judge was saying. "Can you tell me about some of your successes? I think I need to hear some of those."

The Judge laughed. "Well, I won plenty of cases, Clara." He rubbed his hand over his chin and then said, "Here's one you'll appreciate, I think. The District Attorney had an expert witness who testified that he was sure my client had removed bloodstains from his pants using gasoline. This particular testimony was quite damaging toward establishing my client's guilt."

"Oh, what did you do?"

"Well, I was discussing the case with my wife and mentioned that particular testimony. My wife said, 'That's impossible. You can't remove blood from clothing using gasoline.'"

"Really? The man lied under oath?"

"Well, he might not have lied, but his so-called expertise was definitely called into question."

Clara was intrigued by the case. "What happened? Did he go to jail?"

"No, he was cleared of that crime, although I heard he was later shot and killed somewhere in New Jersey."

"That's really an interesting case, and I bet I could turn it into a super story! What else can you tell me?"

The Judge said, "I think that's enough for right now. Time for you to go home."

"Thank you. I guess right now, sir, I'm not so sure about a lot of things. But I do know that I can write, so I'll go home and write Oscar's Story. It's all I know to do at the moment. I am a writer, after all."

The Judge smiled and patted her shoulder. "I think that's an excellent idea. And it just may work. You might be able to pull Oscar back to wanting to learn to read. And for the moment, that's probably the best we can hope for."

Chapter 16

Although his family buried Mr. Brant shortly after he had been killed, they had never held a memorial event for him. The Judge assumed that part of the reason was that Mrs. Brant simply couldn't face it. In addition to bearing the emotional distress of suddenly losing a husband, she confronted the task of rearing four young children alone—with no income and no moneymaking skills. She also had to learn how to access whatever funds were available in her dead husband's bank account so that she could pay for things. She was just not up to seeing other people so avoided holding a memorial gathering altogether.

    The Judge had asked Irene to help her out for a few days. She kept the Judge's books and had a head for business, so she showed the widow how to write a check, deposit and withdraw money from a bank account, and how to pay bills. Jim also performed various chores around the house, such as cleaning the gutters, mowing the lawn, and repairing a broken banister. Neighbors and friends also contributed food and provided babysitting for the children when needed.

    Adding to her stress, however, was an incident involving Billy, her twelve-year-old son. The Fire Chief caught him climbing a one-hundred-foot water tower and throwing firecrackers at the cars below. Some of his friends had dared him to do this, and he accepted but then couldn't get back down, and they had to call the fire department to rescue him. The event happened the day before Mr. Brant was killed, but the Chief concluded it was important for him to attend the boys' club meetings for two months. The Judge concurred. Without a father around to reinforce his disciplining, the boy could benefit from the guidance he'd receive there. However, Mrs. Brant only saw it as an additional burden for her to deal with.

Fortunately, it turned out that Mr. Brant had been a member of a local service club, and when its members heard of his wife's tragedy, they organized several fundraisers, including a door-to-door collection campaign and a bake sale at a local carnival, and managed to raise $500. Then they arranged a memorial event to be held at their meeting hall and invited friends, family, neighbors, and everyone from the store Mr. Brant had managed.

Clara and her parents arrived early, in adherence to her mother's commitment to punctuality. After greeting Mrs. Brant and the children with her parents, Clara huddled together with her co-workers, not sure what to say to the widow. She was still wearing black, as was the custom. The four Brant children clung to each other.

Judge Akers arrived about half an hour later, with Irene and Jim, followed shortly by the Chief. Their arrival must have signaled the beginning of the event because the leader of the organization walked over to a podium and banged a gavel to get everyone's attention shortly after their arrival.

"We'd like to thank everyone for coming. We are here to share our good wishes with Mrs. Brant and her children in light of the sudden and cruel loss of her husband. Mr. Brant was an upstanding citizen who contributed to the community and helped our young people. We will miss him. And I believe that his death was so unnecessary and indicative of the need to get crime under control here in Ventura. We've had robbery after robbery in the area, and I for one was glad to see that someone was finally caught. I see the Chief is here, and I want to thank him for catching one of the criminals. And, Judge Akers, I assume you'll put him behind bars for the rest of his life."

Clara gasped. She looked at the Judge, immediately curious how he or the Chief would respond to this, but his face remained passive as he continued to look directly at the speaker. The Judge had not yet pronounced sentence on Oscar Briarley and many people in Ventura did not understand why not.

Mrs. Brant, standing at the front of the crowd, and others gathered in the room nodded their approval of the statement. The widow said, "Yes, why should he continue to have a life? He took away my husband's and denied him to us. He should go to jail forever!" She started to cry, causing a nearby woman to put her arms around her.

The Judge had heard Clara gasp and was watching her. He wondered how she was affected by the event itself—whether the evening's affair would cause her to recall what must have been a very difficult experience. He knew that she had been spending time with Oscar, which did not seem to upset her. But seeing the widow and her children and hearing discussion of the crime itself might trigger some memories. His concern was confirmed when he saw her run from the room. He was about to join her when he saw her mother pursue her. They re-entered the room a few minutes later, with the mother's arm around her daughter's shoulders. The Judge could tell that Clara had been crying. It bothered him to see this resourceful, inquisitive, caring teenager hurt so much. He hoped her spirit would never be broken.

The Judge went over to them and asked, "Are you all right?"

Clara said, "I thought I was over it. I wasn't expecting to feel this way. I see Oscar almost every day, and it doesn't bother me." She tried hard to resist crying, but did not succeed as tears started to run down her cheeks. "It was truly awful. Mr. Brant looked so surprised; and Oscar, he looked so scared. I couldn't move. I waited for the next shot to hit me."

Her mother continued to hold her and said, "I know, Clara. You've been very brave through it all."

A thought occurred to Clara, and she broke free of her mother and looked at the Judge. "But it wasn't Oscar who shot him. Why do people want him punished?"

The Judge looked at Clara's mother who just shook her head, so he said, "Well, look at it from their viewpoint. He was there. He helped the man who killed Mr. Brant. Don't you think he's responsible—maybe just a little?" He said this gently, like he knew she would disagree and would be disturbed by him saying it.

She responded, "But I can tell you, I'm sure that Oscar didn't know his partner was going to shoot somebody. I'm not even sure at the time that he truly comprehended that what he was doing was wrong. But I truly believe he isn't the kind of person who would kill another human."

The Judge nodded and said quietly, "But Mr. Brant is still dead, and his widow has four children to raise alone."

At that moment, Mrs. Brant walked over to the podium. She was no longer crying and seemed calm. Another woman walked beside her, and Mrs. Brant motioned to her to stay with her. She nodded and smiled.

The widow raised her hand. "Thank you, everyone. I'd like to especially thank my friends for their generous efforts to raise money to help see me through. My husband was a good man, a good husband, and a caring father. We looked forward to living a life together raising our children. We will miss him so much." She swallowed hard and raised her handkerchief to her eyes. Then she looked out over the gathering and said, "I would like to personally thank the Chief for catching the person who helped kill my husband. And thank you, Clara, for identifying and testifying against him. I hope you catch the other one, Chief."

The group applauded. "I also have an announcement. Thanks to Mrs. Nathan here, I now have a job helping out at her real estate office."

More applause. "So the money from that job plus what you have donated should be enough to keep us going until the children are grown. Also, for at least the next year, my widowed aunt from Los Angeles will be living with us off and on to help with the children. Isn't that wonderful?" She smiled and nodded her own approval. "I will miss my husband so much, but I shall be forever grateful to the town of Ventura for all your support. Thank you." She extended her arms to the group. "Now, I would like to invite all of you to enjoy all this wonderful food that you've brought." She even managed to smile and looked quite relieved to now have both a job and someone to help with her children.

The group lined up in front of the buffet table, and Clara saw her neighbor's pineapple upside-down cake with its maraschino cherries in the center of each pineapple slice, which she always ate first. The Judge and the Chief were in line just ahead of her, talking to the organization's president, who was saying, "I hope you plan to throw the book at that Briarley boy, Judge."

The Judge barely smiled and said, "I'm afraid as the judge in the case I can't discuss it."

The Chief interrupted, "But I can. Why do you think we should punish Oscar Briarley? He didn't pull the trigger, you know, and he's only fourteen."

"He was there, Chief. And I know you think you can turn young hooligans into responsible citizens, but you're wrong—in this case especially. The Briarleys are hardly a respectable family. His father is one slippery character, and as they say, 'The apple doesn't fall far from the tree.' And you can't undo the work of a murderer. How is that fair to the victims? How does Mrs. Brant get justice for her husband if you let that boy go?"

The Judge said, "I can't discuss the case, but I can say that there is strong evidence that combining reformation with the appropriate punishment to fit the criminal rather than the crime results in strengthening a person's resolve to do right and reducing his desire to do wrong. That's straight out of our Peace Officer's manual."

"And what would you say is the appropriate punishment for murder, Judge?"

"Like most things, it depends. But obviously, murder is considered the most serious of crimes, and I believe that the punishment should be as severe as we can make it—allowing for accidents and other considerations. But that doesn't mean we shouldn't try to reform the criminal."

"As long as you punish him, you can do all the reforming you want."

The Judge said, almost as if he were delivering a verdict, "When I became a judge, I was immediately weighed down by the unbelievable responsibility given to me, even while realizing in our form of government that someone had to have that power. We've written our laws so that they can be enforced according to their degree of harm to society—at least for the most part. What I try to do as a judge is to look at all the evidence. I listen to all the testimony—even if the witnesses are not knowledgeable about the rules of the court. If I have any doubts I simply ask: What is the right thing to do? Sometimes there is no answer to that question, but when there is, I follow it."

A sudden crash interrupted the discussion. The Judge looked for the cause of the noise and saw Jim Alvarez getting up from a broken table with a large man bearing down on him—and Irene hurrying to reach her husband. The Judge moved swiftly and managed to insert all six-feet-five inches of himself between the two. "What's the meaning of this?" he shouted "How dare you cause such a ruckus at this event!"

Jim did not back down. The Judge suspected that he would attack the other man if he withdrew. "Jim, what's this about?"

Jim stared at the other man and said flatly, "Ask him."

"I'm asking you. What's this about?"

"He accused me of being a Mexican and asked me to leave."

The Judge blinked, said nothing, and then turned to the other man, whom he now held back with a stiffened arm on his chest. "I'm sure, sir, that you didn't really mean to say that, did you?" He studied the man, whose breath smelled of alcohol. He was dressed in a cheap suit that didn't quite fit. His shirt was clean and pressed, but his tie was soiled. His hair and beard both needed trimming.

The Chief was now on the other side of the intruder. Mrs. Brant came running over to Jim. "I'm so sorry, Jim." She turned to the big man and said, "Mr. Blakensfeld, I can assure you that this gentleman has been nothing but helpful to me. Why, he's taken care of many of the household chores that my husband used to do. You should go home now to your wife and son and take care of them."

Blakensfeld grunted but said nothing. Jim continued to watch him carefully, like he didn't trust him. The Chief said, "Why don't I drive you home? Where is your wife, by the way? I'd have thought she would be here."

The big man growled, "Naw, she had to stay at the house in case that brat son of hers decides to come home."

The Judge asked, "Who's your son?"

"Stepson," the man corrected him. "I didn't sire the no-good-for-nothing thief. And his name's Harry Winter."

The Judge narrowed his eyes. Although he had never met Blakensfeld, he now knew he was the stepfather of the boy he'd seen at the L.A. drive-in theater the previous Saturday who had robbed the concession stand. Harry had been missing almost a week since that night. The Judge could understand why the boy was so bitter and spoke out the way he did at the boys' club, given this kind of home influence exhibited by his stepfather.

Irene and Jim both recognized the Judge's look. He had sized up this man and would watch for any sign of him on the criminal side of the law. Jim was sure that the Judge would ask him to investigate him. Jim said, with some satisfaction, "Well, I think you should take the Judge's advice and accept the Chief's offer to go home now." The Chief tugged at Harry's stepfather and pulled him out the door. Jim motioned to the Judge to follow him.

They moved outside through the door where Clara and her mother had recently entered. Jim said, "Judge, do you remember you described an emblem on the shirt of one of the boys at the drive-in theater? You said it looked like a chair?"

The Judge nodded. "Why?"

Jim pulled a crumbled business card from his jacket. "This fell from Blakensfeld's pocket." He handed it to the Judge. In the upper-left corner was a picture of a chair that was exactly like the emblem the Judge had seen on the boy at the drive-in theater. The card said, "Blakensfeld's Furniture," and gave the address of the store.

"Well, that makes sense. I mean, Harry is Blakensfeld's stepson, so he would likely associate with workers from there. So it's likely that he was with some Blakensfeld employees at the drive-in theater. Maybe they drove him back to Ventura. We'll have to look into that, if the Chief hasn't already. That doesn't mean that Blakensfeld himself is involved."

Jim arched his eyebrows. "Everything in me says that he is."

The Judge nodded. "You could be right. What's the latest on the case with Hiram Chissum's mother and son?"

"The Chief is definitely on board with our plan. I hope to speak with the mother tomorrow. We're moving carefully. She works as a bookkeeper at a company that loans farm equipment. We want to approach her alone—outside of her workplace and with no police. I was hoping she'd be here tonight, but I haven't seen her. She sometimes has lunch at the downtown café, which is also an option. I can arrange to be seated next to her in a quiet booth. I'll let you know when we connect."

The Judge sighed. "Make sure the Chief knows about the chair emblem and Mr. Blakensfeld. He may want to initiate a surveillance team for him." He stared at Jim. "I fear we have a long and difficult way to go before we've solved this crime. And many lives will suffer the impact."

Jim nodded. He hoped, for the Judge's sake, they could solve at least that part of the mystery involving Oscar Briarley. "Judge, by the way, the Chief and I don't believe that the Briarley case is related."

"Nor do I. I'm hoping Clara Wilson can help with that."

Jim, who never much believed that she would be helpful, still wasn't sure. But he had another idea, which he didn't want to share with the Judge just yet. He needed to do some additional research.

Chapter 17

The next day, Jim's patience and perseverance paid off. He followed Hiram Chissum's mother to the restaurant and nodded to the waitress with whom he'd made an arrangement. She escorted the woman to a back booth and put Jim in the one next to her so that they were back to back.

He waited until they had both ordered, glanced around the restaurant to be sure no one was looking, and with his hands in front of his mouth, told her, "Mrs. Chissum, please don't respond to what I'm going to say." He couldn't see her face so he didn't know how she was reacting. "I'm here representing the Chief. We want to help you and your son. Hiram and his friend Eddie approached Judge Akers a few days ago and said you needed help. But we know that your lives have been threatened so we're doing what we can to assure no one sees us. Can you tell me if you understand?"

He waited for several seconds before he heard a woman's thin voice. "I understand. But, please, they've threatened my son, and I know someone's been following me. Please be careful. How can you help me?"

"With your permission and assistance, we believe we can follow your son the next time they ask him to do something for them, and catch them in the act. They won't know where or how we got the lead, and our hope is to shut them down. Do you think you could get word to us the next time he's approached?"

"Maybe. It depends on when and whether he lets me know."

"Could you put something outside when he's contacted— like a ribbon on the doorknob, or a chalk mark on the door even? We'll keep your house under surveillance so that no one can tell we're there but we don't want to give away that we know about your son. So—"

"I'll put out a box of old clothes on the stoop. I gather clothes for my church for charity so it will not be suspicious."

"All right. I'm going to drop my card on the floor. It has my name and the Chief's phone number. If you need anything, call that number and they will get me as soon as they can. Or you can ask for the Chief himself."

"Thank the Judge. I know he sent my son to jail, but he may have saved him from a life of crime. And if he can help my other son, I will be very grateful."

"Do you have any idea who's doing this?"

There was no sound from the other booth, and Jim hoped that she might know. She said quietly, "I fear my boss might be involved, so please don't show up at the store."

She dropped her money on the floor, leaned over to pick up the money and his card, got up from her booth, turned to leave, looked directly at him, and placed some cash on the table to cover her check. Then she left the restaurant.

Jim stayed for another fifteen minutes, nursing his coffee. He wanted to be sure that if anyone were watching her, they wouldn't connect him to her. He now had two names to be investigated as possible suspects: Blakensfeld, Harry's stepdad who ran the furniture store, and Franklin, the manager of the farm equipment store where Mrs. Chissum worked.

He paid his own check and left the restaurant, eager to get to the Chief with this latest information and his speculation. He had intended to go directly to see the Chief, but as a precaution took a route toward the courthouse instead. He wanted to check to see if anyone was following him. He noticed a boy on a bicycle who stayed close to him. He determined that the bicyclist was indeed following him and decided not to go to the Chief's office or the courthouse. Instead he walked in the opposite direction and eventually entered a barbershop. His hair did need cutting, so he spent the next half hour in the chair. When he came out, there was no sign of the boy. He again started toward the Chief's office. He went a circuitous route to see if anyone was shadowing him, but detected no one.

When he reached City Hall where the Chief's office was located, he again looked around carefully. He opened the door and walked quickly to the Chief's office, entering without knocking, then sitting down next to his desk.

The Chief said somewhat sarcastically, "Come in and help yourself to a chair." Then he noticed the look of satisfaction on Jim's face. "You got to her?"

Jim responded, "I did. And you know what else? I believe a boy on a bicycle was following me today. I lost him, but I was surprised that they're on to me. Anyway, Mrs. Chissum has agreed to help. I met her at the restaurant, and we sat at different booths. She's definitely scared. But if anyone saw us, we were just two people having lunch."

"What's the plan?" the Chief asked. "How will we know if her son's been approached?"

"She'll put a box of old clothes on her porch. Apparently she does that fairly often as part of a charity with her church, so it won't be suspicious."

"Regardless of whether she puts out a box of clothes, I think we should keep her house under surveillance."

Jim nodded. "I agree, but it will be difficult. The only place to hide is across the street and down a few houses behind some bushes and trees in front of an unkempt lawn. Whoever goes will have to lay low and won't have a clear view of her house."

"Did she have any idea who's doing this?"

"Yes, she did."

"Blakensfeld."

"No, her boss, Mr. Franklin. He runs the farm machinery rental company. I'll start looking into him, with your permission. Quietly."

The Chief nodded. And Jim saw the same concern on his face that he and the Judge had expressed—the realization that this crime ring was far-reaching and would involve more people, and perhaps more teenagers, than originally anticipated. He was not looking forward to the next few weeks.

Chapter 18

Clara checked in with Irene daily to keep her updated on her progress with Oscar, and Irene kept the Judge appraised. For that entire week, Oscar refused to see Clara. But she kept going back every day and gave the deputy something new that she either printed or typed for Oscar to read. And she kept adding new words that would be more challenging for him, which would cause him difficulty and might spur him to want to see her in order to learn the new words.

In the meantime, in addition to his investigation into Mrs. Chissum's boss, Jim had had an idea of his own to help Oscar Briarley. On Wednesday of that week, he made an appointment with Oscar's attorney. He had done some research at the Ventura County Library on the incarceration of minors and wanted to go over some possibilities with Attorney Alberts before checking with the Judge. He wasn't sure of the correct procedure, but since he was investigating on his own, he figured he could proceed without the Judge's permission or approval.

He met the defense attorney in his office on Main Street and quickly outlined his idea. "I read about a case up north where they kept a twelve-year-old at a county jail until he turned sixteen so that he wouldn't have to mix with hardened criminals. Do you think we could get that for Oscar? I mean, staying at the Ventura County Jail until he's sixteen?"

Alberts nodded over and over. "It's possible. I'll have my law clerk check out the actual case to see if we can use it as precedent. Will you have time to do additional research?"

"I'll make time, but I'm not sure how much more is available at the library."

"Never mind. I think what's more important is to find case history, and we're more able to find that. What you can do is try it out with the Judge. See how he responds. He can't give you a definite answer, but you can tell if he's positive about the idea. In the meantime, I'll see what we can find out. It's something, at least. This boy doesn't deserve doing hard time. I just wish we could talk him into telling us who was with him at the store that night."

Jim was hopeful. At least they were doing something that might help Oscar, which would offer the Judge some way to mitigate a tough sentence for the boy.

The next day he walked into the Judge's chambers just after lunch. He greeted his wife with a kiss on the cheek and asked, "Is the Judge available?"

Irene responded, "I believe so. We're getting ready to go listen to the Martinez case. Do you want to come, too?" Jim nodded.

"Judge," she called, "Jim is here to see you. Then he's going with us to listen in on the Martinez case."

"Come on in, Jim."

"Hi, Judge. How's the Briarley case coming?"

The Judge shook his head. "There isn't much more time. I was able to respond positively to his attorney's request to postpone a decision for a week based on the death of Oscar's brother, but I need to state a verdict and a sentence in two weeks. I will take into account his age, but I can't promise where he'll be jailed. Murder is murder, and without some reason to reduce his sentence, I'm constrained in what I can do."

Jim knew that the Judge kept repeating this situation because he felt helpless to do anything about it. Jim had considered how to present his proposal to the Judge and was prepared. This was the perfect opening. "I have an idea that I want to run by you. Of course, Alberts will have to prepare the real proposal. But why can't you appoint Briarley a ward of the county to be remanded in this county jail at least until he's sixteen? It's been done before, you know, in California."

At first the Judge looked startled. Then he thought about it and said, "How do you know about this?"

"Well, you know I'm taking courses that require research. Whenever I can I relate my research projects to the law, so I'll be better prepared when I apply to law school. I did some research at the Ventura County Library and found a newspaper article that talked about a teenager who was kept in a county jail in the San Francisco area until he turned sixteen. I checked with Attorney Alberts, too, and he said it looked like what he called a '*bona fide* case on which to base a motion.' But we weren't sure, so I said I'd float it by you. In the meantime, his law clerk is doing more research for precedence."

The Judge nodded. "Tell him to continue. So long as he can find case history, it's a possibility. I'll also do some searching, but I need a motion before I deliver a verdict so I can incorporate it into my sentencing, regardless of the outcome."

Jim nodded. "I'll let him know."

Irene stuck her head in the room. "We should go now if we want to hear this afternoon's discussion. As it is, we'll be walking in on a session already underway."

The three walked out of the Judge's chambers and into the courtroom and then proceeded about half way to the front and sat down at the end of a row. They looked around and noticed Mrs. Martinez and her children sitting in the front row just behind Mr. Martinez, who was on trial for killing a cow. Irene and Jim had never met the defendant, who they saw was a slim man with dark hair, who bent over the table, only glanced up occasionally, and never looked directly at the presiding judge. Irene had only met Mrs. Martinez the day she and her children had visited the Judge in his chambers, asking for his help.

They also noticed a row of men dressed in black suits who sat on the other side behind the prosecutor's table. Irene and Jim both knew they were members of the local Cattlemen's Association. The Judge leaned over to Irene and whispered, "That's Judge Hawkins. He'll side solidly with the Cattlemen's Association and their law. Martinez doesn't stand much of a chance."

The defense attorney, a lanky fellow with sparse hair and a squeaky voice, was speaking. "Your Honor, my client, Mr. Martinez, fully admits to shooting and killing a cow. He brought it to the Chief and told him willingly what happened. He did not intend to kill a cow. He was hunting for a deer to feed his family. Surely you can appreciate that and take it into account."

The prosecutor stood up and said, "Your Honor, Mr. Martinez is a convicted felon. Why should we believe him? He has gone to prison for thievery. We know that he was seen shooting his rifle by several people, so of course he was bound to get caught. He simply tried to minimize his punishment by taking the cow to the Chief."

"But, your Honor," countered the defense attorney, "Mr. Martinez has been a hardworking member of the community for the past ten years. He is married and has a family. You heard from his current boss. You heard from others that he is an honorable man and a good provider for his family."

After about ten minutes of listening intently, the Judge got up and walked to the gate separating the public area from the courtroom itself. He leaned over to the defense attorney's assistant sitting next to the defendant, who smiled when he recognized him. The Judge whispered something to him. Then, with almost everyone watching him, including the sitting judge, he walked back and sat down next to Irene and Jim. The defense attorney stopped mid-sentence and walked over to his assistant who whispered to him. He glanced back at Judge Akers, and then said, "Your Honor, I'd like you to hear from one more person. I promise it won't take long but I think you should get to know her."

The presiding judge asked, "And who is that?"

"I'd like to call the defendant's wife."

Mrs. Martinez gasped, but when the presiding judge granted the motion, she stood up and walked slowly to the witness chair, her long hair caught in a large comb. Her dress was the same one she had worn a few weeks earlier when she approached the Judge for his assistance; and she wore flat shoes that surely must have had holes in them, for they looked so well-worn. When she turned to be sworn in, her tired eyes showed fear and concern.

The defense attorney waited until she was settled and then said, "Mrs. Martinez, thank you for agreeing to testify. I think you know your husband better than anyone."

The poor woman looked down at her hands, which were folded in her lap. She said quietly, "Yes, sir."

The presiding judge said, "You'll have to speak up so we can hear you."

She nodded and said more loudly, "Yes, sir."

The attorney then asked, "On the day in question, can you tell us what your husband was intending to do? Just like you told me when we first met, all right?"

She nodded. "Yes, sir. We hadn't had anything much to eat for several days. A coyote had gotten our chickens. We still had some tomatoes and squash in our garden. But my husband said he was sure he could get us a deer. We've had deer before, and it's good."

She stopped and looked at the attorney. He nodded. "Go on."

"So, he got his rifle and went out. I don't know where it was, but he said it was all right to hunt there. He came home later, very upset. He said he accidentally shot a cow. He came to get a friend with a truck to help him take it to the Chief. He said he knew it was wrong. He didn't know what else to do."

"And what about your life with him during the past ten years? Has he ever stolen anything? Or broken the law that you know of?"

She opened her mouth and eyes wide, and shook her head violently. "No, no, no. We go to church. He would never do anything that would hurt his family or go against the church. I tell you, he killed the cow by accident. I know it. He is a good man." She looked at the presiding judge and said, "Your Honor, he did not mean to do this. You must believe me. He is a good man. He loves his family. He would not do anything that might hurt us."

Irene, Jim, and Judge Akers saw no empathy on the presiding judge's face. The attorney must have had the same reaction. He tried one more time. "And you say that during the ten years you've been married, he never did anything that might be considered a crime?"

"No, nothing," she said firmly. She had been energized by her own outburst and added, "He works hard for all we have. I do sewing. We are a hardworking family. If the coyotes hadn't gotten our chickens, we would have had eggs to eat. He would never have gone hunting. But he was after a deer, not a cow."

The attorney turned to the prosecutor, indicating that the witness was his, and sat down at the defense table. The District Attorney stood up and rolled his eyes. "Of course, Mrs. Martinez," he said. "You would defend your husband. He puts food on the table, even if he has to steal it."

The defense attorney stood up. "Your Honor—"

The presiding judge interrupted by stating, "That will be enough. Just ask your questions."

"All right, Mrs. Martinez, let's assume you're telling the truth. You don't know for a fact that your husband didn't kill the cow deliberately. After all, I'm sure the family would have enjoyed beef for dinner rather than venison."

The frightened woman said, "Actually, my children prefer venison."

A few people in the courtroom laughed.

"Oh, I see. But my point is that you don't know for a fact that he didn't kill the cow on purpose, and then when he realized that someone had seen him, decided to take the cow to the Chief."

"I know that my husband would never lie to me, and he said that he killed the cow by mistake."

The woman, who could hardly talk at the beginning of her testimony, now spoke firmly and without hesitation. Irene was surprised. She had questioned how wise it was to ask the poor, tired woman to testify. But when she glanced at Judge Akers, she saw a slight smile on his face. He knew her. He must have known she would speak well.

The prosecutor shook his head. "I'm sure that's exactly what a wife would say. Your Honor, I have nothing more for this so-called 'witness.'"

Neither the presiding judge nor the prosecuting attorney seemed impressed with her testimony. However, the Judge, Irene, and Jim proudly watched as Mrs. Martinez started the walk back to her children. She stood up straight, her head held high, and she looked right into the eyes of that prosecutor and then those of the men in the first three rows with no hesitation. Some of them even looked away. It was a moment to remember.

But that sense of triumph was short-lived. The presiding judge said, "I have enough to make a ruling now. The law is very clear. Killing cattle is a felony. Mr. Martinez is sentenced to one year in a state penitentiary without benefit of probation or parole." He looked directly at the defendant and said, "I'm sure you'll think twice about killing someone's cattle ever again."

The group of men in the front cheered at the sentence. Judge Akers leaned over to Irene and confided, "My friends from the Cattlemen's Association. I warned Mrs. Martinez. This is wrong. I've told them repeatedly that the punishment is too severe for the crime. They know exactly how I feel."

He got up and immediately walked up to Mrs. Martinez and put his arm around her. The group of men from the Cattlemen's Association simply shook their heads at the Judge. He ignored them and shook hands with the defense attorney. He then patted the defendant on the back and watched as he was taken away. He and the attorney, along with Irene and Jim, helped Mrs. Martinez lead the children out of the courtroom.

He said to her, "Don't worry. They'll appeal. In the meantime, my assistant—you know, Irene Alvarez in my office?"

Irene smiled at her and said, "Hello, Mrs. Martinez. I'm going to help you get some sewing jobs that you can do at home, so you can still watch the children while you earn some money. I've already lined up three new customers in addition to the Judge and us."

The woman looked at Judge Akers with her very tired eyes and smiled. "You are so kind. But why is the rest of the world so against us?"

Chapter 19

On that Friday, when Oscar again refused to see Clara, she handed the deputy her latest lesson page. He smiled and winked. "It's working. He's reading everything you bring. I bet he'll see you Monday."

"Seriously?" His support encouraged her. The deputy seemed interested in helping Oscar, and she found that heartening. He was her comrade and ally.

He nodded. "Yes, seriously. He reads everything over and over. You'll see, if not Monday, then Tuesday. But I think he'll miss getting your written lessons during the weekend, and he'll want to see you on Monday."

She left the jail and walked over to the courthouse, cheered by the deputy's words. She wanted to alert the Judge to what was happening. Even small encouragement might be useful. She had read the morning's paper about the outcome of the Martinez trial and suspected that he might be discouraged. Irene had told her how he felt about Mr. Martinez and his family and his inability to prevent a long prison term for something that he believed didn't merit it. Given his pride in the justice system, he would not appreciate its blemishes.

She was pleased to have even the slim hope offered by the deputy of reaching Oscar. She was fearful, however, that the Judge was more focused on his need to deliver Oscar's sentence, which could cause him to be moved to another prison as part of his punishment.

When she arrived, she found Irene typing and waited respectfully until she looked up. "No lesson again today. I'm sorry. Let me check if he can see you now."

"His door is closed. Is there someone with him?"

"Yes. He's talking to the Chief. Hold on."

She knocked and entered upon hearing a gruff "Come in."

"Clara is here, sir. Can you see her now?"

"No. Tell her to wait. It will probably take us about ten more minutes."

Irene pulled the door closed and looked at Clara. "You heard?"

"Yes. That's fine. I've got homework and lots of stories to write. Have you worked for the Judge very long?"

Irene smiled. "I used to work with him at his law firm. He brought me here when he became a judge."

"Oh, how did you get the job at his law firm?"

She said, "Well, my mother abandoned my father, me, and my brother when I was quite young. We were never sure why. My father did his best to raise us, but he died when I was still in high school. The Judge knew my father through his work—he had helped him with an insurance investigation. Anyway, when my dad died, the Judge arranged for me and my brother to live with a family so I could finish school, and then he hired me to work at his firm."

"And you've been with him ever since?"

"Yes." She stopped and looked up at the ceiling. "I think it's been more than ten years. I've learned much about the law and can help him because of that. He pays me well, which is good because we don't make too much money growing lima beans on the farm." She laughed. "Although the war in Europe is certainly helping—the price and demand have really increased this month."

"Oh, you have a farm?"

"Yes, with my husband and our two children."

"How old are they?"

"Five and eight."

"Do they like to read?"

Irene laughed. "Well the eight-year-old does. The five-year-old, not too much yet."

Clara heard someone at the Judge's inner door and said, "By the way, what kind of mood is he in today?"

"Oh, I'm not too sure. He was discouraged with the outcome of the Martinez case—poor Mrs. Martinez." Irene shook her head, "But he was relieved with what happened with the Rodriguez case. The two men pleaded guilty."

"The Rodriguez case was the murder from ten years ago, right?"

"Yes. At first, they pleaded 'not guilty,' but the Sheriff had enough evidence to convict them, I think, and their attorney must have believed he couldn't win. Just goes to show that you shouldn't step out on your spouse—that's how they caught them, you know!"

"It would have been an interesting case to follow. But I sure wouldn't envy the Judge having to decide about putting someone to death."

Irene shook her head. "We've never discussed it. I tried once, but he refused to go into it. But I don't think the Judge supports the death penalty. But if the District Attorney called for it and they were pronounced guilty, the Judge would have had to sentence them, I think."

The door opened and the Chief came out. "Hello, Clara. I understand you're trying to help teach Oscar Briarley how to read." He shook his head. "Good luck with that. You do know that Oscar Briarley comes from a family of hardened criminals, don't you?"

"Well, his family might be, but Oscar isn't. At least not yet."

He nodded. "Yeah, I have to admit, I don't think Oscar is like the rest of his family. Well, good luck with that one." He turned to the Judge and said, "See you tomorrow."

The Judge told her to enter and then asked, "What's happening with Oscar? Have you been able to get him to say who his partner was?"

"He hasn't been willing to see me all week, but Deputy Brown thinks he will see me on Monday. I've been taking him written lessons with short stories every day about him and me, and the deputy says he reads them over and over, and he thinks Oscar's ready to talk to me. So maybe when I see him on Monday."

The Judge stayed silent, and because Clara had run out of anything else to say, she said nothing, not something she did easily. Finally, he asked, "So what kind of stories have you been writing that have caused Oscar to want to see you again?"

She smiled. She believed she had won something if he wanted to know about Oscar's reading progress. "Well, mostly I just keep asking him questions, you know, 'Who are you?' kind of questions. 'What's your favorite color? What do you like to do when you're not eating or sleeping?' Then part of the lesson is to help me write his story. And every now and then I tell him something about me, and what I like. But in each lesson, I give him new words that are harder or that he doesn't know. That way, he'll want to see me so I can help him learn those new words. He really basically wants to learn, so I'm just using that to get him to the next step."

The Judge smiled. "Good for you."

"Now I just need to get Oscar to see me again."

The Judge looked at her, shaking his head. "You read a lot, don't you? Are you familiar with a character in Voltaire's *Candide* named Pangloss?"

"No, I've never read anything by Voltaire. Should I read it?"

"Yes, I think you should. *Candide* is basically a criticism of a philosophy of optimism popular in his time."

She tried to make the connection. "You mean that I am too optimistic?"

"I think you jump to the side of optimism too quickly, but in the end I believe it serves you well, unlike Pangloss."

She decided not to respond.

He stood up and started to pace. "But let's put that optimistic problem-solving brain of yours to work. We're still searching for Harry Winter. I'd like your opinion as a teenager who might know things we adults don't."

She said, "Yes, sir."

"You know that Harry's father died several years ago of pneumonia. His mother remarried. Harry's stepdad was not happy about supporting a child that wasn't his."

Clara interrupted. "Yes, that was obvious with the way his stepfather acted at Mr. Brant's memorial. He doesn't seem to be a good father or even a nice man. I didn't like him."

The Judge's Story

The Judge nodded, "Well, apparently he is very stern with Harry and has been known to beat him quite severely with a belt. The doctor at the hospital told the Chief he's treated Harry several times for wounds and bruises consistent with a beating."

She said quickly, emboldened by his trust in her, "But that's probably why he's the way he is! Can't you do something? Can't you get him out of that house?"

"The Chief is still investigating. He takes quite an interest in helping boys, you know. He lost his own teenage son as a result of his involvement with a gang—that was before the Chief arrived here. But that's neither here nor there. What I'm wondering is if you might have any idea where he might go to hide."

"I wish there was something you could do to get him out of that house. Of course, I guess the Chief has to find him first." She realized the Judge probably concurred, and that what he had asked her implied his agreement. "Well, he must be able to take care of himself. But will he have to go to jail since he robbed the drive-in theater?"

"He's sixteen, and this would be his first arrest, although the Chief caught him hanging around some stores with windows broken by someone throwing bricks through them. That's why he comes to the boys' club meetings—the Chief made it part of his punishment."

"But what can I do?"

"I need you to think like a teenager trying not to be found. Where would you go? Who would help you?" He hesitated and then said, "Someone pilfered the garbage one night outside a couple of the downtown restaurants, and maybe that was Harry looking for something to eat, so we think he might be back here in Ventura, although no one knows how he might travel back and forth to L.A. The Chief has visited Harry's home several times, but he's convinced the stepfather would definitely not hide him. No love lost there. Someone must be helping him, but so far we haven't figured out who."

"I can't think of anywhere other than maybe a church, or what about that old school that was shut down a few years ago?"

"We've alerted all the churches in the area, and the Chief checked out that abandoned school already." The Judge stood up and paced.

Clara said, "You might want to check with the boys at the Chief's boys' club meeting. They might know something. Some of them seemed quite friendly with him."

The Judge nodded. "You're right. That's a good idea. We're serving food tomorrow—one of the mothers suggested it and several of them got together and are bringing things for the boys to eat. And I bet Harry is having difficulty getting food. One of them might try to steal some to take to him. Thanks, Clara. Did you need anything else today?"

"No, sir. I'm glad I could help."

Irene knocked on the open door. "The District Attorney is here, sir, for your next meeting."

"Thanks, Irene." He turned to Clara. "I need to speak with District Attorney Bilkins now. Thank you for stopping by."

Irene glared at the Judge, and he knew she was concerned about the responsibility he was putting on Clara and was displeased that he asked her for more help. Irene felt sorry for Clara. She had just endured a fifteen-minute meeting with the Judge that had jerked her from praise about her accomplishments to criticism as overly optimistic and then to usefulness when asked for help.

Irene waited for Clara and when the Judge closed his door said to her, "He can be a little harsh sometimes. He thinks he's supporting you."

Clara cocked her head and gave an expression of disbelief that Irene appreciated.

Clara smiled, and then remembered that she had been curious about Irene's husband. "Does your husband ever visit here? I've never met him, you know."

"He was here yesterday for the Martinez trial. And he's been studying at the library. He's been around. You're just missing him."

"Oh. I see. I thought maybe the Judge had him searching for Harry Winter."

Irene smiled. "I think that's the Chief's job."

Clara wanted to pursue her questioning but the phone rang. She waved good-bye as Irene picked up the handset, and then she walked home for the weekend.

Chapter 20

That Saturday the Judge pulled up in front of the meeting place for the Chief's boys' club with a goal in mind—to see if he could get any of the attendees to give him information about Harry. He had alerted the Chief about what he wanted, and the Chief had likewise advised his deputies.

The Judge found it frustrating that they had not found the boy yet. How easy was it for a sixteen-year-old to just disappear? Maybe he went back to L.A. It would make sense. He could get lost in that large city. No one had seen him, nor was there even a trace of him following the sighting of someone pilfering the garbage at the downtown restaurants. The Judge had become more concerned about Harry's welfare after meeting his stepfather, who was a bully and certainly not a loving parent. Harry would not likely return to his home, given the treatment he would probably receive there.

The Judge carried his papers into the boys' clubroom and then joined the deputies to prepare for their arrival. The mothers were already in the room, and the Judge helped to set up a table for the food. As the boys started filing in, he pointed to the food and invited them to help themselves. They were excited to do so and piled up platefuls of bacon, potatoes, eggs, grapes, and oranges before starting their various projects. The Judge had to admit that the food certainly smelled good. But he decided to wait to see what was left over rather than filling his own plate. He knew that this food had cost these families some sacrifices.

He circulated from group to group for more than an hour. The boys were unusually subdued. He had anticipated comments from them, but perhaps they were intimidated by his presence. He noticed the boy who had joined with Harry in criticizing Clara for "ratting" out Oscar weeks before. When he saw the Judge, he quickly averted his eyes and pretended to be going in the opposite direction. This caused the Judge to follow him and ask, "How have you been doing? Are you reading any books?"

"No. I gotta go."

The Judge watched him head toward the food and decided to check out the table where several boys were building a bridge with an erector set. As he approached, he heard one of the smaller boys tell an older boy, "We need to get some extra food to take to—"

When he saw the Judge, however, he stopped talking, and the group dispersed to different parts of the room. He suspected they might be gathering food for Harry but also knew that many families still were unable to get enough to eat, so it was possible that the boy was just taking some extra food home to his family. But, he decided to watch them, just in case. If Harry were close by, they might take the food to him. He could follow them and, if they led him someplace suspicious, he could get the Chief. It would do no harm if they didn't lead him to Harry.

He didn't want them to think he'd overheard, so he stayed out of the way and watched the building of the bridge from a distance. A few minutes later, he saw the two boys who'd been discussing the food go to the table and fill a ten-pound empty cloth flour bag when they thought no one was looking.

He searched the room but didn't see the Chief anywhere, and the only deputy was busy with a group of boys. So he picked up a book that was lying on a table and pretended to be leafing through it. While peering at the book, the Judge watched the boys, who were making their way to the back door. He walked toward the front door with the objective of going outside and then retreating to the back door where the boys were leaving. He hoped they wouldn't suspect his plan.

While the two boys left through the back door, he went out through the front. When he thought that they could not see him, he hurried around the corner to find out where they were going. He started after them. His broad stride enabled him to catch up and, several blocks away, he saw the two boys go into a well-kempt warehouse that stored farm equipment. He followed them through the same door as quietly as he could and stopped just inside.

The structure had no windows, and the Judge waited for his eyes to adjust to the dark. The only light came from somewhere ahead off to the right, revealing several tractors, which explained the smell of rubber coming from their tires. It was difficult to see, and he wasn't sure what to do next. He didn't want to startle them into running again, but he didn't want to lose them either. He started to move toward the lighted area when he saw Harry sitting on the concrete floor pushing food into his mouth, as if he hadn't eaten in days. The sounds of his chewing seemed unrealistically loud in the quiet warehouse, which shielded the interior from any outside noise. The other two boys were emptying the bag of food on the floor next to him. The Judge contemplated turning around and getting the Chief, but then Harry saw him and stood up, ignoring spilled food, getting ready to run.

The Judge said, "Harry, don't go. I want to help you. Now what's this all about?"

"What's it to you!" Harry did not seem afraid of the Judge. His eyes were more blank than anything, almost lifeless.

"Look. You're in trouble, I know, but it's not hopeless. Tell me what I can do to help. Should I get in touch with your mother?"

Harry laughed briefly. "Don't bother. She doesn't give a damn what happens to me. And my stepfather—that king of respectability—well, he seems to win no matter what I do." Again, Harry responded listlessly, with no energy, almost toneless, perhaps from little food and/or sleep.

The Judge wasn't sure what to do. Harry's low energy concerned him, but his instinct told him to match it. He feared that if he got excited, Harry would bolt. So when he responded, he did not raise his voice. He spoke slowly and calmly. "I understand you feel that way. But even if they don't care, you have to. You don't want to spend your life in prison. And you won't have to. Robbing the drive-in was your first offense. We can probably get you probation, if you're willing to listen. Are you listening?"

The Judge's Story

The two boys who had delivered the food remained in place and poised to respond when Harry started to creep toward the door. He told the Judge, "All right, all right. I'm listening."

The Judge turned with Harry's movements so that he always faced him, and he continued to speak calmly with little emotion. The Judge knew that he had to convince Harry to give himself up, but the teenager was far too savvy to believe that surrendering would mean he would go free. "What you did at the drive-in is a mistake. And it's one that you'll have to pay for. But I want you to remember that it's not the end of your life. You can change the way you live. You won't always be staying with your mother and stepfather. While you're going through this, keep remembering that you can still get an education, earn a living, maybe buy a house, get married, and live a better life than what you've had so far. Do you believe that?"

"Sure, whatever you say." The Judge could tell from his tone and his posture, which was poised to run, that he neither believed nor cared about anything he had just said.

"No, it's more than what I say. It's true. Your life can be different."

The boy looked at the Judge like he was the stupidest person on earth, shaking his head and sneering. The Judge told Irene later that he would never forget that look. His expression had changed from disinterested blank eyes to reflecting what the Judge could only describe as hatred. His eyes seemed to turn almost red. "How the hell would you know? You don't know anything about my life!"

Although concerned by this new reaction, the Judge quickly said, "Because I was you once. When my parents got divorced, my stepdad wanted nothing to do with me. Then my real father didn't want me either. It took me a long time, but I managed to make it. You can, too. But only you can do it, but we're here to help if you want it. One day at a time. Do you hear me?"

Harry shook his head and smirked. "I hear you, but I don't believe that your life was anything like mine." Then he laughed, a dry laugh that sounded forced and even ominous, like it was intended to hurt someone. He faced the Judge full on, and for a few seconds the Judge feared that the teenager might attack him.

Instead he said, "Let me try this on you. My stepdad likes me for how tight my ass is. Got it? My mother's so weak she does nothing to stop him. He's been on me for years—since I turned thirteen. And do you know who's the leader of the crime gangs here in Ventura? Bingo. You got it. My stepdad. He's got us all organized so we can go out and rob whatever place he sends us.

"So you tell me, Mister Judge. How am I ever going to make it in this world? My stepdad controls whatever I do. When I tried to tell on him, he told the cops I was a problem juvenile. The cops want to lock me up. My mother is so stupid—she lets my stepdad walk all over both her and me." As he was talking, he moved slowly toward the door, which the Judge was trying to block. Although he started his discourse in an animated voice, by the end of his confession his speech had returned to a monotone, almost like an alarm clock running down.

His words stunned the Judge. He wasn't sure how to proceed, but knew he had to say something. He continued to speak quietly, but tried to add concern and urgency to his tone. "Harry, I didn't know all that. But I promise you I'll look into it, and so will the Chief. Regardless, you need to look beyond your current family life and surroundings. And the first step is to give yourself up, so we can help you. Try to think of a life without your stepdad, like you're starting all over. What do you like to do, Harry?"

The teenager looked at the Judge with expressionless eyes. "Maybe I just like to do nothing. Maybe I just like to sit around and—do nothing. Maybe I don't know what I want to do because just plain being alive is too damn hard." He was almost to the door. If the Judge were going to stop him, he would have to do it physically. Harry was going to push his way through the door.

The Judge now raised his voice and said almost frantically, "Please, Harry. Think. You're a bright boy. Why do you think that your life has to stay this way? You can change it. You can make it different. You have choices."

But Harry wasn't listening. He pushed against the Judge, who tried to hold on to him with little success. Just then the other two boys, whom the Judge had overlooked, yelled loudly and ran at the Judge enabling Harry to wiggle out as they pushed him hard to the floor with a thud that could have signaled broken bones. All three teenagers then ran out the door. The Judge managed to get up, tested a hurt leg, and started chasing Harry. He saw one of the younger boys and yelled at him to go get the Chief or a deputy, but the boy just smiled and ran away. Then he saw a young man on a bicycle, and he pulled out a five dollar bill and told him to go back to the boys' club building and tell the Chief that he was chasing Harry Winter and to come to the warehouse as fast as possible.

He started running in the direction where he last saw Harry. He caught a glimpse of him a block ahead. He continued in the same direction. When he reached the railroad tracks, he saw Harry running toward a parked freight car. The Judge shouted, "Harry, wait! I want to help you."

But Harry kept running. He stopped briefly and looked at the Judge, who also stopped but kept shouting, "Harry, we can help you! I promise. We can get you into a home where people will care for you."

Harry shook his head. "Then what, Judge? What do I do then? I'm damaged goods!"

The Judge shouted, "You learn to live your life without someone like your stepfather. You learn what it means to live a different life—one that you choose."

The Judge watched Harry move toward the parked freight car. When Harry saw the Chief pull up, he started to climb the ladder attached to the car. The Judge continued to shout, "Harry, stop! We will help you."

The Chief and the deputy got out, walking toward the teenager. Then, they all heard the whistle of an approaching train, causing Harry to stop and the Judge to wave at the Chief. The space between the freight car where Harry was climbing and the track for the oncoming train was only a few feet. The Judge feared that if he didn't hold on tightly, the force of the oncoming train could pull him off.

"Stay away from me!" Harry yelled.

The Chief stood still and looked at the Judge for guidance. The Judge nodded and yelled, "Harry, the Chief and I want to help you. We have always tried to lend a hand. Think of the boys' club. We created it to make it easier for you." But Harry kept climbing and quickly reached the top of the freight car. He looked out over the yard full of trains and then at the group below. He smiled like he had a secret.

Meanwhile, the oncoming engine had not slowed down. The Chief ran toward it waving his arms and screaming to stop the train. He wasn't sure if it would hit Harry, who was now facing the moving train and yelling, "I'm not going to go to jail! There's nothing I want to do, Judge. I don't want to do nothing. But I don't want to go to jail. That much I do know. I want to do what I want to do—even if I don't know what that is." And he laughed and pointed at the Judge and said, "Get it?"

The Judge screamed back, "I understand that, Harry. And we'll all work with you to do that—what you want to do. And we'll help you figure it all out. You have time. It's not unusual for someone at your age not to know what you want yet."

The noise from the oncoming train dominated their reactions. The engineer had started to brake, and the sparks raised an ominous burning odor.

Harry was pacing back and forth on top of the freight car. The Chief continued to wave his arms at the oncoming train, which despite the application of the brakes, was barely slowing down. The deputy was edging closer to the freight car's ladder, while watching the oncoming train. He realized he needed to get out of the way of the moving train.

The Judge's Story

Meanwhile, the Judge was reaching out to Harry, trying to motion him to hold on tightly.

The braking freight train started to slow, but was still approaching at a relentless rate. The Chief had turned and was hurrying back toward Harry, who paced on top of the parked freight car not caring about his safety. The deputy started to climb the ladder Harry had just used, but grabbed hold of the rungs as securely as he could, as the moving train grew closer.

In an instant, Harry threw himself in front of the oncoming engine.

The Judge was screaming, and the train was screeching.

The Judge looked away. It was almost as if a strong wind had turned him away, but somehow he knew he'd always remember the sight of Harry falling toward the train and he, yards away, with his arms in the air hopelessly trying to catch the falling boy to save him.

It was over in a brief moment.

The authorities spent the rest of the day removing poor Harry's remains from the tracks, treating the train's distraught engineer, and trying to talk to the Judge. The Chief had tried to get him to sit, but the Judge pulled away. It took the Chief several attempts but finally the Judge allowed him to lead him to the nearby patrol car and he got in. He mumbled over and over, "I failed him. I had him, and I couldn't convince him. Why did he think he couldn't change his life? Why?"

Meanwhile, one of the deputies pulled up to the scene, along with a wagon from the county morgue. The Chief talked to his deputy and shook his head, then walked back to the Judge. He said, "We've learned some very disturbing things about the boy's stepfather and how he treated him. One of my deputies is talking with his somewhat rattled mother back at the station now. If my deputy understands her correctly, not only was he beating Harry, but also apparently he was—" The Chief looked around to make sure no one could hear him, but the Judge already knew what he was going to say.

He nodded, "I know. He told me."

The Chief said, "He told you that, well, his stepfather was having sex with him—you know, how a man does to another man. Only Harry was a boy." He looked down at his shoes and moved his lips but no words came out. He remained quiet for a few seconds and then managed to say, "It's been happening for a few years." He couldn't help himself. His face turned red and he slammed his hand against the car. "Son of a bitch. I'm gonna get that guy. We're looking for him."

The Judge stared at the Chief and said, "Are you saying that his mother knew and didn't stop it?"

The Chief nodded.

The Judge shook his head and mumbled, "I hope you catch him."

The Chief was relieved that the Judge was speaking. He asked, "How did you find him, by the way?"

"I wish I hadn't. He might still be alive."

The Chief shook his head. "You don't know that. But I need to know how you found him. Did someone at the club tell you where he was?"

The Judge managed to say, "The two Franklin brothers started loading a bag with food, and I followed them to that warehouse nearby with tractors and other farm stuff inside. Who owns it, by the way?"

"I think the farm equipment rental company. We didn't think to check it out because it was locked and the rental people go in and out of it all the time, so if Harry had been hiding there, they would have noticed him. We'll check it. Maybe there's a place to hide, but I guess it doesn't matter much now."

"You should talk to the Franklin brothers to find out how they were connected with Harry."

"That's a good idea. They might know how he was getting back and forth between here and L.A., too, and if he did any other robberies."

Suddenly the Judge remembered what else Harry had said. "Chief, Harry also told me that his stepfather was the one who organized and ran the robberies. Can that be true, or do you think he was just making it up to get even with him?"

"I don't know, but we'll check into it. I can't believe Blakensfeld's smart enough to have pulled off all these robberies without us catching on to him."

"I'm just telling you what Harry said, and I don't think he'd lie, quite frankly. He seemed quite sincere. He had nothing to lose at that point."

"We'll look into it."

The Judge looked at the Chief, closed his eyes, and sat shaking his head.

Chapter 21

The Judge returned to his home at dusk, parked the car that he'd picked up at the boys' club, and entered his house—trying hard to convince himself that things were normal. However, when he sat in his chair in the parlor, he kept seeing flashes of Harry talking to him in the dark warehouse, running down the street, climbing the railroad car, and then, over and over, falling to his death in front of the looming engine. He hardly noticed when it got dark in his room and made no move to turn on a light. He just kept going over and over what he could have done differently.

His fatigued body took over, however, and he fell asleep in his chair. Unfortunately, his mind clung to the scenes of that afternoon's tragedy, and he woke up in a few hours sweating and shaking as he saw Harry's face again and again on its way to the train engine. He stood up to get a glass of water and thought about going to bed, but instead returned to his chair, fearful that falling asleep again would bring back the nightmares.

"All right," he told himself. "You've felt sorry for yourself long enough. What the hell are you going to do about it?"

His years of tending to the lives of criminals and innocent victims demanded that something instructive come from the situation. He was unwilling to allow Harry's death to pass without understanding why the boy had been so distraught that he preferred to die rather than solve his problems. Of course, he now factored in the boy's home life, which must have been horrific. What else had he endured? Why had no one cared enough to help this boy? How could his mother have allowed it to happen? Who else was involved? The Judge wanted to catch and punish whoever had caused this boy to hate his life so much that he threw himself in front of a train.

As the sun was rising that morning, he had explored what he needed to know to proceed. And first, he wanted to know who owned the warehouse where Harry had been hiding; and he also wanted more information about his stepfather.

He waited to drive to Irene and Jim's home as late as he could on Sunday morning so as not to disturb them. His restless night had produced a plan, but both Irene and Jim recognized as soon as they saw him that the Judge was upset. His eyes had dark circles, and he was shaking. They had heard about Harry Winter's death, and Irene, especially, knew that the Judge would take the suicide personally, particularly given that it occurred so soon after Oscar's brother's death.

Before they would listen to his request, Irene made him sit down for coffee and biscuits. She was relieved to see that the food helped to revive him, so pushed some bacon at him as well.

While she forced food down him, Jim told him, "It wasn't your fault. Nobody knew what his stepfather was doing to him—nobody except the stepfather and his mother, that is, and they're the ones to blame. I can't believe that his mother didn't put a stop to it."

The Judge nodded. Talking with his friends reinforced his intention to find out the truth and why it had happened.

"Thanks, Jim. I will always feel some responsibility. If I hadn't chased him, he might still be alive." He put up his hand to stop Jim's interruption. "Regardless, I'm here to hire you to find out any information you can on Blakensfeld, that's Harry's stepfather. And, although this may have nothing to do with his situation, can you find out who owned the warehouse where Harry had been hiding; and who might have had access to it? The Franklin boys led me there, and I don't know who they are other than their last names, but the Chief might."

Jim nodded. "Of course. I'll see if I can find out anything else today and let you know in the morning."

The Judge looked around suddenly realizing they were alone. "Where are your children?"

Irene smiled. "They're next door playing with the neighbors' children. We alternate on Sundays."

The Judge stood up. "I'm sorry. I've interrupted your time alone together. Listen, thank you for the food. It really helped. I think I'll go try to get some sleep. I didn't get much last night."

Irene and Jim both protested and tried to convince him to stay. But he had felt like he absorbed enough of their energy to return to his routine of walking around Ventura and out on the pier. He expected it was clear enough for him to see the Channel Islands, and he felt the need to surround himself with the sounds of the surf and the sea gulls screeching along with the feel of the damp sea air.

Chapter 22

The Judge walked into the courthouse the following Monday, welcoming its familiar sense of endorsement. Irene had not yet arrived so he unlocked the door to his chambers and entered. He expected her and her husband to arrive shortly and wanted to talk to them before going to Court that day.

He sat down at his desk and stared at the calendar Irene had placed there on Friday before departing for the weekend, but nothing got through to him. Instead what he continued to see was Harry jumping from the freight car. Then his mind carried him to the last time he had visited Tommy Briarley who, as a young man, was struggling to understand who he was and why what he had done was wrong. Both decided to end their lives.

To the Judge, who had overcome many problems to succeed, the choice of suicide had never been an option. He tried to recall over and over what Harry had said, something about not knowing what he wanted, but he knew he didn't want to go to jail. He wanted to do what he wanted to do, but he didn't know what he wanted to do. It made little sense, and yet it made a lot of sense.

"Good morning, Judge." Irene startled him. "Are you all right?"

"Thanks, Irene. Yes. Is Jim with you?"

"Yes, sir," said Jim. "And I have some of the information you're looking for." He sat in the chair in front of the Judge's desk. "The Chief was correct. The farm equipment rental company owns the warehouse. So I checked to see who had access to it, and discovered—are you ready for this?—that the father of the Franklin brothers manages it. The Chief picked up the boys and is still holding them, by the way. He asked them how Harry got into the warehouse. They said that they got hold of the key from their father's office and let Harry in. There are several hiding places in the building that both boys knew about, so Harry could hide whenever anyone entered the building. They used to play there until their father caught them."

"What about the father? Is he someone we should check out?"

Jim nodded. "Oh, yes. The boys claim their father was not aware of what they'd done, but the Chief asked me to check him out anyway. Besides, he's Mrs. Chissum's boss, and I was already looking into him given her suspicions. This is just too big of a coincidence—that the person who she believes threatened her son to intimidate him into helping with robberies is the *same* person who manages the warehouse where Harry was hiding. I believe that the Franklin boys' father and Harry Winter's stepfather are somehow connected. Anyway, I'm going to try to see Franklin later today. I'll let you know. In the meantime, the Chief is searching for Blakensfeld and will arrest him for what he did to Harry."

Jim looked at a small notebook he kept in his pocket. "Oh, and the boys said that they didn't know how Harry got to and from L.A., but then they said he knows how to drive so maybe he just stole a car."

The Judge looked puzzled. "How did he learn to drive? I thought the Chief said his stepfather didn't own a car."

"That may be incorrect. That's something else I'm checking. I think Mrs. Blakensfeld may own some property that her husband manages. I want to check it out to see if there might not be a car on it. Also, I'm wondering how Blakensfeld delivers his used furniture. Maybe he has some kind of small truck somewhere."

"Good, Jim. Did you find out if Franklin and Blakensfeld are acquainted?"

"Not yet, but I'm checking into that, too."

"Did you learn anything else about how the stepfather treated the boy?"

Jim looked at the Judge. "Are you sure you want to hear it?"

"Hell, yes, Jim! I've got to understand why he killed himself."

"I went to the hospital where he's been treated at least a half-dozen times. His mother would bring him in." He checked his notes. "All total, both of his arms were broken at different times; and he had broken ribs, a concussion, burns, and lacerations."

"My god. How could that have gone unnoticed?"

"The doctor said that the mother claimed the boy was very clumsy. She claimed a new accident every time—he fell off his bicycle, he tripped down the stairs, he slipped on a rock and fell over waterfalls. You get the picture."

"All right. See what else you can dig up. I've got to get to the courtroom. I'm so disgusted that I pity the criminal who faces me today."

He grabbed his robe and left.

Jim turned to his wife. "That was not an easy report to give."

She said, "You knew it wouldn't be. I just hope Clara can get Oscar to tell us what he knows. I can't imagine what one more failure will do to the Judge right now."

"You know I never put much faith in her. I just don't think the boy has any idea what he's facing and he has only one thing to cling to—his belief that squealing is wrong."

He turned and left Irene to ponder what was next.

Chapter 23

Clara approached the jail on Monday afternoon with mixed emotions. Friday she'd left with the hopeful words from the deputy that Oscar might see her. Since then, however, the Judge had called out her optimism and she learned that Harry had killed himself. When she heard about Harry, she found it difficult to prepare Oscar's lesson. She recalled the day he questioned her about writing a story that told how someone else felt. But no matter how bad life got, she could not imagine not wanting to read a good book; or see the ocean and hear its pounding surf; or feel a breeze on her face; or hear music. She simply could not imagine ending her life.

Clara recalled that the Judge had questioned if Oscar knew Harry. Given the death of both his brother and now Harry by suicide, she hesitated to ask him—if he was even willing to see her. With the two suicides on her mind, she had prepared a lesson that contained five of her favorite things, thinking that might cause Oscar to consider his favorites and maybe motivate him to imagine what his life could be outside of jail.

When she arrived, Deputy Brown greeted her with a smile. "Well, let's see if he's ready for you today. He certainly has been poring over the lessons you gave him last week."

One of the other deputies left to bring Oscar to the meeting room. After putting her bag away, Clara walked to the door and waited for the deputy to either let her in or tell her that Oscar was not available. She was rewarded when the door opened. She entered just as Oscar sat down at the table, with all of the papers from the previous week in front of him. He looked up at her and grinned as if nothing had happened.

She smiled back, and almost laughed. He looked very much like a boy. She hadn't noticed his freckles before, but they were prominent that day. Someone had cut his hair, so it was almost tame. The prison clothes were clean, but too large for him, which probably made him appear smaller than he really was. He was sticking his tongue out and bowing his head—like he had done something mischievous.

She sat down across from him. "How have you been?"

He said, "Swell. I need you to tell me some of the words on these papers."

"Do you want to talk about why you didn't see me last week?"

"No, ma'am. I understand what you're trying to tell me, I think. You know, Tommy tried to help me. That's why I didn't want to see no one. One time he'd been drinkin' some'a Pa's hard cider, and he was feelin' low, I guess. Anyway, he told me to get out of there. He told me to run as fer from Pa as I could get."

"Why did he say that?"

"Pa ain't a good person."

She held up her hand, and he said, "'Isn't.' But I don't want to talk about Pa. I want to learn what these words are. Do you think you could get me a pencil?" They both looked at Deputy Brown.

He shook his head. "Not likely, but I'll see what I can do."

"Yes, sir. It's hard doin' my lessons without something to write with."

The deputy nodded. "I'll see what I can do. Maybe I can arrange for you to spend time in here with a pencil and me for a half hour or so a day. That way, it won't go back to the cell."

Clara said, "Meanwhile, let's review all of these lessons and catch up. I have a new one for today and a new book for you."

They worked their way through each lesson. She was rewarded with his lists of why reading was important. "So I kin know why the wind blows and why it rains. Isn't that somethin'? And I'd sure like to know where a baby cow comes from. I went with Pa to a barn once and saw a little tiny baby cow come out of its ma. That's really somethin'." And it turned out he liked to hear the surf. "I only been to the beach once, but, Clara, when them waves hit the sand, it's somethin'. Why do they do that?"

That day, by telling her about his favorite things, Oscar gushed about who he was, and it seemed to Clara that at that point, he might have known himself better than she knew herself. He didn't know all the right words, but he had spent time exploring his likes and dislikes. Now he wanted help to explain himself and to discover the world around him through reading.

She shared her feelings with the Judge later at a meeting in his chambers. "It was one of the best moments of my life. I can't believe how I felt. I wanted to jump up and yell, 'Hooray!' Then I remembered Harry."

The Judge looked at her with a new expression that day that she didn't quite understand until he said, "We can't always be successful. We just have to keep working at it. We missed out helping Harry, but it sounds like you're well on your way to showing Oscar how to welcome and, to some degree, direct the life he's been given. We all need support from each other."

She looked at the Judge and said, "Yes. Thank you for giving me credit for helping Oscar, but, you know, it just occurred to me that I didn't do as much as Oscar did. He found whatever it takes to learn, but he was Oscar before I ever came along. He had some kind of strength in him to reject his father's influence. I may have given him guidance on how to build on it through reading, but he had it in him. Maybe that's what I've been missing."

The Judge shook his head. "Maybe, but that sounds a little deterministic, like if someone doesn't have it in him, then he can't change. I don't believe that."

On that day sitting with the Judge, she remembered in later years that she felt like she was the one who was being mentored and that she'd already traveled to many different places guided by the Judge. She felt like, thanks to him, she had changed maybe even more than Shaggy had transformed into Oscar.

Chapter 24

Right in the middle of the burglaries, Harry's suicide, and the investigation of Harry's stepfather, the Judge's family arranged a party for his sixtieth birthday. Irene and Jim were relieved for the interruption. They believed that the Judge needed a reminder of his family and his successes. Clara, on the other hand, was curious about attending the Judge's birthday party not because it offered food, fun, or entertainment, but because it would give her the opportunity to explore the Judge's personal life. She figured she would write about him some day, and yearned to fill out his character with more personal details.

She and her parents arrived at his home on the day of the party at the exact time it was to begin. A young woman, who turned out to be his daughter, greeted them and showed them into the parlor, where cut flowers were arranged in vases. The table in the dining room was full of food, including a birthday cake that said "Happy Birthday, Judge." The Judge was dressed as always—black suit, vest, and tie. When Clara and her parents entered, he was standing in a small circle talking to District Attorney Bilkins and the Chief. Clara heard the District Attorney say, "We can't keep him in the county jail forever. It's not an orphanage. You need to sentence him."

She saw an expression she had come to recognize as anger on the Judge's face. "This is my birthday party. It is not appropriate that we discuss a case here."

Bilkins tried not to look embarrassed, but his face betrayed him and turned red. The Chief looked away with a slight smile. Clara was curious about what the Chief thought of Oscar. He had never seemed to want to prosecute him. She figured the Chief knew something that the rest of them didn't. Or else maybe he just felt the boy was too young to go to prison.

Her parents walked toward an acquaintance of theirs. And the Judge seemed busy. She saw Irene standing by herself and went over to her. "Hi, Irene. Is your husband here?"

Irene smiled and said, "He is now." She pointed to a good-looking, young dark-haired man about five feet ten inches, dressed in dark slacks, a jacket, and white shirt who was just entering. Although Clara had never met Jim Alvarez, he looked familiar, but she couldn't quite place where she'd seen him.

Irene said, "Let me introduce you." She pulled Clara toward him. "Jim, this is Clara Wilson, the girl who's been teaching one of the teenagers in jail how to read." She glared at him to make sure he didn't say anything negative, given how he felt about Clara's reading project.

But he smiled and said, "Pleased to meet you," and held out his hand, which he shook just like she was an adult. Then she remembered. Jim was the lone person who had sat behind Oscar at his trial.

The Judge had broken away from his group and interrupted. "Jim, could I talk to you for just a moment?"

She watched as the Judge pulled Irene's husband aside. He kept his hand on Jim's arm and leaned into him so that his ear was close to Jim's mouth. She was surprised that Jim did all the talking. The Judge simply nodded and then re-joined Irene and Clara. He said, "Excuse me, Irene. I'd like Clara to meet my children. And could you check with Jim? He needs some assistance." Clara watched as Irene walked quickly to Jim, who said something to her and then walked over to the Chief and pulled him aside.

Clara's observation of Irene, Jim, and the Chief was interrupted as the Judge steered her across the room to a tall, slender young man with thinning hair—unlike his father—wearing a light-colored suit. He turned out to be his older son, Edward, who didn't resemble the Judge at all.

"I'm so pleased to meet you," she said. "Where do you live? How far did you have to travel?"

The man did have his father's laugh, however. "I came from New York. I actually flew to Los Angeles on a DC-3."

"Oh, wow that must have been exciting! How long did it take?"

"Only seventeen hours. All the way cross-country. Can you believe it?"

Clara was impressed. The same young woman who had answered the door came up and asked, "Edward, you're not boring Clara, are you?" She introduced herself as the Judge's daughter, Florence. Clara thought she was very attractive with her thick brown hair pulled back in a bun and wearing a flowered dress.

Clara said, "Oh, you're the teacher. You must meet my mother. She's a teacher, too."

Florence smiled. "I know. My father introduced us right away. We're getting together tomorrow for lunch. I want to ask her about some problem students."

"Oh, she's really good at helping. She's given me ideas for the boy I'm tutoring when I thought about giving up."

Florence laughed and said, "From what Dad says, you're persistent and seldom give up."

"What else did he say about me?" Clara was anxious but curious.

"Well, perhaps the word 'stubborn' came up." But Florence shook her head as soon as she said it. "Just teasing. He likes your persistence and says you are making a difference in the lives of some of the boys. He was very distraught over the death of the boy last week. He didn't say so, but I know he blames himself. You helped him overcome that with what you've been able to do with the boy you're tutoring."

"Yes, I know he blames himself for Harry's death. But your father has done so much to help people here in Ventura. And none of us knew what a horrible life Harry had."

Clara decided this was as good an opening as any to learn more about the Judge. She asked, "What was it like growing up with him as a father? Sometimes he can be, well, sort of stern." She was recalling the discussion where he called her overly optimistic. "Was he like that as a father? And did he change after he became a judge?"

The Judge's daughter studied Clara for a few seconds, and Clara feared she'd been too forward. However, Florence said, "Well, all of us were out of the house by the time he was appointed a Superior Court judge. So I don't know if he's changed." She hesitated and studied Clara again before continuing. "I'm not sure how much he'd want you to know, but he seems to care about you."

Clara said, "Oh, I know. I promise I won't divulge anything you tell me. I just want to understand him better. I want to be a writer, you know. And it helps to hear about people's feelings so I can create real people, like Mr. Steinbeck does. Besides, the Judge has influenced my life so much this past month."

She nodded as if she'd made a decision. "I'm sure he's affected your life. He does that these days. But I can tell you what I remember most about him was how much my mother's death changed him. I guess it had an impact on all of us, but mostly him. He used to laugh a lot. He would tell silly jokes. He was constantly looking for things to bring my mother to make her happy—like this vase, for example." Florence pointed to a cut-glass vase about a foot tall holding chrysanthemums from their garden. "She always kept it full of flowers from the garden, when they were available. I don't think he welcomed my bringing them here today."

"How else did he change?"

"The best way I can describe it is that he withdrew somewhere inside."

Edward interrupted and seemed more than willing to talk about his father. "He became stern and almost joyless. He stopped participating in our lives."

"Edward, that's harsh," Florence said. "But he's partially right. Dad did reduce the amount of time he spent with us. We were in our teen years, and attention from him would have helped us cope with our mother's death, but he didn't seem to have the capacity. Just remember that if you ever have your own children."

Edward said, "He seemed to have time for his clients, but not us."

Another young man, whom Clara hadn't noticed until he walked up, said, "It's Dad's birthday, and you're both harping on his shortcomings. He threw himself into his clients as a way of coping. When Mom passed, it was like half of Dad died, and he increased the efforts of his other half to fill the void," he said. He turned to Clara and said, "Hi, I'm Johnny, the youngest of the three Akers children. And I understand you're Clara, one of Dad's new friends and the one who's teaching a young hooligan how to read."

"He's not a hooligan, actually. But I am teaching him to read," Clara said. "Your brother and sister were simply answering my question about what it was like to grow up with the Judge as your father. It's hard to get to know him personally. I'm afraid maybe I stirred up some unhappy memories. I didn't mean to."

Johnny said, "Good luck getting to know him. He's a private person and believes it's his responsibility as a judge to keep his personal opinions to himself. The best way to get to know him is to study how he decides his cases and how he used to handle his clients."

Florence jumped in. All three Akers children now seemed eager to talk about their father. "For example, I remember one time he came home after a day in court defending one of his clients. There were three accused all being tried together for the same crime—I can't even remember what it was. But one of them was being represented by a different lawyer."

Edward interrupted. "Oh, I remember that. He was angry because the lawyer came to court without having anything prepared. He had no information about his client or even seemed to know what he was being accused of. Dad was furious. He reminded us all that being prepared is the least we can do in order to defend a client, or to do anything."

Clara looked at Johnny and asked, "Does he ever get discouraged? I mean with a case?"

He looked at his siblings and then said, "Yes and no. He's told me he believes our justice system in the U.S. is the best in the world—even if it does seem to have faults. And speaking of faults, he cautioned me about the jury system—how a crowd mentality can infect a whole town and that can be reflected in a jury." He looked around the room as he said quietly, "He's particularly concerned here in Ventura about how Mexicans are treated. I know that for a fact."

Florence said, "I agree. If you look through his past cases—a good way to get to know him, I might add—you'll see that he represented a lot of Mexicans. We were never well off, by the way, because he was not overly thorough about collecting fees. I'm sure there were many clients who never paid. Growing up, I resented not having more money. Now, I respect him for it."

The Judge walked up to the little group. Clara had been hanging onto every word of the Akers children, wanting to know more, but assumed the Judge had no intention of her hearing too much. He said, "What's going on over here?" He looked at the group and smiled. "I hope you three aren't giving Clara too much information. She's a writer, you know, and I'd hate to see anything about me in her stories."

Despite their minor complaints about their father, the Akers children all looked at him with respect and adoration. They smiled back. Edward said, "Actually, I was filling Clara in on my plane ride from New York."

"Yes, for a railroad man, you decided to travel by air. Interesting, son." The Judge laughed along with Edward.

"I wanted to spend as much time with you as possible, and I could only get so many days off, Dad."

The Judge smiled and put his hand on his son's shoulder. "And I really appreciate it, son. Thank you. All of you. It took a special effort for you to come here today." All three Akers children were blinking. Clara was pleased to see their emotion.

Florence was the first to leave the group, "Oh, I see an old friend. I'll talk to you later, Clara, and I'm looking forward to comparing notes with your mother tomorrow."

Before she could get away, however, the Judge said, "What about that fiancé of yours? Is he going to make it?"

Florence nodded. "He should be here any minute. He was just going to get some ice cream. You can't have a birthday without ice cream!"

The Judge looked at his sons. "What about you two? Has either of you met anyone yet?"

Both young men rolled their eyes and walked away. The Judge turned to Clara, who rushed to say, "Not me. I don't even have a boyfriend. I'm too young."

The Judge laughed, took her arm and guided her to Jim, who was standing alone. "Where's Irene?" Clara asked.

Jim answered, "I think she went out to the kitchen to help with the food."

"Oh, that's nice of her. I really like Irene. How long have you known her?"

"Let me think. We've been married for ten years, and I guess I met her a few years before that."

The Judge interrupted, "Excuse me, I see some new arrivals I need to greet." And he left them there to talk.

"How did you meet Irene? She said the Judge helped her after her parents died, I believe."

"Yes, and that's how I met her. I was a client of the Judge's. He was a lawyer then, of course. He helped me. I had broken a store window, just for fun, not to steal anything. He got my punishment reduced to attending school. So I got an education, which made all the difference in my life. That's why Irene and I are so interested in what you're doing with Oscar Briarley. We know firsthand what it means."

"So was Irene working for the Judge at the time? I guess he would have been a lawyer then."

"Yes she was. I fell in love immediately, but figured it was hopeless—me being a Mexican and her not."

Clara looked startled by his frankness and by the realization that what he said was a problem. "How did you get over that? What did the Judge say?"

He smiled. "I think the Judge forgot to teach Irene to distinguish between Mexican and non-Mexican, because it didn't seem to bother her. And he gave her away at the wedding."

"Oh, what a great story! And you've been together ever since?"

"Yes, I fear it's been difficult for our children, but we believe if they're educated they can learn to deal with it and maybe even help to change the bias—which I understand is what you also believe."

"Yes I do, although the Judge scolds me sometimes and says that I'm overly optimistic."

"The Judge is careful to assure that optimism has a good dash of realism associated with it. He warned me before Irene and I got married that there would be problems. He said we could most likely overcome them, but only if we were prepared. So maybe that's what he's also trying to teach you."

Clara studied him as if he'd just given her clear insight into her relationship with the Judge. "You could be right. What other advice did you get from the Judge?"

"Well, he is the godfather of our children, so we obviously think he's a very special person."

Irene joined her husband and Clara. "I second that. What about you, Clara, what do you think about the Judge?"

Clara was surprised at her question. She always assumed she should be the one doing the asking, but after a moment's thought she responded, "He's taken me places I'd rather not have gone but once I visit them I realize I'm—" she searched for the best word to describe the results of sharing unpleasant events "more prepared or a more complete person. Does that make sense?"

Irene looked puzzled. "I think so, but so long as you know what it means. I can tell you that he's patiently helped me to learn about the law so that I can support him and earn a living doing it."

Jim said, with pride in his voice, "I bet you know more about the justice system than most of the lawyers in this town."

Irene smiled. "I don't know about that. I haven't gone to school and studied. I've just watched the Judge and read his briefs and his judgments. They're very revealing."

Clara looked at Irene and said, "That's probably a great way to get to know him, isn't it? I've been trying to get to understand the Judge as a person. Maybe the best way to do that is to read how he thinks."

Jim nodded. "Maybe. It's one way. Certainly talking to others, like us, is another. But why do you believe you don't know him?"

She looked bewildered, but could not think of an answer.

He continued. "I mean, you know he's fair, because of his judgments in court. You know he cares, because of how he used to fight for his clients, and now how much he is concerned about those who need support, like Oscar Briarley. Irene and you both saw how broken up he was over the young man who committed suicide, and how much he tried to help the boy who threw himself in front of the train. He is a caring man who believes in justice. What more do you need to know?"

"I guess I want to know what makes him happy, and who are his heroes. What does he like to do when he's not working? I mean, for example, I know he likes to walk. But he likes to do that because it enables him to think and solve problems. What does he like to do just for fun?"

Jim looked at her and squinted. Then he said quietly, "Well, let me tell you some advice he gave me. As part of my studying to become a lawyer, the Judge often counsels me, which is further indication of the kind of person he is. For example, he recommended that I never take a case representing someone who has truly hurt a victim deliberately and without remorse. He says that one's reputation as a lawyer will be tied to those cases. But, again, you only have to look at his cases to really get to know him."

She nodded. "Yes, of course. But—"

Irene interrupted. "Have you ever asked him?"

"No, I haven't, and actually until Jim just questioned what it was I wanted to know, I guess I hadn't actually thought of exactly what I wanted to know. It's just my habit as a writer to try to understand people. And maybe you're right. Maybe it's what he does that is who he is. But if I were trying to describe his character in a book, I wouldn't know what to say about him personally, and that's what I'm trying to get at."

Irene shook her head. "Well, I agree with Jim. You only need to watch what he does—his actions—to know who he is. Think about everything you've been involved with since you met him. Doesn't that help? Beyond that, I'm not sure that who he is personally is something you have a right to know, Clara. Maybe he saved that part of himself for his wife."

Clara thought about that and replied, "I think you're correct about one thing, Irene. I don't believe I should intrude on that part of him."

She turned to Jim and said, "By the way, you attended Oscar Briarley's trial the day I testified. Was that part of your efforts to become a lawyer?"

Jim looked puzzled, and then wary. "Not exactly." He did not elaborate, which only raised Clara's curiosity about exactly why he was there. And what was it that he had told the Judge earlier that day that caused the Judge to listen so closely?

Chapter 25

Jim left the Judge's birthday party with a purpose. Following his conversation with Mrs. Chissum leading to the possible connection of the Franklin brothers with Harry Winter, the Chief requested that he pursue the lead. As a result, he had approached three of Franklin's employees at their workplace. He always assured no one saw him talk to any of them. Finally, one of them agreed to meet with him, although he, too, was reluctant. It was only after Jim promised that neither he nor the Chief would divulge his name to anyone that the worker agreed to meet him at the same warehouse where the Judge had encountered Harry.

Jim had disclosed the fact that he'd scheduled this meeting to the Chief and the Judge at his party, which was the conversation that Clara had witnessed with such curiosity.

He arrived a half-hour early for the meeting. The warehouse was locked so he searched for a corner behind some tractors parked outside where he could hide his bicycle and wait unobserved. He removed his coat, bemoaning the heat. Surely it would break soon. Even the children were minding it.

Jim heard the arrival of the employee before he saw him. He drove up in an old Ford and stopped around the corner from where Jim was hiding. He got out of his car and walked to the door, carrying a briefcase. He pulled some keys out of his pocket and unlocked the door. Jim waited for another five minutes before approaching the entrance. He wanted to make sure that no one was following.

At exactly the time they had agreed to meet, Jim knocked on the door and waited for a response. When the door opened, he entered and was greeted by a slightly round, short, nervous, sweating, bald man. Jim tried quickly to reassure him by saying, "Thank you for seeing me. I don't mean to get you into any trouble. We're just trying to understand Harry Winter's situation. Mr. Franklin's sons helped him, and he was found here. Please understand that we just want to follow up."

He offered his hand to shake and the uneasy employee took it and said, "Nestor. My name is Nestor Morgan."

"Thanks for meeting with me, Nestor. What can you tell me about your boss? Anything at all. Does he know the Blakensfeld family?"

Nestor nodded. "Yes, I believe so. I've seen Blakensfeld at the store a couple of times, and they seem to know one another."

"Do they seem friendly or just business acquaintances?"

"Well, as far as I know, Blakensfeld has never bought anything at the store, and I don't believe he would have a reason to rent any farm equipment. Usually he and Mr. Franklin would just meet and then go out to lunch. Sometimes they'd talk in his office."

"Who else visited Franklin who you'd say wasn't a customer?"

Nestor thought for a few seconds. "Well, his sons, of course, and sometimes their friends. Harry stopped by at least once a week. Sometimes he'd drop off some boxes—he and his friends who worked for Blakensfeld. Sometimes they'd even bring some pieces of furniture."

"Boxes? Furniture? What kind of boxes?"

"I never saw what was inside. Mr. Franklin would put them in his car, so I just figured it was personal stuff. Mr. Blakensfeld has his own business, you know. He sells used furniture and things like lamps or dishes in his store. So I just assumed maybe Mrs. Franklin liked to shop or maybe Franklin was helping to deliver stuff for him."

Jim nodded. "I see. How did Harry get the furniture and boxes to Franklin?"

"Oh, he drove them in his pickup truck."

Jim shook his head. Neither the Chief nor he had located any kind of vehicle associated with Blakensfeld. This could explain how Harry had traveled to and from L.A. He asked, "His pickup truck? Can you describe it?"

"I sure can. It was an old black Ford. I wasn't so sure it would make it. The boy had trouble getting it started a couple of times. I remember thinking that his father should see to it that he had a decent vehicle to deliver stuff."

Jim thought, *Where did the pickup come from? Where did Blakensfeld keep it that they hadn't uncovered it?*

He asked Nestor, "Do you know for sure the pickup belonged to Blakensfeld?"

"Nope, but whose else would it be?"

Jim shook his head. "I don't know." He planned to let the Chief know, just in case. Maybe someone else had been involved in Harry's life that they didn't know about yet.

"By the way, how do you know that the boys were delivering stuff from Blakensfeld. Is it possible they worked for someone else?"

"Well, they wore shirts with the Blakensfeld emblem— you know, it looks like a chair."

Click. Another piece of the puzzle fell into place. Jim recalled the Judge describing an emblem like a chair on the shirt of one of the boys he had seen at the drive-in theater Harry Winter had robbed, and he had found Blakensfeld's card at Mr. Brant's memorial event with that same emblem. It was looking more and more like there was definitely a connection between Blakensfeld and Franklin—and maybe the robberies.

Nestor asked, "Is there anything else? I need to get home to my wife."

Jim said, "Can you think if there was anyone else you know who associated with Mr. Franklin."

"Nope. I just know he sure likes to use boys to do work around the place. They'd help Harry sometimes. He didn't pay them very much, I can tell you. Probably cheaper to use them than adults."

"What about Franklin himself? Did he ever do something that maybe was unusual?"

"Franklin? Mostly what's unusual is that he does nothing to promote this business. I've given him lots of ideas on how to grow it, but he just ignores me. It seems a shame. It could be a great business. People around here need tractors especially, and he could be renting many more."

It occurred to Jim that perhaps the reason Nestor was willing to talk with him was because he was an unhappy employee. Nonetheless, his information was useful.

"Thank you, Nestor. I really appreciate your help. And I promise that the Chief will not in any way implicate you or let on to your boss that we spoke with you."

Nestor nodded. "I like to help out when I can. But I need this job, so please keep your promise not to tell on me."

Jim said, "I promise. And thanks again."

Jim opened the door far enough to look outside and, seeing no one, squeezed out, walking quickly to his bicycle, which he'd left behind the tractors. He mounted and rode out, constantly checking for anyone who might be interested in his presence.

He was looking forward to an evening with Irene and the children. He hoped the uneasiness he was feeling would not intrude.

Chapter 26

The next day, the Judge was sitting at his desk reading a motion on why an employee at a State Mental Hospital should not be sentenced for thirty days following his two-week trial that proved his guilt for drunkenness and disorderly conduct. He expected Jim at any minute to report on his investigations. Irene was typing away when the phone rang. The Judge heard her scream and said, "What do you mean? I'll be right there!"

The Judge jumped up and ran to her. "What's happening?"

Irene was grabbing her purse and dashing toward the door. She said, "Thomas was in a fight at school. I need to get to him!"

The Judge responded, concerned about the kind of fight an eight-year-old might be involved in. "I'll drive you. It will just take me ten to fifteen minutes to get home and pick up the car, but we'll get you to the school faster that way. Wait outside for me to pick you up. Watch for Jim. He's due here any minute."

She nodded and watched the Judge rush out of the building. She decided to stay in the office for a few more minutes in case Jim might try to reach her by phone. But she was too anxious to sit still. The principal had told her that her eight-year-old son was involved in a fight and would probably need medical attention. He did not offer any details other than to say that he had separated the boys and had them in his office, and they would wait for her arrival and that of the other boys' parents—apparently two others were involved.

Although she was thankful for the Judge's offer, she grew impatient waiting for him to retrieve his car from his home. Where was Jim? She needed to get to the school. She locked the door and started down the stairs and into the lobby when Jim walked up. "Where are you going?"

Irene said, "Come with me. Thomas has been in a fight. The principal said—"

"Is he all right?"

Irene nodded. "I think so. But we have to get there right away, the principal said. The Judge went to get his car to drive us. He should be here by now."

Jim opened the door for Irene and they both searched the street for the Judge's blue Chevrolet. They were relieved to see him driving up the hill and ran out to meet him. When they got in, the Judge said, "Good, I'm glad you're here, Jim."

Jim asked, "Do you know the way, Judge?"

"Yes, I went there with you to the Christmas show." The Judge had already started driving toward the school.

"Who called you, Irene?" the Judge asked.

"The principal. And there was noise in the background, like children yelling. He said to get there as soon as possible."

The Judge drove as quickly as he could and they arrived at the school within ten minutes. Irene and Jim were out of the car and charging toward the principal's office before the Judge could park. He secured his car, ignoring curious looks from a group of young boys playing stick ball and followed his friends by locating the sounds of screaming boys and orders of a man yelling, "Quiet down!"

When he reached the principal's office, he was met with Jim holding his son, who had a bloody nose and a long bleeding cut on his left arm. The cut caused the Judge to question whether a knife had been involved. Irene was placing some bandages on it from a first aid kit. A man, who the Judge assumed to be the principal, stood between Jim and two boys who looked slightly dirty but did not seem to be bruised or bloodied. The Judge recognized them immediately as the Franklin brothers, who had inadvertently led him to Harry that fateful day.

Jim was saying, "How could you let this happen?"

The principal responded, "I can assure you, sir, we did not 'let' it happen. Your son must have said something to cause these boys to attack him."

The Judge felt anger. He interrupted before Jim could say anything, understanding quickly that the last name of "Alvarez" was influencing the principal's assessment of the situation. "What do you mean?"

About then, Mr. Franklin burst in. The Judge knew that he was the Franklin boys' father, but Jim was confused by his arrival. He was acquainted with Franklin but not the boys. However, he learned quickly that the two boys who had attacked Thomas were the sons of the man he'd been asking questions about. Their father approached them both and patted their heads proudly, almost applauding them for fighting.

Jim sputtered, "You—"

Franklin smiled and said, "I guess my boys didn't appreciate having some Mexican ask around about their father."

The Judge was relieved that Jim was holding his son. Otherwise he might have attacked the older Franklin. Instead, Irene grabbed hold of him and pushed him out the door. The Judge said, "Using your boys to attack a child. How courageous of you, sir."

The principal stood still and said nothing. The Judge moved toward the principal and looked down at him. "You, sir, need to examine your own prejudices. You are an educator and should know better. But given that is not the case, please be aware, that if anything more happens to that boy, you will be in front of my court within a day for negligence in regards to protecting a minor. Am I clear?"

The principal nodded, his eyes wide.

The Judge turned but had one more parting remark. "I am ashamed of all of you."

Chapter 27

That same day, Clara eagerly approached her meeting with Oscar. She had received permission to leave some books with him, so he could start to enjoy them on his own. The deputies were still uneasy about allowing him to have a pencil unsupervised, but Deputy Brown said he would be willing to sit with him for fifteen minutes a day in the visitor's room when available, if he wanted to write something. What he had discovered was that Oscar could not print much, and he could barely sign his name. So he helped him practice writing.

Both Clara and Oscar were more interested in reading than writing, although Oscar would sometimes forget his questions when he was reading alone and told Clara and the deputy that he wished he could write them down so he could remember to ask for Clara's help. And now that Deputy Brown had agreed to sit with him, he had the opportunity to practice.

Deputy Brown sat with them during most of their sessions. He usually was reading himself, and Clara tried hard to see what books he had. She was disappointed to discover they dealt with law enforcement. He was studying various texts. However, he also listened to the lessons. That day Clara noticed that occasionally Oscar would look over at him as if to ask if what he said was correct. That's when Oscar told her that Deputy Brown was helping him to read, too. From then on, she consulted Deputy Brown about Oscar. She felt like he understood him and wanted to help.

But she was ecstatic that she could leave some books with Oscar, and had brought three: a Hardy Boys mystery, *Little House on the Prairie*, and *The Yearling*. She knew that these were probably beyond what he could comprehend, but she wanted to see which one would interest him the most and planned to help him understand them.

He greeted her with his smile and a nod. He wanted to first talk about what was happening. She had not mentioned anything about Harry Winter's suicide, although she was curious if Oscar knew him. She was concerned that the suicide might upset him. However, he seemed to have grown more confident and sure of himself over the past week, so she decided to risk it.

"Oscar, did you know a boy named Harry Winter?"

She saw no recognition or interest in Oscar's eyes. "Nope," he said. "Who's he?"

"He robbed the drive-in theater in L.A. a while back, and I just wondered if you knew him."

"Nope. What happened at the Judge's birthday party?"

She said, "My mother made me wear a really frilly dress."

He responded, "I bet you was real purdy."

She laughed, too embarrassed to correct his grammar. "Anyway his children are all grown and very nice. There weren't any other teenagers there. I was the only one."

Then she produced the three books she'd brought. "They said I could leave these with you. First, though, I want to talk about each of them. I got them from the library, so I'll have to return them in a few weeks."

She reviewed the books' covers and explained the plots. He chose *The Yearling* to start with. He read a few pages but then closed the book and said, "I can keep these in my cell and read them myself?"

"Yes, isn't that great?"

He nodded. "Yes, it is. But I was wondering. Could you tell some things to me? I was talkin' to Mr. Alberts—he's my lawyer, you know—and he was tellin' me about what I done and why the Judge may have to send me to jail. It's because, well, it's because that man in the store got kilt, isn't it?"

"Yes, Oscar. Murder is very serious. This is why it's so important that you tell the Judge or the Sheriff who was with you."

"But, Clara, I didn't shoot nobody. I don't understand."

"We know you didn't shoot anyone, but the law says that because you were doing a crime—and that was robbing the store—when a murder was committed, that you are as guilty as the person who pulled the trigger. Do you understand?"

"So I'm gonna go to jail because I was there when it happened?"

"You were there and you were helping to rob the store, which is what caused the death of Mr. Brant. You were committing a crime. If you had just been standing there, like as a customer, you wouldn't be guilty. But murder is a very serious crime, and the Judge can't excuse you."

"Oh." He seemed to be thinking about what that meant. "So why will it help to tell who done it?"

"It will give your attorney a reason to petition the Judge for leniency. What that means is that because you co-operated, he can give you less time in jail."

Oscar stood up and picked up the books. "Thanks for these," he said.

"Don't you want to read some more?"

"No. I want to think. I just needed to understand better, and you are good at helping me do that. I know you tried to tell me before. But I think I understand now."

She was disappointed that he didn't want to spend more time on the lesson, but was encouraged that he might be considering his future and possibly deciding to divulge the name of his partner.

She left the room to use the extra time to talk with the Judge. She wasn't sure what she'd say to him, but it seemed like a good idea to let him know the latest state of Oscar's thinking.

However, when she got to the Judge's office, no one was there, and the door was locked. She looked into the room through the glass in the door and saw that Irene's desk appeared disorderly—like she'd left in a hurry. The Judge's door was open, but she didn't see him.

She started to leave when the Judge appeared. "Oh, hello, Clara. Did I have an appointment with you?"

"No, sir. I finished with Oscar early and thought you'd be interested to know that he's really thinking about what it means if he tells the name of his partner."

"Oh, that's good."

"I think he really understands now, sir. Where's Irene? She isn't sick, is she?"

"No. Her son was beat up at school."

"The eight-year-old? Is he all right?"

"Yes. I drove her and Jim to pick him up. Then I dropped them off at the doctor's. His arm will probably need bandaging, and he'll have a black eye, but I think he'll be all right."

She looked at the Judge. He didn't appear angry, but he did seem sad. She said, "What happened? You said he got beat up. Who did it?"

"The two brothers who led me to Harry. Apparently their father didn't appreciate being investigated by a Mexican. And the principal blames Thomas for saying something to irritate them."

"What?" At first Clara didn't understand. Then she comprehended that the principal blamed the victim because of his ethnicity. "I'm sorry that they had to go through that."

The Judge nodded. "Me, too. Someday, maybe, we'll learn to live together, and that just because we appear different doesn't make anyone less of a person." He smiled. "Irene's husband is studying to be a lawyer. I think he'll help to overcome some of the prejudice against Mexicans. And I'm sure that some day they'll be judges, mayors, and governors." He looked at her and remembered why she was there. "I'm glad Oscar is finally starting to understand his situation."

"Me, too. Sir, I was thinking, do you suppose his younger brother might know something? Or maybe his mother? I don't think his father would be helpful, but maybe one of them would tell us something if we could make them realize how we could keep Oscar from spending more time in jail. If Oscar won't tell us, maybe one of them will. I'm worried that we're getting close to when you have to make a decision, and I just don't know how soon Oscar will tell us anything."

"What are you thinking, Clara?"

"I was wondering if maybe you and I could go out to the family's place and talk to them?"

"You've heard Oscar talk about his family. Do you really think they sound like the kind of people who support each other? I cannot imagine they'd be helpful."

"I don't know. But maybe since Tommy killed himself, maybe they'd be more willing to lend a hand to Oscar."

The Judge said, "Clara, I doubt very much that his family will want to help him."

He stopped and stared at the ceiling, his eyes betraying concern and pain. "But I think maybe I should visit them. I couldn't save Harry, but maybe I can help Oscar. It might be the last chance we'll have to keep him from a long prison term. I haven't spoken to them since Tommy's death. When Irene gets back, I'll see if she can arrange my schedule so I can drive out there. But if I do this, only I will go. Not you."

"But I'm your best hope to get them to talk. I'm just a girl who's trying to help their son. I know Oscar better than anybody. I can talk to them. Besides, what harm can it do if I go?"

She waited while the Judge considered her plea. She really did believe she could help. "No, Clara. I appreciate the suggestion, but it's not a place for you to go. Oscar's parents and life are nothing like yours."

"But my dad always tells me that if I don't see what's bad, how can I change it? Right?"

The Judge shook his head, but he didn't smile. "No, you're not going. Maybe some day you'll be ready for that kind of exposure, but not yet."

She decided to change the subject. "Have they caught Harry's stepfather?"

"No. That's part of the reason that Irene's son got beat up. You may not know it, but Jim helps me out doing research and he also helps do investigations for the Chief. Sometimes he checks out people I want to know more about. He was trying to find information about Harry's stepfather's friends, and apparently was checking out Mr. Franklin, who was not pleased to have an investigator of Mexican ancestry ask questions about him. We believe he got his sons to beat up Jim's son as a possible warning."

For a few seconds, Clara was speechless. Then she said, "Can the Chief arrest both father and sons?"

The Judge shook his head. "He's already had the sons into the station regarding their part in hiding Harry. Their dad got them out and even threatened the Chief, saying the boys hadn't done anything wrong. So I doubt it, especially since the principal claimed that Irene's son picked the fight."

Clara said, "It's not right. We need to do something."

The Judge shook his head. "*We* don't need to do anything. The most helpful thing *you* can do is to get Oscar to identify his partner. For now, the Chief needs to protect Irene and Jim's children. I would prefer that they take them out of school, but Jim will have none of that. He won't be intimidated. So I'll make sure the Chief asks one of his officers to watch them as much as possible—without Jim knowing."

Clara bit her lip and shook her head. "A few weeks ago I might not have believed that Jim's children were in danger, but after all that's happened—. For that matter, what about Jim? Will he continue to look into Mr. Franklin?"

The Judge nodded. "I couldn't stop him now if I wanted to. He believes that there is more to Franklin's reaction than just bigotry, and he is sure it has something to do with Harry Winter and his stepdad."

She looked around the room as if questioning whether she could ask something and then blurted out, "Why do you think Harry's mother didn't do something to help him?"

The Judge hesitated and then answered, "I guess it's all right to tell you. The Chief says she acts like someone who's been beaten repeatedly, so it's possible she knew but just was too afraid to say anything. She seems to really miss Harry."

The Judge stared at Clara, reflecting that he was relieved to talk to her at that moment. Her caring reinforced his trust in people.

Chapter 28

The day the Judge arranged to drive out to see Oscar's family was a Saturday and the eighth day of another scorching heat wave. Ventura had broken an all-time record for water usage. The beaches were crowded. Everyone was hoping for a storm to help cool things down. The day started out the same, but had become overcast by mid-morning, so there was hope for rain and a break in the high temperatures.

Before starting his trip to the Briarley place, the Judge decided at the last minute to stop by City Hall and talk to the Chief. At first, he wasn't going to talk to the Chief or the Sheriff about the idea Clara had proposed to see if any of Oscar's family could help figure out who accompanied him to rob the store. He anticipated that the Chief would try to talk him out of it, especially since he and his deputies had already interrogated the father.

He also was regretting his decision not to send Jim, who was far more equipped than he to handle this kind of interrogation. However, he doubted that anyone in the Briarley family would speak to an "Alvarez," given their stated bigotry. Besides, Jim was preoccupied with his son, who was recovering from his beating—both physically and emotionally. So when Jim had offered, the Judge shook his head. "You'd be in danger, Jim. My god, their son killed a Mexican for no good reason. He didn't get that prejudice on his own. I'm sure his father spawned it."

But the more he thought about what he was doing, the uneasier he grew. It didn't occur to him that it would be dangerous. After all, if they didn't want to talk to him they just wouldn't let him into their house. Rather, he wanted to be sure that his thought process was logical, given his emotions surrounding how guilty he felt about Harry's suicide and his resistance to facing another failure. He didn't want the time and effort to visit the Briarley home not to be successful because of his own emotional state.

So he decided to talk it over with the Chief, who was a good sounding board. There was no boys' club meeting that Saturday morning due to the Chief scheduling a special meeting that night to mourn Harry Winter, and Jim had told him that the Chief was at the jail interrogating a suspect.

He walked into the city jail and waited for the deputy to locate the Chief, who came out of a small room looking puzzled. "Hello, Judge. Is something wrong? I wasn't expecting to see you today."

The Judge shook hands with the Chief and said, "I need you to listen and give me some advice. You know I'm going to have to sentence Oscar Briarley to a long term if he doesn't help us. I don't want to do that. I failed with Harry Winter. I just can't face another one."

He stopped and took a breath. "So I'm considering a trip out to the Briarley place today to talk to the family about Oscar. I'm hoping that maybe one of them might know something about who partnered with Oscar and killed Mr. Brant. Or at least maybe they might know some of their son's friends who might be able to help. I was on my way out there when it occurred to me that I should check in with you to see what you think of the idea."

The Chief at first looked surprised, then concerned. He was about to advise the Judge not to go when he thought better of it and said, "Why do you think they might tell you anything? We've talked to them several times and got nothing."

The Judge nodded. "I know. I think they might be more willing to talk to someone who's trying to help Oscar and is less threatening. I'm not the law coming to arrest anyone. And they might be more willing to help save Oscar since they lost their oldest son."

"But you are the person who convicted their other son, who died in jail. They might blame you for that. Anyway, I'm just not sure what they'd tell you. Let's think about this for a minute. What you're looking for is a name. You think that one of them might actually know who went with Oscar that night?"

"That would be great, but maybe just the name of someone Oscar knows. I mean the boy must have some friends somewhere. You and Jim—even Clara—haven't turned up anyone, so I'm hoping that at a minimum, I'll get the name of someone the boy's acquainted with."

"You know we think his partner was probably a grown man, or a large boy, given Clara's description."

"Yes, so I'll ask them if he has any adult friends."

The Chief raised his eyebrows and nodded. He said, "I hate to say it, Judge, but you might be right. If the mother is sober, you might get through to her. I'm not sure about Oscar's father. I wouldn't turn my back on him. When I went out to tell them about their son Tommy's death, he actually lowered his rifle on me. My deputy had to remove it from him. And I never saw the Missus, although she listened at the door and when I delivered the news, I thought I heard her cry out. His father said it was our fault for putting him in jail for a no-good reason. So beware."

The Judge took a deep breath, again questioning his own decision to make this visit. "I don't recall any of the family being at Tommy's or Oscar's trial, but Clara said the father did visit Oscar in jail once. What about the younger brother?"

"Goes by the name of Frankie. You'd have to get him away from his folks before he'll talk. And I'm not sure if he's right in the head. But he might know something. He's pretty much beat down by his pa though, and, as I said, I'm not sure he's all there." He pointed to his temple. "And none of those boys has had much looking after. Without Oscar and Tommy around, I doubt that Frankie stands much of a chance."

The Judge sighed. "So you don't think it's worth my time to go out there?"

"Actually, I do." The Chief had known the Judge for many years. The two of them had joined frequently to help out juveniles who they thought deserved a break. He believed that Oscar Briarley was one of them. He added, "But I'd like to send a deputy with you."

The Judge quickly said, "That will work against my advantage of not being the law. It's what I'm trying to avoid."

The Chief nodded. "Yes, I know. I understand, although I'm not sure that Claude Briarley will distinguish between a judge and a deputy. But here's what I suggest. You go ahead. I'll send my deputy in an hour. That way, if anything goes wrong, you know to stall them and that help's on the way. Is that reasonable?"

The Judge asked, "Do you have any idea if they're at home? Or does the father work somewhere?"

The Chief laughed. "Mr. Briarley does a lot of things, but work isn't one of them. It's hard to say if he'll be there, but the Missus doesn't ever leave the house, so she'll be there. Don't know about the boy."

The Judge smiled. "Thanks for the advice, and for the offer of the deputy. Now it looks like I've got weather to fight, also. But I have to go today; I'm running out of time before the final hearing. If we don't find extenuating circumstances, my hands will be tied."

The Chief nodded. "I know, your Honor, I know. And I believe he's actually a decent boy. He's just never had a chance." He looked out the window. "Regarding the weather, the report says the storm's not supposed to come up this far north, so we might get the tail end of it or something, but not the worst of it."

The Judge looked doubtful. "All right. I'm on my way."

"Good luck. I hope you're able to get what we need. Do you need directions, by the way?"

"No. Irene took care of that for me. Thanks."

The Judge trudged back to the car and re-launched his journey. The Chief had reassured him that pursuing the trip was worthwhile. And although he didn't think it was necessary, he was also relieved that a deputy would show up in case he needed someone. He hoped that the precaution would not be required and that he would pass the deputy on his return trip.

The weather had begun to turn more threatening. The wind was blowing, the skies were darkening, and thankfully the temperature was dropping. The Judge was sure they would see rain before the end of the day.

He searched his own motivation for taking this extra step to help Oscar. He recalled when he first heard about the case. Irene told him, "A boy was caught as part of the robbery that killed Mr. Brant, the store manager. He didn't pull the trigger, but he was definitely involved."

She had stopped mid-sentence and said, "I think I know this boy, Oscar Briarley. When Thomas was in first grade there was a dog chasing him at the school. Oscar got between the dog and Thomas and chased it away. He couldn't have been more than eleven or twelve himself. He even asked Thomas if he was all right and helped him up. He ran away when a teacher arrived, but she had seen what he did and just wanted to thank him. We tried to give him a small reward or something, but we could never reach him."

Jim also told him another story about Oscar that they had not been able to corroborate. When talking with neighbors of an elderly woman who had died a few months prior, he heard about a boy who had taken food to her in the last few months of her life. They were sure it was food because one of them looked in on her and also dropped off what they could spare. They found remnants of bread and apples. The woman had identified him as the son of Mr. Briarley. They knew about Briarley and suspected he helped himself to some of the woman's furniture while doing a chore for her. They succeeded in scaring him away. But they said that they saw Oscar there once or twice a week, and he continued to bring food to her.

The Judge had known both of these stories going into the trial. Then when Clara said in court that he had refused to beat up someone being held by his brother, he began to question what kind of boy this was. He seemed to care about people, which was not a typical characteristic of most criminals.

The Chief agreed with this assessment. He had spoken with Oscar, who was shy, not belligerent; curious rather than assertive; and full of wonderment at new surroundings. The

Sheriff and his deputies at the jail where he was being held said he helped fellow inmates by sharing his food or allowing them to go ahead of him for exercise or meals. He never pushed, hit, spit, or shouted at his fellow inmates.

And, thought the Judge, he'd never had a break in his life. His mother was a drunk, his brother a murderer, and his father a n'er-do-well. So that's why it was important that he try to do whatever he could to help the boy.

He returned to figuring out a game plan. If the mother were sober, he'd focus on her. After all, mothers are supposed to care about their children. If she wasn't sober, maybe the Judge could get the brother Frankie separated from his parents, and maybe he could tell him something. He would heed the Chief's advice and stay clear of Mr. Briarley if he could.

As the Judge drove away from the town, the day darkened and the wind blew the car. He had to hold on to the steering wheel very tightly to stay steady, and he stared unwaveringly at the road. Then the rain started—hard. The car's wipers could barely keep the windshield clear enough for the Judge to see where he was going. He was not looking forward to the less-than-adequate road he had to turn onto next. He guided the car with some effort. The wind was blowing fiercely. He questioned the weather report, which said the storm would not get this far north. The rain was so heavy he could hardly see the road, and when the car ran over a large rut, it caused his head to hit the roof of the car as it jolted.

He estimated that the Briarley place was at least another two miles, which on the muddy road could take a while. The sound of the wipers and the wind caused quite a commotion. Despite his commitment, he was worried that he wouldn't be able to reach the Briarley house and might instead get stuck on the narrow, muddy road that must have been created as a trail for donkeys. He was now relieved that the Chief had insisted on sending a deputy. If he got stuck, at least he could count on being rescued eventually.

He spied a fairly large rock in the road and managed to avoid it. But he believed he was getting closer. He was barely creeping along, like some kind of injured animal. He stared at the road to avoid any additional rocks or potholes. However, the rain was now pouring and the wind roaring so it appeared as if he were driving through a waterfall. It was difficult to see a few inches, much less several feet.

Then he saw it. The Briarley place. He pulled the car up to a part of the road that looked less muddy, and turned off the engine. He tried to see the building, which was only about twenty feet from the car, but could view only some kind of wood structure in the shape of an A. It looked more like a shack than a house. The roof appeared to have some kind of covering attached to it—most likely put there to block holes and prevent rain from getting in. However, one of the covers was flapping and must have pulled loose from its anchor. There were buckets of various sizes scattered about on the ground full of rainwater, and the Judge assumed that the Briarleys didn't have running water, a theory reinforced when he saw a well off to the left.

He pulled on his parka and decided to knock on the door to see who was there. He assumed everyone would be inside due to the storm. About then, the rain let up a little, enabling the Judge to see more of the place. There was an outhouse to the right—he didn't envy them the walk, especially in the current inclement weather. He didn't see any other structures, but debris was scattered about—an old bed frame with the springs sticking up; a bicycle with one wheel; a table with three legs; a couple of chairs with no backs; and bottles everywhere, many broken.

The Judge opened the car door, which allowed the wind to blow inside momentarily. He closed it quickly and pulled his hat down and parka up to protect himself from the weather. He ran to the front door of the house where there was a small front porch of sorts, but the wood didn't look too sturdy. He approached the door carefully and knocked. He saw the door open and called out, "Mrs. Briarley? It's Judge Akers. May I come in?"

He heard what he interpreted as a "yes," and walked through the door. He was accosted by such a foul odor that he instinctively reached up and covered his mouth and nose, hoping to stop it. The inside was dark. The one window had a dirty sheet covering it. The room was cluttered with clothes and garbage scattered about. There was a mattress of sorts on the floor in a corner but it did not have any sheets or blankets, although buckets catching the water pouring from the ceiling surrounded it, causing the sounds of splashing water that competed with the rain falling outside. He saw no other rooms or beds, and agreed with those who concluded that Oscar probably was better off in jail. If nothing else, at least the roof didn't leak.

The Judge saw Mrs. Briarley scurry to sit in a rocking chair, which she moved back and forth violently. What little he could see of her indicated she was lanky. Her sparse hair hung loose in patches, like a child had pasted it on her head randomly. Her face and what he could see of her arms had multiple sores. She was wearing a foul-smelling, gray nightgown that managed to cover her legs, but her feet were bare and filthy. There were dozens of empty bottles on either side of her chair.

She rasped, "That you, Claude?"

"No, Mrs. Briarley. It's Judge Akers. I've come to ask you about Oscar and whether you know who might have helped him rob the five-and-dime store and kill Mr. Brant."

The rocking chair stopped moving. "What? Who is ye?"

The Judge feared it was hopeless to reach her. She did not seem sober. He then asked, "Where's Claude? Where's your husband?"

"Who is ye?" she repeated.

"I'm Judge Akers."

Just as he was responding, the door blew open and the Judge was now staring at Claude Briarley's .22 rifle aimed directly at his chest. He vaguely noticed that the round-shouldered man was dressed in farmer's overalls, which were wet from the rain, along with his long brown hair and beard.

Briarley pushed the door closed while still pointing the rifle at the Judge.

Again the woman said, "Is that ye, Claude?"

"Yeah, Lila, it's me. Who be this?"

To the Judge's surprise, she answered, "He sez he's Judge Akers."

"You ain't been telling the Judge nothin', I hope," he hissed.

She started rocking again. "What would I be tellin' him? Is there somethin' I shouldn't tell him? If'n there is, then I'll tell him that. Where's Frankie?"

On cue the door opened and a short, distorted version of Claude stood there confused at the presence of the Judge. "Who is ye?" he said.

Claude smacked the boy across the head, "Close the door, you dumb shit. You think we live in a barn?"

Frankie closed the door, but not before the Judge noticed his crippled leg, which became more visible when he limped over to a kerosene lamp and lit it, providing some light in the dim room. Then the Judge observed his face—most noticeably his protruding gums and teeth, pockmarks, and lazy eye that wouldn't stay open. His eyes betrayed a lack of awareness, and the Judge surmised that he was hardly as smart or as aware as his brothers.

Claude continued to point the rifle at the Judge. "What are ye doin' here, Judge? Tryin' to kill all three of my sons?"

Lila, who continued to rock, said, "He killed my sons? Then kill him, too, Pa!" She literally screeched.

The Judge said, "I didn't kill your son. I tried to save him. And I'm here to help Oscar. I'm hoping you can tell me who his friends are, and maybe even who helped him with the robbery. We believe Oscar is basically a good boy. We even have someone teaching him to read so he can get a good job eventually."

Claude waved the rifle, causing the Judge to focus on him and speak quickly but distinctly. He continued, "Look, Mr. Briarley, I'm here to find out if you know who might have helped Oscar with the robbery. If I can find out who actually killed Mr. Brant, then I might be able to give Oscar a lesser sentence. Do any of you know anything? If you don't, I'll just leave." He started to move toward the door.

The sound from Lila was something between a crow's caw and cat's meow, but it apparently was how she laughed. Although she never stopped rocking, she laughed for a long time, even though Claude said, "Stop it, Ma. That's enough." He threw a bottle at her that he'd been carrying. "Here."

She caught it in both hands, unscrewed the top, and started to drink. There were no labels on the bottle, but the Judge assumed it was alcohol. When she'd finished, she wiped her mouth with the back of her hand and looked at them. "You come all the way out here just for Oscar, did you, Judge? Well, then mebbe you didn't kill Tommy."

Claude crept toward the door and motioned to the Judge to stand back. The Judge started to walk toward Lila, and Claude moved to where the Judge had been standing.

Frankie said, "What should I do, Pa? Do you want me to hide his car?"

Claude looked at him. "Naw, we kin wait. What makes ye think ye can move that car?"

"I kin, Pa." He stuck out his chin even further and caused slobber to spew around him.

The Judge looked directly at Frankie and said, "Do you know if any of Oscar's friends might have helped him that night?"

Lila cackled again. "How the hell would he know? He don't never leave here. He cain't walk. Even the truant officer don't make him go to school."

"But maybe Oscar said something to him," the Judge reasoned.

"No, siree," Claude said. "Who do ye think it 'twas, your Honor, sir? Ye must have some idea."

The Judge shook his head. "All we know is that the person was probably older. He was taller than Oscar. Do you know if Oscar had any friends like that?"

Frankie seemed to appreciate the Judge asking him such an important question. He ignored his father's interruption and said, "Mebbe I know, and mebbe I don't. What's Oscar sayin' about me?"

Stalling for time seemed like a good idea, so the Judge welcomed Frankie's question. "He says you're a very smart boy, and that you could learn to read, too."

"Pshaw! Me, read?"

Both parents laughed—Claude in a kind of sneering way and Lila as if the crow had died. But even if it was at Frankie's expense, the Judge decided to keep him talking to stall for time until the deputy arrived. "No, really, Frankie. You could learn to read just like Oscar. He likes reading books now."

But Claude was not willing to allow anything positive to be said about reading or education. "It's what kilt your brother Tommy. It got into his head and made him hang hisself. He was happy 'til he started readin' them books."

The Judge noticed that the chair was no longer rocking. Lila was actually standing, although she was swaying on her feet. "You sayin' that the Judge here kilt my Tommy?"

The Judge yelled, "Of course not! But your husband is going to be responsible for your other son going to jail for a long time if you don't help us." He took a breath, realizing that he had yelled, and said more quietly and firmly, "Mr. and Mrs. Briarley, I was very sorry about Tommy. You know that I was able to get him special things at San Quentin." Given Claude's outburst about the detriment of book-learning, the Judge thought better of telling them he was responsible for getting books to their son. "I did whatever I could to help him. Why do you think anything different now? And I can assure you that I am here to help Oscar."

Lila was still standing but swaying less. She said, "I remember you." She now started blinking rapidly. She studied the Judge, almost as if she knew who he was. He wondered if she ever was aware of her surroundings and their reality.

The Judge looked at her. "I'm afraid Tommy killed himself, Mrs. Briarley. Do you remember the Chief coming out here to tell you? He used a sheet somehow."

The Judge's Story

The blank and weepy eyes between the disheveled, stringy hair expressed something. She said, "Oh, yes. I remember. I was so sad. He was my first born." She looked at the Judge.

The Judge continued to watch the rifle. But he was talking to Lila. He said, "Mrs. Briarley, do you know who helped your son, Oscar, rob the five-and-dime store?"

"Mebbe I do, and mebbe I don't. What's it to you?" She had returned to her prior place, somewhere where they weren't with her. She seemed to have forgotten they were there.

The Judge then said, "Frankie, do you know who was with your brother when he robbed the store?"

"Naw. Why would I know?"

"Well, do you know any of his friends? Does he go with anyone else to do things, like to the movies?" The Judge continued to ignore Claude Briarley, while keeping the rifle in view. He believed that it was the only way he might escape. Briarley continued to point the rifle directly at the Judge's chest.

Frankie shook his head, and the Judge almost expected the slobber to spray out like a dog's when it shook its head, but thankfully the slobber stayed somewhere on the deformed boy. "Naw. He don't do nothing with nobody. He's like a girl. He's no man like me 'n Pa 'n Tommy."

The Judge asked, "Why do you say that?"

"He let all the animals go—let them out of their cages, after Pa and me trapped them." He shook his head and spit.

Lila interrupted, "Well, at least he kept the place clean. Look at this mess. Nobody's touched it since he went to jail." She was back with them again.

The Judge had managed to maneuver so that he was now closer to Claude. He was clenching his fists like he did before a fight in his youth. Although it had been years since he'd hit anyone, he figured he might need to do so now.

The Judge said, "Look. I want you to know that we'll do everything we can to give Oscar as fair a jail sentence as possible. But if we don't learn who killed Mr. Brant, then

Oscar will have to pay for that crime. It's the law." The Judge was focused on Mrs. Briarley, who had locked eyes with him. She was definitely back with them. He continued, "If we catch the person who actually did the killing, I might be able to give Oscar a lesser sentence, since we know for sure he didn't pull the trigger. He'll have to do some time, but we'll help him get an education and learn a skill so that he can support himself. He might even be able to help you after he's finished serving his sentence." He was now facing Lilia. "Wouldn't you like that?"

Lila licked her dry lips, which were also full of sores. "Oscar was always my favorite, you know. He brung me flowers and helped me into bed when I wasn't feelin' so well." She turned to her mate and said, "Pa, you need to let the Judge go. He's gonna help Oscar, and then he'll help us. You hear me? And ye gotta tell him about ye killing that store man so's Oscar—"

"Shet yer mouth, woman!" Claude screamed.

The Judge had deduced that Lila was his best hope, but was surprised and concerned for his life when she revealed her husband as the killer. That explained why Claude had stayed away from the trial. If Clara had seen him, she might have identified him. The Judge realized that Claude would now be even more inclined to kill him, given what Lila had just told him. He decided the time for him to attack was now, while Claude focused on Lila. However, it was about then that they all heard something crash against the shack. The wind had picked up intensity and must have picked up something and blown it against the thin walls. Claude turned back to the Judge and pointed the gun at him again.

The Judge couldn't see outside, but it sounded like the rain was coming down again in sheets. He became concerned about the state of the road and troubled over whether the deputy could drive on it. What if he couldn't reach him? Or even if he should escape from the Briarleys, could he drive back on it? He hadn't seen any vehicles parked around the place, so he assumed if he could get to his car after disarming Claude, then he might have a chance of escape. He could send the Chief back after Claude later. Stalling to wait for help was becoming less of an option.

Lila was moving slowly—swaying again—toward Claude. The Judge focused on the rifle. Frankie started to cry. "No, Ma, no!" And, to the Judge's surprise, he ran out the door, leaving it open to the rain and wind. The Judge took advantage of the interruption, using the sounds of the storm to mask his movement, and jumped at Claude, reaching him a split second after Lila, who was screaming like a hurt crow. He couldn't believe that the swaying, sick-looking woman could move so fast. Not only did she beat the Judge to Claude, but she got her hands on the rifle and yanked it. Unfortunately, Claude held onto it and pulled the trigger. The shot was loud, and the Judge unconsciously covered his ears before he grabbed the gun away from Claude, who released his grip on the rifle when he realized he had just shot his wife and gasped as he watched her fall to the floor.

He screamed, "Why did you do that, Lila? Are you all right?"

She opened her mouth and stared at her husband looking surprised and in pain. "Why?"

Claude started to go to her, but saw that the Judge was pointing the rifle at him. He took one look at his wife and then ran from the room into the wall of rain.

The Judge bent over the crying Lila. Although bleeding onto her gray nightgown, Lila's eyes were opened wide, and she was clutching at the Judge. "I don't wanna die," she moaned over and over.

The Judge focused on her but kept the rifle close by. He looked for anything to place on her chest to stem the bleeding, but all he could find was a dirty old shirt. He drenched it with what was left of Lila's alcohol and then placed it on her chest.

He tried to comfort the deranged woman. "All right, Lila. Stay quiet. I'm going to take you to a hospital, but I'm going to have to carry you to my car." He worried that Claude might return and get the rifle. So he grabbed it and using the attached strap hung it on his shoulder. Then he picked up

Lila, who weighed less than a hundred pounds, and carried her as carefully as he could out the door.

They were almost blown over. The noise of the wind moving through the trees and carrying rubbish about heightened the ringing in his ears he still felt from the rifle shot. He looked around for any signs of either Claude or Frankie, and not seeing either one, pushed his way to the car. Opening the door proved to be a challenge, but he managed by holding Lila mostly in one arm, freeing a hand to unlatch the back door. He laid her on the back seat, as gently as he could. She moaned and was barely conscious. By then, her nightgown was red with blood and was plastered against her thin body, and her wet hair had almost disappeared. He could see that her eyes were yellow. Her appearance concerned the Judge. He put his car blanket over her.

He placed the rifle on the floor on the passenger side in the front and continued to scan for Frankie or Claude, but it was difficult to see anything.

He turned to see Claude just in time. He had some kind of hammer and was preparing to bring it down on the Judge's head. The Judge turned and moved out of the way. Claude's momentum pulled him down, and when the hammer hit the car, he cried in pain.

The Judge grabbed him, and hit him hard in the jaw, knocking him the rest of the way to the ground. He prepared to hit him again, but Claude stayed down. The Judge yelled, "Frankie, are you there? You need to take care of your pa. I'm taking your ma to the doctor. Do you hear me, Frankie?" He doubted that the boy could hear him above the noises of the storm.

He got into the driver's seat and started the car. Claude managed to get part way up, but appeared dazed. The Judge decided to worry about Lila rather than try to catch Claude, so he drove away, leaving Claude on his knees in the sheets of rain. He stopped to check on Lila to see that she hadn't shifted when he pulled out so abruptly. She remained on the seat.

Given the wind and the rain and the conditions of the muddy road, he had no choice but to drive slowly. The noise of the wipers and the wind hitting the car intensified his tension. He got stuck once, but by driving back and forth got unstuck, and was on his way again. Throughout the drive, he searched for any cars coming his way, in case the deputy had managed to get through. When Lila moaned, he stopped to check on her, but she didn't open her eyes. The wind never let up blowing the rain against the car. The windshield wipers could hardly keep up.

The Judge had seen many cruel things in his life, but he was shaken by a father who would, first, involve his son in a murder and then let him pay for something he didn't do. He'd see that Claude Briarley would be arrested. He could testify what Lila had told him if she didn't survive to tell the Chief herself. Or, perhaps now, Oscar would admit it was his father who killed Mr. Brant.

He reached the paved road and even though it was full of standing water and the rain still made it hard to see the road, it was a huge improvement over the trail he had just left. He checked on Lila repeatedly, but realized that the best he could do for her would be to get her to a hospital as soon as possible.

When he arrived at the community hospital, he ran inside to get help. When he couldn't find anyone, he wheeled out a gurney to the car and put Lila on it, then took her back inside. A nurse saw him this time. He identified himself and explained Lila's situation. She ran and got some orderlies, who arrived within a few minutes.

The Judge warned the medical attendants that she could be dangerous and that she was a drunk. They nodded and clamped restraints onto her arms. While they were taking her away, three more cars arrived at the emergency area. The nurse explained, "We're getting a lot of victims from the storm. That's why no one was here when you arrived. You better move your car." The Judge surmised that the severity of the storm was also why the deputy had not reached him.

The Judge asked her to alert the Chief about Lila. She said, "The phones are all down, so I don't know when we'll talk to him. But he and the deputies are out taking care of people hurt in this storm, so it's likely he'll show up here eventually when he drops off more injured people."

"All right. I'll go move my car and then see if I can help out here or get in touch with the Chief to help."

The storm did not let up. People continued to pour into the hospital. The Judge went wherever he saw a need. For a while he stayed at the emergency area and helped unload incoming victims. When there was a break, he went to the areas where victims were piling up and ran errands for the doctors. The phones remained out of order.

Sometime after midnight, a nurse found the Judge and asked, "Are you the one who brought in the shooting victim?"

When he nodded, she said, "We managed to stop the bleeding, but she's not in very good condition. What do you know about her?"

He said, "Not much. Only that she drinks too much. I doubt that she eats properly, if at all. She doesn't seem to be totally aware of her surroundings."

The nurse nodded. "Even if we save her from the rifle wound, the doctor doesn't think she has long to live. If you know her next of kin, we should notify them. Did you want to see her?"

He must have looked puzzled because the nurse said, "She's calling for someone named Oscar. She keeps saying he's the only one who ever cared."

"I'll speak to her. I'm not sure she'll know who I am, but maybe I can let her know that Oscar's all right, at least. Have you seen the Chief?"

"I'll take you to her and then see if I can track down the Chief. I think I saw him just a little while ago. He's been dropping off people and then going out for more."

"Good. He'll want to question Mrs. Briarley, if he has time."

He followed the nurse and saw Lila lying in a bed looking more comfortable than he'd previously witnessed her. Her arms were restrained but the doctor had succeeded in stopping the bleeding. What was more remarkable was that her face was clean and her thin hair combed. She wasn't exactly pretty, but she looked far more human.

And looking at her lying there almost peaceful, he experienced the strangest thoughts: how did this woman meet up with Claude Briarley? Who were her parents? And what kind of wedding ceremony did Claude and Lila have? Did she wear a wedding dress? Did they ever really care about each other? Did they even ever get married? He started to think of them as real people, not as the caricatures they'd become. He literally shook his head to bring him back to the present moment. But maybe he'd see if Jim could find out anything about this pathetic woman.

He walked over to her and stood there waiting for her to see him. She looked up and said, "You." She closed her eyes and licked her lips. He suspected she was craving alcohol. She opened her eyes and struggled to keep them open. "Please. Help Oscar. He's a good boy."

"I will. I promise." She seemed lucid, so he asked her, "It was your husband who killed Mr. Brant, wasn't it?"

"I think so. He said so. He didn't mean it. Accident. Oscar didn't want to go. Claude made him." She closed her eyes. He was getting ready to leave when she said, "Frankie's a good boy, too." She took a breath and closed her eyes. He looked at the nurse, who had re-entered with the Chief.

"Did you hear her?" he asked the Chief. "She said that Claude forced Oscar to participate in the robbery and that he was the one who shot Mr. Brant. Can you testify to that?"

The Chief nodded. "I heard her."

The nurse also nodded. "So did I."

"You were right to go out there. You couldn't have known about this. But if you hadn't gone out there, we might never have known it was the father who killed Mr. Brant."

The Judge lowered his head, and the Chief patted his arm.

Chapter 29

The next day was full of news about the weather—one of the most destructive storms to ever hit Southern California. Record rainfall caused floods, road and railroad washouts, and the loss of power and phone service. Houses were actually washed out to sea in Belmont Shore near Long Beach.

In the Ventura area, most of the damage and loss of life occurred at sea or at the pier. An old barge got loose and crashed into one of the piers and destroyed it. It turned out that the deputy who was supposed to help the Judge had been busy helping to rescue people off a boat. He swam out to it with a line to help bring them in. The Chief had called out all of his deputies and other capable men to help.

Another fishing boat was not so fortunate. It was seventy-five yards from shore trying to dock when it was overturned by large waves. There were only two survivors out of twenty-six on board—a man and a woman who swam to shore and then walked five miles to Oxnard.

Although electricity was restored, the day progressed without phones, which hampered emergency communication. The emergency system relied on the police being summoned using a series of traffic lights implemented by a telephone operator-generated message. Without benefit of the phone system, they had to be reached using other methods, mostly people running to the station or simply looking to find someone. Many stayed at home listening to the radio for any news of the storm, including Clara and her parents.

It was after 10:00 in the morning when they heard someone knocking on their door. Judge Akers, dressed in pants, shirt, jacket, and long muddy hip boots, and in need of a shave stood there and said, "Hello, Mr. Wilson. I'm sorry to bother you. I don't have much time, but I just wanted to let

Clara know the outcome of my trip to the Briarley house yesterday."

"Come in, Judge. You can take off your boots here. Would you like some coffee?"

"Oh, that would be wonderful." He removed his boots and joined them in the parlor. "I've been helping some of the neighbors clear out the debris from wind damage. That's why I look like this."

Clara walked up to him and said, "Did you go to the Briarley place? What did they say? Did you find out who Oscar was with?"

The Judge nodded, "Yes and yes. It was a difficult visit." He hesitated, not sure how to proceed. Then he said, "First, the person who was with him and who shot Mr. Brant was his own father."

Clara was stunned. "What?"

Mr. Wilson put his arm around his daughter and stared at the Judge.

The Judge responded, "Yes. Mrs. Briarley told me."

"I don't believe it! How could he do such a thing to Oscar?" Clara almost screamed, causing her father to hold her more tightly.

The Judge motioned to Clara's father and said, "Not everyone has great parents like you."

Mrs. Wilson entered the room with coffee, which she handed to the Judge. She checked out Clara to see how she was taking the news, just as she pulled free from her father's grasp.

"So is Oscar's father in jail?" Clara asked.

The Judge said, "Not exactly. While I was there, he pulled a rifle on me and accidentally shot his wife, Oscar's mother. She's at the hospital now. We don't know if she'll pull through. I haven't had a chance to go see her yet today. And both the Sheriff and the Chief are busy helping people caught in the storm, so I doubt they've had much time to go looking for Mr. Briarley."

"But he killed Mr. Brant, and we know that now, and he tried to kill you, and he shot his wife. He's dangerous!" Clara did not understand why it wasn't top priority to catch such an evil man.

"Clara!" Her mother's tone suggested she had said too much.

"I'm sorry, sir," she said.

The Judge looked at her and said, "Just so you know, I talked to the Chief and then went to the police station myself and to the Sheriff's office and gave them that information, so everyone has been briefed. But Clara, right now people are depending on our officers to help them—and in some cases, lives are at stake. This was a really ferocious storm. Besides, I doubt that Claude Briarley is going far. He doesn't have the means to travel. I'm more concerned about his son, Frankie. That boy might not survive on his own."

The Judge's words calmed her. She said, "Do you think he'll go to the hospital to see his wife?"

The Judge looked at her and frowned. "I doubt it. Although he might rationalize that he wasn't responsible for shooting her since if I hadn't been there, it wouldn't have happened. I'm just not so sure he cares much about her."

Clara responded, "But she's all he has."

Mrs. Wilson watched the Judge closely and said, "Have you been up all night?"

"Yes, ma'am. That's how I know that the officers are out there helping folks."

"I'm fixing you some breakfast. You sit down, and I'll bring it to you."

The Judge must have been tired because he did exactly what he was told. Mr. Wilson followed him and also sat. "Is there something I could be doing to help? I planned to go check on the oil derrick barge to make sure it stayed put, but afterwards I'm available."

"Yes, it's best to go see the Chief at the station. He's coordinating from there. The two-way radios are working between the police cars, so that's helping. He's even mobilized the boys' club to help."

He continued to drink his coffee. Mrs. Wilson handed him a plate with toast, an orange, and oatmeal, which the Judge gulped down.

Clara said, "I should go to the store to see if anyone needs deliveries."

Her mother nodded. "That's a good idea, but isn't it closed today?"

The Judge said, "It's open. I saw a sign when I passed it earlier." He paused for a moment and asked Clara, "If you get a chance, could you check on Lila Briarley—that's Oscar's mother? I just won't have time, and with everything that's happening I'm not sure they'll be able to look after her much. She's also suffering from alcohol withdrawal, so she's really in a bad way. A friendly face might help her, and you could also let Oscar know that you looked in on her."

Clara nodded enthusiastically. "Yes, of course." She appeared pleased that the Judge had asked her to do something. Besides, she was eager to meet Oscar's mother.

Mr. Wilson, who had gone into his bedroom to change, came out carrying his boots. "I'm leaving with you." The two men departed, and Clara and her mother finished dressing and then they, too, left—Clara to see about running errands for the store and Mrs. Wilson to check on the school.

The sun was shining, and the sky was blue, which seemed at odds with the damage of fallen trees, stalled automobiles, and debris-littered streets. As she was walking, Clara yearned for some kind of "normal" to come back, but at the moment wasn't sure what that would be.

After checking into the store, making deliveries, and asking a co-worker to help out, she started to walk to the hospital, which was probably a mile from her last stop. When she reached it, she was not surprised at how busy it was, given the destruction from the storm. There were dozens of cars outside the emergency area. When she entered, she was met by the smell of antiseptics which she assumed from her reading was surgical alcohol, along with hurried activity from scurrying doctors and nurses treating injured men, women, and children in chairs, benches, or stools spread throughout the lobby.

She wasn't sure where Mrs. Briarley would be, and there was a line in front of a poor woman seated at a table who looked like she hadn't had much sleep. Nonetheless, she was providing capable assistance to those waiting, a result Clara assumed was due to a group of volunteers who were circulating and bringing paperwork to the receptionist's table. Clara waited patiently for her turn. When she gave her name, the receptionist asked, "Are you a relative?"

"No, ma'am. Judge Akers asked me to look in on her."

The woman studied the papers in front of her. "What is your name?"

"I'm Clara Wilson."

"Yes. Your name is here." She gave Clara the room number with directions. After wading through even more patients waiting for care in hallways, Clara approached the room carefully. She heard moans and screaming before she saw the woman thrashing in the bed and pulling against her restraints. The antiseptic smell overpowered the room. A nurse was standing over Lila trying to calm her down, but without much success. Clara wasn't sure what she could do, but entered the room regardless. At first, the nurse didn't notice her.

Then Lila opened her eyes, which were yellow, and she tried hard to focus on Clara. The nurse looked at Clara and said, "I gave her something to calm her, but it will take a few minutes. Can you talk to her and try to keep her from moving? I've got so many other patients to see. We just don't have any spare doctors to help right now. Can you just try to hold her down? I'll go see if I can find help."

"I'll do what I can." Clara walked over to the bed and said timidly, "Mrs. Briarley, can you hear me? You may not know me but I'm here to tell you that Oscar is going to be all right. You did a good job raising him. He is a good son." The nurse nodded in encouragement, and then left the room.

"Mrs. Briarley, do you know what Oscar told me about you? He said that you are quite a woman."

Clara was sure that she smiled, but she was so far gone. The thrashing about had caused her wound to re-open, and Clara noticed blood seeping through the hospital gown. She panicked and ran out in the hall for someone to help, but found no one. She heard Lila scream again so returned to her bed and continued talking.

While trying to hold down the struggling woman, she said frantically, "He's learned to garden, too. He helps out at the jail. He likes the food there."

Clara did her best to hold Lila down, but she was strong, despite her wound and the damage caused by her drinking. Continuing to try to calm her, she said, "And do you know Oscar never once said that it was his pa who made him rob that store nor would he ever say it was his pa who killed Mr. Brant. He said it was against who he was to tell on him."

Lila's face started to twitch, then her whole body. Clara watched, shocked, as she twisted and turned with no relief. She swallowed hard and then repeated, "You can be proud of your son Oscar. You did a good job with him. He'll be all right."

She was relieved when the nurse re-entered with a doctor behind her. She happily turned her over to them and ran from the room.

On her way home, she stopped by the Judge's house. He wasn't there so she left a note that she had stopped by to check on Mrs. Briarley, who wasn't doing well.

She felt sad and disturbed. She hoped her words about Oscar had helped.

Chapter 30

Phone service was restored the following day, and most businesses re-opened—as did school. Not all of Clara's teachers were able to get to school that day, so several of her classes turned into study periods. She used the time to prepare a lesson for Oscar. She wasn't sure what to tell him that day. He seemed to care about his mother. And how could she tell him that they now knew his father had been his partner and that his own father had shot his mother?

She decided to discuss with the Judge how to approach him, which is when she learned Lila Briarley had passed away. She sat across the desk from the Judge, as she did so often.

He told her, "She died about ten this morning. I'm not sure she ever had a chance."

The Judge noticed that at first Clara didn't respond. She appeared confused. Then she started blinking, followed by putting both hands on his desk, removing them, and putting them in her lap. She said in a thin voice, "I did tell her over and over that she had done a good job with Oscar and that he would be all right. Is that true? Will you be able to be more lenient with the sentence now that we know about his father?"

He gave her his I'm-the-judge-and-can't-discuss-it look. She said, "I know, I know. You can't talk about it. But can you help with what I should tell Oscar about his mother?"

He got up from his desk and walked out to Irene. "Can you check with Attorney Alberts to see if he's informed Oscar Briarley about the death of his mother? And how much did he tell him? Does he know his father shot her? Let me know as soon as you reach him. Tell him Clara is getting ready to see the boy and needs to know how to proceed."

He walked back behind his desk and said, "It will help to know what Mr. Alberts did. You should wait to hear from him before visiting Oscar."

Clara said, "No, I believe I should go as soon as possible. He'll want to talk about it. He likes to have help figuring things out."

The Judge sighed. "You may be right. By the way, the Chief and a deputy went out to the Briarley place today, but there was no sign of either Mr. Briarley or Frankie. They're getting notices out to local law enforcement to be on the lookout for Claude Briarley."

Irene hung up the phone and walked into the Judge's inner office. "Mr. Alberts says he talked with Oscar about his mother's death and told him that his father shot her. He said the boy just stared at him and said nothing."

Clara asked, "Did he tell him that we know it was his father who shot Mr. Brant?"

"I don't believe so. He said that Oscar just stood up and wanted to go back to his cell. He thinks he wanted to cry but didn't want him to see it. He said to tell you, Clara, to try to talk to Oscar."

She stood, ready to go. The Judge held up his hand. "What are you going to say?"

She shook her head. "I don't know. I'll start by asking him how he is. He's less likely to be concerned about crying in front of me." She smiled. "I'm just a girl, you know." Then more seriously, she said, "Also, he's had a little time to get used to the news. I'll tell him how I spoke to his mother in the hospital after you saved her. What I'm not sure about is telling him we now know it was his father who killed Mr. Brant. I'm hoping he'll volunteer that information and offer some details. Maybe he'll know where his father might be hiding."

"That would help," the Judge said. "But let me tell you what else she said about Oscar. It might help." And he told her what Lila had said about Oscar keeping the place clean and bringing her flowers.

She headed to the jail armed with the hint that Oscar's helping to find his father would influence the Judge's verdict and more likely, the sentencing. When she arrived, Deputy Brown looked doubtful about whether Oscar would want to see her, but told her to wait so that the guard could check. She was rewarded with the return of the deputy, who put her bag in its usual place.

She entered the room and sat down at the table, waiting for Oscar to appear, unsure how to proceed but believing she should be there. Usually Oscar arrived before she got to her chair, but today it took him longer. Although the temperature had dropped and the room was cool, she found herself perspiring—perhaps because she had almost run from the Judge's chambers to the jail. She found herself tapping the table, kicking the chair, and biting her lips. Finally, she heard the buzzer and the door opened. Oscar stood there, his eyes red, looking down, hunched over. He walked to the table slowly, his usual grin replaced by a passive face. He carried a copy of *The Yearling*. He handed it to her when he sat down and said, "I really liked this. I need to know a few words." He spoke in a monotone, not like his usual full-of-life bravado.

She took the book and said, "I'm so sorry, Oscar. I just heard."

He pinched his lips together firmly and nodded. "She was my ma."

"I know. Listen, I want to tell you. I went to the hospital yesterday and talked to her. I told her you were learning to read. And that she had done a good job raising you. I think she understood. She told the Judge you were the only one she ever cared for."

He looked down at the table, but couldn't stop the tears, which at first he ignored and then wiped off on his sleeve. Clara hoped that the deputy would pretend he didn't notice. She was relieved that he buried himself in his own book.

She said to Oscar, "She cared about you. She tried to get your father to tell the Judge who was with you that night in the store. I don't think he meant to shoot her, Oscar. I think it was an accident. But I can tell you I'm pretty sure he meant to shoot the Judge. Your ma didn't want that."

"I sure wish the Judge didn't go out there, Clara."

She thought he believed that the Judge was responsible for his mother's death. "Oh, Oscar, it wasn't the Judge's fault. He tried to stop your father. The Judge took her to the hospital. He did everything he could."

Oscar looked up, tears now fully flowing down his freckled cheeks. "No, I know that." He sniffed. "I just wisht' he didn't see my place. And I bet it was all dirty, 'cuz I was the one that kept it clean."

Clara smiled and nodded. "The Judge said that's what your mother told him."

He asked, "Did she?"

"Yes, and she said you brought her flowers, too. Did you do that?"

Now he started to return to some of his normal enthusiasm. "Yes, I did. She loved flowers. I'd pick 'em—you know, them purple and yeller flowers. They grow everywhere."

"Yes they do." Clara continued to smile, waiting for Oscar to go to the next topic.

"I remember once't I had a little puppy I'd found by the road. Someone musta left it there. I was only about mebbe six or seven. Ma didn't drink as much then. Anyway, I really wanted to keep that little puppy. He licked my hand and my face like he liked me. I was scar't that Pa would hurt him—even then I knew about him and Tommy killin' animals for fun. I tried to hide him. I locked him up in Harper's barn. I took him whatever food I could find.

"One day my pa musta followed me. He grabbed my puppy and me and hauled us back to our place. He pulled on it the whole way, and it screamed and yelled. Clara, I can still hear it. And it started to bleed. When we got to our place, Ma saw the puppy and me. Then Tommy came out and I knew they was gonna pull it apart like they liked to do. I started to yell and scream. Pa slapped me and tied me to a tree so's I'd have to watch. But Ma, well, she went inside and came back out with a rifle, and she just shot and kilt that little puppy so's I wouldn't have to watch it suffer none."

Clara listened to that story and wanted to strike out at all the Claude Briarleys on Earth who bullied and tortured. Oscar had come to accept it as the real world. Worse, he had associated his mother with an act of kindness that involved killing his only friend.

"How's Frankie?" he asked.

Clara hid her anger and said, "I think he was scared about what happened. The Judge said he ran out the door into that awful storm."

Oscar stood. "What do you mean, he ran out? Where is he?"

Clara noticed the deputy was looking up from his book and appeared to be ready to stand. She said, "Oscar, I think you need to sit down." As he was sitting, she said, "The Chief and the deputies are looking for both Frankie and your father. The weather was so bad when the Judge was there, that he couldn't find him."

"Clara, he cain't take care of hisself. He just ain't, I mean, isn't very smart."

"But he's probably with your pa. Won't he take care of him?"

Oscar looked at her and shook his head with great force. "No, ma'am, he won't. Not without Ma being there to make him. You've got to tell the Chief to find him."

She looked over to Deputy Brown and said, "Can you alert the Sheriff and the Chief that Frankie Briarley is in danger?"

The deputy said, "Just a minute." He pushed a button and waited by the door until he saw another deputy, then motioned to open the door. He spoke to him for a few minutes, nodded at Oscar, and the second deputy left.

Deputy Brown said, "He's going to talk to the Sheriff, who will notify the Chief. We think the Chief knows about Frankie so is probably already aware of the need to find him, but he's going to make sure." The deputy walked over and peered at

Oscar, whose eyes looked close to frantic. "Oscar, we'll do everything we can to find him."

The boy nodded. "He's so helpless. And, Pa, well, he don't care."

"We know. We're looking for your pa, too, but every deputy will be told that Frankie hasn't done anything wrong, and he should be treated as a victim."

Uh oh. Clara knew Oscar would pick up on that. He would catch that the deputy was implying that his father had done something illegal. "You looking for Pa as some kind of criminal?" he asked.

The deputy looked at Clara and then said, "What's important is that we're looking for Frankie to help him."

Oscar looked at her. "What ain't you tellin' me, Clara?"

She didn't even think about correcting his grammar at that point. "Your pa shot your mother, Oscar. Even if it was an accident, he still shot her and she died. That's a crime."

He accepted that explanation, but she couldn't leave it there. His life was full of people who either deceived or bullied him. She had always tried to tell him the truth. To her, it seemed important to maintain that trust so that he would believe whatever she told him. So she said, "Oscar, I know it was your pa who shot and killed Mr. Brant. Your ma told the Judge and then confirmed it in front of the Chief. When they bring him in, and if I recognize him, I'll have to testify against him. Do you understand?"

At first, she thought he was upset. He seemed almost angry. But that emotion didn't last long. He looked at her and said, "I'm glad, Clara. Pa, he's not real nice. He shoulda not killed my ma nor Mister Brant."

She watched Oscar that day as he tried to process the pieces of his life—a drunk for a mother, a murderer for a father, a brother dead by suicide, his retarded brother missing, and the prospect of spending a significant part of his own life imprisoned. Given her own background filled with parental love and support, she could not comprehend how he managed to move forward. Worse, she questioned how useful she could be in bettering his life. All she could say was, "I'm so sorry, Oscar."

He looked at her and tried to smile. "Yes, ma'am. I do believe you are." He wiped his nose on his hand and took a breath. "We need to do this lesson. I gotta learn to read so I can go learn how to work."

She used every ounce of energy she could muster to give Oscar the best lesson possible. He didn't wait for her to direct him. He pulled *The Yearling* from her hands and pointed out the words he didn't understand. Then he started to read aloud, with no breaks. He read that day with an earnestness that went beyond a student wanting to please his teacher. And the deputy allowed them extra time, but finally he interrupted. He said, "I'm sorry ma'am, but I really do have to get him back to his cell. He'll miss dinner if we don't."

Oscar stood up, looked directly at her, and nodded deliberately. "See you tomorrow?"

"Yes, and for as long as you're here."

He started to walk to the deputy and then turned to her and said, "You might tell the Chief that Pa sometimes hides out at the old Harper barn. But if'n he has his rifle, be careful. He has a lookout place and he kin shoot most anything."

She asked, "Does he have more than one rifle?"

"Oh, yes. He's got mebbe three." He took another step and then stopped again. He said, "And he was the one that kilt Mr. Brant. It was wrong. He didn't need to do it. That's why it's all right for me to tell on him. He didn't need to kill him. We could have got away without that. He's just plain mean. And mean is wrong."

Clara wanted to say something more, but Oscar turned and walked quickly through the door before she could. Deputy Brown said, "I'll let the Sheriff and Chief know what he said."

She nodded. She would also contact Attorney Alberts. She hoped that what he said would be enough for the Judge to consider special extenuating circumstances when sentencing Oscar.

If ever there was an example for the merits of rehabilitation, Oscar was it.

Chapter 31

The next morning the Judge arrived at his chambers, where Irene and Jim were waiting for him. Irene said, "I got a call from the Chief this morning, and they're on their way out to the Harper barn to see about rounding up Claude Briarley. Clara got Oscar to tell her that his father was responsible for the Brant murder, and then he told them where he might be hiding. The deputy told the Chief that the boy is really broken up about his mother."

The Judge nodded. "That's good news that he's co-operating—and just in time, too. I assume Attorney Alberts has been informed and will expect a motion from him to consider leniency. What else is happening? Why are you here, Jim?"

"I'm still trying to track down Blakensfeld and find evidence that he and Franklin created that gang of boys responsible for the round of robberies. The Chief had to pull deputies away from Mrs. Chissum's house when the storm hit, but no robberies were reported. He's reassigned someone so we still might find out something from that. I've been watching the Blakensfeld house and I'm meeting with Mrs. Blakensfeld later this morning. I'm not sure how co-operative she'll be, but she was willing to talk to me, and that's something."

"What will you ask her?"

"Well, I thought I'd ask her where she and her husband went either for business or pleasure; and about any property they might own; who his friends were, besides the Franklins."

"Don't you think the Chief has already grilled her on those things?" the Judge interrupted.

"I don't know. I checked with him that it was all right to talk with her, and he said it was. He said she can be frazzled and he wouldn't be surprised if she knows more than she says. He thinks I might be able to get some information."

"Good luck."

Jim started to leave and then turned back. "You know, sir. There's something about all this that just doesn't add up."

"All what?" the Judge asked.

"I'm not sure, but so much is happening at once. You've got Oscar Briarley and his father robbing the five-and-dime store and then all the other robberies in the area. Then there's Harry trying to rob the drive-in. And the Franklin boys—why are they so involved? Why does Mr. Franklin care if we talk to his employees? Maybe that's what bothers me the most, that he wants to stop us from talking to them."

The Judge said gently, "You don't think it was just because your last name is Alvarez?"

Jim shook his head. "No, I don't. And believe me, I'm sensitive to bigotry. His is real but his actions go beyond what I'm accustomed to encountering."

"Have you talked to the Chief about your suspicions?"

Jim shook his head. "No, not yet. I don't have anything solid. I just don't get it."

"Your instincts usually prove solid. By the way, when you get a chance, can you find out who owns the Harper barn? I understand it's deserted, but someone must own that property."

"Yes, I'll stop by City Hall on my way back from seeing Mrs. Blakensfeld."

Jim left the office, Irene started her daily typing, and the Judge put on his robe and headed for the courtroom.

Later that afternoon, the Judge waited at his desk expecting a call from the Chief's office about the capture of Claude Briarley. Clara entered, or more accurately, burst into the chambers where Irene was sipping coffee. She asked, "Did they catch him yet?"

"We're waiting to hear from the Chief," Irene said. "The Sheriff sent some of his deputies along with the Chief's men. The last we heard, Claude Briarley had barricaded himself in the barn and was shooting at them. But they had surrounded the barn and expected he would either run out of ammunition or fall asleep, and then they'll get him."

"Did they find Frankie?"

Irene shook her head. "I don't know. I haven't heard anyone mention him."

The Judge's door opened. He saw Clara and Irene and heard Clara's question about Frankie. "Let me call the Chief's office and see what's happening." He picked up the handset and asked for the Chief's office. "What's happening, Carrie? Have you heard anything?"

He listened, said thanks, and then hung up. He told them, "The Chief hasn't returned yet. They haven't heard anything since the earlier report that they had the Harper barn surrounded."

Jim rushed into the Chambers and said, "You're not going to believe what I found out today!"

"What?" the Judge, Irene, and Clara all spoke at the same time.

"You know the Harper barn where Claude Briarley is hiding? You won't guess who owns it."

"Oh for goodness sake, Jim. Just tell us." Irene spoke as a wife accustomed to her husband's guessing games.

"None other than Mr. Harold Franklin."

The Judge smiled. "Now we're getting somewhere. Your instincts were right. It couldn't be a coincidence that Claude Briarley is holed up there. This is all somehow connected. What else did you find out?"

"Mrs. Blakensfeld—you know, Harry Winter's mother—can hardly form complete sentences, but I do believe she wants her husband caught and punished. I talked to her for more than an hour. She definitely blames her husband for her son's death. She claims that she didn't know all that was going on and that her son did work for his stepdad delivering furniture. She'd forgotten that he could drive a pickup truck."

"She forgot?" The Judge arched his eyebrows. "Right. Did she know whose pickup truck it was? And, for that matter, where it is?"

"I thought you'd never ask. She said they keep it at the Harper barn."

The Judge stared at the room without focus. "More and more curious. So we know that Blakensfeld, Franklin and now Briarley are connected somehow. I think we should make sure that the Chief thoroughly checks out that barn after they capture Briarley."

Jim called the Chief's office again and repeated what he had just learned and requested that the Chief be notified.

The Judge turned to Clara. "Do you think Oscar knows Harry or the Franklin boys?"

She shook her head. "I thought about that earlier, but I don't think so. When I mentioned Harry's name, Oscar didn't know him. I mean, he did not recognize the name at all, I'm sure. I'm on my way to give Oscar his lesson today. He has become more motivated since his mother's death, and he is also more co-operative. He's the one who told us to check out the Harper barn for his father. I can ask him about Harry and the others."

The Judge nodded. "I think that's a good idea. If you learn anything, let the Sheriff or deputies know right away."

She picked up her bag and headed to the jail. She followed her usual procedure, pulled out the lesson for the day, and waited patiently for the door to open. Oscar must have been ready—and she was about ten minutes later than usual—because he entered about the same time as she did, and they sat down at the table simultaneously.

He immediately asked, "Have they found Frankie yet?"

She shook her head. "They found your father in the barn, like you said, but he won't come out. They don't think Frankie's with him."

Oscar started to jiggle and sway. He bit his lips. "Oh, Frankie needs me, Clara, he needs me."

She looked at the distraught boy, who was in jail facing sentencing for murder, but whose main concern was his disabled brother. She said, "Oscar, I need you to think. We have to figure out where Frankie would go without you, your mother, or your father. What did he like to do more than anything?"

Oscar stopped jiggling, but continued to bite his lips. He looked at the table, then at the ceiling, then at his shoes, and then at her. "He liked to walk in water. I used to tell him it was 'cuz it made him feel gooshy—you know, good and ooshy."

She nodded. "So is there a pond or a creek nearby where he might go to make himself feel better?"

Oscar nodded. "Yes. I took him to a creek about a mile from our place to the east. But now that creek will be full of water from the storm, Clara. He'll drown if'n he tries to wade in it. And he don't know no better."

Deputy Brown sensed the boy's agitation and stood up. He said, "Oscar, I need to tell the Sheriff so that they can search for him there. Can you be more specific about the place?"

Oscar looked at the deputy. "Sir. Yes, Deputy Brown, you go past the Harper barn where Pa is. There's sort of an old road to follow. That road ends and you go this way," he held out his left arm and then continued, "for about almost another mile." He turned to Clara and said, "Pa taught me about how far a mile is. Best thing I ever learnt from him." Then he looked at Deputy Brown and said, "Do you think you can help, sir?"

She was surprised that Oscar was asking the deputy for help, which the officer must have sensed, because he turned to her quickly and held up his hand, then he looked at Oscar intently and asked, "Do you think that's where Frankie might be?"

Oscar's eyes grew wide with hope. "Yes. If he ain't with Pa, and he ain't at home, that's the only other place I can think of where he'd be."

Deputy Brown smiled. "Good, Oscar. I'm going to let the other deputies know, and they'll organize a search party. Is there something we can say to him when we find him so that he won't be scared?"

"Tell him that you know that he likes to feel 'gooshy' and that Oscarootie sent you to bring him to me. Then bring him here as fast as you can. Please, sir."

Deputy Brown said, "We'll do our best. Now stay seated." He buzzed the door and spoke to the deputy there. He explained the need to search for Frankie and what to say. Then they closed the door and he returned to his perch.

Clara said, "Oscar, I have a question. We need your help. I know you told me you didn't know Harry Winter, the boy who tried to rob the drive-in, but I'm wondering if you know the Franklin brothers or any other boys who might pal around together."

"No, not really, but Frankie might."

Clara was surprised. "Why Frankie?"

"Pa took him one time to some kind of meetin' at the Harper barn. I couldn't go on account of Ma. I had to take care of her, so jest Frankie went."

Deputy Brown sat up straight and looked at Oscar closely. Clara asked, "When was this?"

"Oh, a few months back. Frankie come home all excited like he was important or something."

She could see that Deputy Brown wanted to join in the questioning but feared Oscar would stop confiding if he intervened. She asked, "Did he tell you who was there?"

"Yeah." He leaned forward and whispered to Clara, "He said there was a 'sir' there."

Uh oh. Her heart started to beat faster. Was it possible that a policeman was involved? What was going on? She was confused but decided not to follow up with that line of questioning in front of the deputy until she talked to the Judge. Instead she shook her head slightly to warn Oscar not to say anything more about the "sir," and then said, "Did your pa or Frankie ever go back?"

Oscar seemed to understand not to talk about the "sir" part of the story because he quickly said, "I think Pa did." He crinkled his face in a puzzled expression. "You know, I think he went the day 'afore we robbed the store. He said he'd get Ma a new dress if'n I helped him."

"What else did Frankie say about the meeting? Were there other boys there?"

"Oh, yes. But Frankie don't know nobody. He never went to school or nothin'. He jest knew Pa and Mr. Blaken, er, Blakensfu, Blakens—I could never learn how to say his name."

Clara gasped. Oscar looked at her. She said, "Do you mean Mr. Blakensfeld?"

Oscar nodded. "Sure. He come to our house a couple times. He and Pa knew each other from way back."

She glanced over at the deputy, who was nodding. They both recognized the name of Harry's stepfather. It hadn't occurred to her to use the stepfather's last name because she had assumed Oscar would know Harry by his biological father's last name, Winter. She indicated to the deputy with a quick shake of her head that he should not move. She said to Oscar, "Tell me about Mr. Blakensfeld. How did he know your pa?"

"Oh, they was in some kind of home for bad boys together." Oscar actually giggled. "Mr. Blakensfeld, he married some rich lady and would bring Pa some money now and then. Pa, he would do things for Mr. Blakensfeld. I didn't like him. He tried to look in my pants. Ma caught him one time and hit him with one of her pots. He didn't try that no more."

"One time you told me that your pa would sometimes put things he got from old ladies into his barn. Where is that barn? Is it on your place?"

"Oh, I meant the Harper barn. Mr. Blakens—you know, said it was all right for Pa to keep things there. I didn't like it that he took things from old lady Rakin. She was kind to me. Once't she gave me food when I hadn't 'et for days. Later I helped her when she couldn't get out no more."

"What was in the barn? Do you remember?"

"I went there one time when Pa wasn't around. It was full of all kinds of purdy things—tables, chairs, jewelry, radios. But I couldn't find no dress for Ma."

"Did your pa ever meet with Mr. Blakensfeld anywhere else besides the barn?"

Oscar nodded. "Oh, sure. They liked to go to a place up in the hills—some huntin' cabin. Frankie and I was not never s'pose to go there, but I followed Pa once't."

Deputy Brown couldn't stay still. He stood up and said, "Oscar, can you tell us where that cabin is? Or maybe draw a map?"

Oscar smiled broadly. "Oh, I like to draw. Can I have a pencil and paper?"

Deputy Brown smiled back. "You bet you can. Hold on." Again he pushed the buzzer. He spoke to the other deputy quietly, who turned and left for a moment and then returned with paper and pencil. Deputy Brown handed these to Oscar. The boy drew a small version of his dilapidated house.

Clara looked at the deputy. "How did you know he could draw?"

The deputy shrugged. "I didn't. But he sure can. He's an artist! Look at the details."

Oscar grinned. He opened his eyes wide and stuck out his tongue while he put pencil to paper. Then he drew arrows with left and right turns. At the end of the final arrow he drew a cabin with trees behind and beside it, a front door and windows. A path led to it.

He turned to Clara and asked, "Can you write the numbers for me?" He told her the number of miles to write by each arrow. She did as he directed.

Then he eagerly presented the drawing to Deputy Brown, his face and eyes smiling.

The deputy studied the drawing and said, "Oscar, that's wonderful. I'm going to see that you get as many pencils and as much paper as you'd like. We'll figure out how."

Oscar started to jiggle and then grinned. "Pa don't like me to draw stuff. He says it's girly-like."

Deputy Brown and Clara said at the same time, "Oh, no. It's wonderful!"

The deputy went to the door again and pushed the buzzer. He gave the map to his colleague and pointed to his watch. Clara realized that it was well past visiting hours at the jail.

Oscar said, "We didn't get much reading done today."

"No, but we will. Don't you worry. We will."

Deputy Brown said, "Oscar, we need to go so that you get dinner. I think it's rabbit stew tonight."

Oscar stood and followed the deputy with that peculiar gait that Clara had noticed the first visit she had made. She waved good-bye and waited for the door to open, grabbed her bag, and ran for the Judge's chambers with the hope that he would still be there. She wasn't sure what she'd do if he wasn't because she had so much to tell him. And she was concerned that Oscar might be in danger if indeed there was a "sir,"—a police officer—involved in whatever was going on.

Unfortunately when she arrived, she tried the door to the Judge's chambers and found it locked. She stood outside his chambers for a moment pondering her options when Jim startled her as he opened the door and came out of the Judge's office. He said, "Sorry, I didn't realize Irene locked the door. The Judge wanted me to wait for you in case you came back here. He went home early. Come on in."

She said, "You won't believe what I found out!"

Jim smiled, appreciating his own method of revealing important news.

She explained in a lowered voice, "Oscar said a police officer was part of something going on in the Harper barn. Harry's stepfather and Oscar's father know each other. Oscar told us another place where Mr. Blakensfeld might be hiding and drew a fantastic map to it."

Jim grabbed her by the arm and guided her into the Judge's chambers. He nodded, "It's starting to make sense now. But if there's someone from the Sheriff's or the Chief's office involved we have to move carefully."

Clara looked at Jim. "What do you mean 'it makes sense'? I'm so confused. And I'm worried about Oscar. If he knows about a policeman being involved in something, isn't he in danger?"

Jim nodded. He picked up the phone and gave the operator a number, which Clara assumed was the Judge's. He talked quietly and quickly. She could only catch an occasional word: "Oscar Briarley, Clara, police officer—"

He replaced the receiver. "Let's go. The Judge wants us both at his home—now."

She was relieved that the Judge was involved with this latest development, but still concerned for Oscar. She said, "Should we go back to the jail to make sure Oscar is protected?"

"We can't do that. The Judge is handling it. He'll probably arrange some sort of protective custody and make sure at least two officers are guarding him at all times. We need to leave right away. He wants us out of this building and with him."

She followed Jim through the door and started down the stairs. It was now starting to get dark. She realized her parents would be worried that she was late. She asked, "Do I have time to call my folks?"

Jim looked concerned, but returned and re-opened the door. "Go. Do it quickly. Tell them the Judge needs you at his house."

She picked up the handset and asked the operator for her number. Her father answered. She said quickly, "Hi, Dad. I need to go to the Judge's house. I'm with Jim Alvarez, you know, Irene's husband. So I'm not alone. I'll call you from there."

Her father said, "Are you all right? What's going on?"

"Yes, I'm fine. Oscar told me some things today that I need to tell the Judge, and we think it might help to catch Oscar's father."

"Call me when you get to the Judge's. You hear?"

"Yes, I promise."

She replaced the handset and hurried out to Jim, who re-locked the door. He led her out down the stairs, through the large doors from the lobby, past the statue of Father Junípero Serra, onto the street. He searched the area before signaling her to follow. They walked that way to the Judge's house—he scanned everywhere without letting up. She followed him without question or conversation, moving with determination and her face showing a mixture of concern and satisfaction that Oscar might be in danger but she had helped him. They walked that way for about fifteen minutes, until they reached the Judge's house. Jim knocked on the door, and the Judge opened it almost immediately. He looked relieved.

Before she was even in the door, he said, "Clara, I need you to tell me exactly what Oscar said that suggested a policeman is involved in whatever is going on, and anything else he said."

"He whispered to me about there being a 'sir' involved, so that Deputy Brown couldn't hear him. He said that Frankie went to a meeting with his father at the Harper barn and Mr. Blakensfeld was there. He didn't know that Blakensfeld was Harry's stepfather. I had asked him about Harry Winter. Anyway, when I asked if there was anyone else there, he leaned over and whispered that there was a 'sir' there—that's how he refers to policemen. I changed the subject, and he caught on right away that he shouldn't say anything more. I don't think Deputy Brown or anyone else heard him."

The Judge said, "Good thinking. All right. Any ideas, Jim?"

"Have they found Frankie Briarley yet?" Jim asked.

"I don't know. Let me call the Chief's office. He's still out there at the Harper barn. They won't leave until they either catch Claude Briarley or kill him. The Sheriff and his deputies are still looking for Frankie."

Jim said, "Before you call, here's what I'd suggest. Find a place in one of the jails to isolate Oscar and, when they find his brother, bring Frankie to him. And somehow we have to get Clara to them. She has managed to get more information from Oscar than he even knows he knows! She might be able to get through to Frankie as well." The Judge smiled but did not choose that moment to mention to Jim that his plan to get Clara to talk to Oscar had worked—despite Jim's belief it wouldn't. However, he would bring it up at an appropriate time.

Clara said, "I don't know Frankie. But I might be able to help Oscar get through to Frankie." Then she remembered, "Oh, I have to call my dad. I promised."

The Judge picked up the handset and asked for her number. He said, "Hi, Mr. Wilson. This is Judge Akers. I wanted to let you know that Clara is here with me. I just need her help for another hour or so. I'll try to keep you informed. She has been extremely valuable at getting information from the Briarley boy. I promise that she's safe."

The Judge replaced the handset onto the receiver. He said, "Clara, can you give Jim and me a few minutes to figure some things out? If it weren't for your talent with reaching Oscar, I'd have sent you home right now, but I think we might need you."

Clara nodded. "Sure." She was pleased that she could be useful.

"Jim, it's time to check in with the Chief's office to see what's happening." He gave the operator a phone number and listened to whoever answered at the city jail. "What's happening out at the Harper barn? So they finally caught him? Good. I assume they'll take him directly to the county jail? And have you heard anything about whether the Sheriff's deputies have found Frankie Briarley? All right. I'll call the Sheriff's office."

He hung up and then lifted the handset again and asked the operator for another number. "This is Judge Akers. Can you tell me if you've found Frankie Briarley? No, no luck yet. Yes, I know it's dark. Will they start again in the morning?"

He replaced the handset onto the receiver and said to Jim, "Some good news. They've caught Claude Briarley. They're taking him directly to the county jail, and he'll be in the adult maximum security section, so there's no chance he'll run into Oscar."

He continued, "It got dark before they could find Frankie, so they'll start to search again in the morning."

Jim asked, "Does that mean the Chief will be coming back tonight?"

The Judge responded, "Yes, right now he's helping take Briarley to the county jail."

"I think we should go over there to meet with the Chief and the Sheriff and tell them what Oscar told Clara. And I think Clara needs to come with us in case we want to talk to Oscar again."

Clara sat up, ready to go.

The Judge nodded. "I agree. I'd prefer not to take Clara but, you're right, we might need her." He couldn't resist. He grinned at Jim who caught the sign and just rolled his eyes. He turned to her. "Have you eaten anything tonight?"

She shook her head. He said, "What about you, Jim?" He, too, shook his head. The Judge said, "Me neither. It will take the Chief a while to get to the jail. I think we should eat something."

Jim laughed. "And I suppose you have something in your refrigerator?"

"Well, no." The Judge smiled. "But we can stop by the café and pick something up. I'll call Molly." He ordered three chicken potpies to go. Then he said, "I'll get the car. I don't want Clara walking any more tonight."

He left the house, and Jim turned to Clara and said, "Let's go. Food will help you, I bet." The Judge drove up and they got in—Clara climbing into the back seat. They stopped by the restaurant to get their dinner and, with the smell of chicken and fresh baked piecrust permeating the car, proceeded to the courthouse. They said very little in the five-minute drive. The Judge focused on his driving. Jim seemed to be thinking.

When they arrived, the Judge parked the car in front of the courthouse, unlocked the doors, and decided they should go to his chambers first, where they could eat before walking over to the jail. As soon as they entered, he called the Sheriff's office to let them know they were coming. Apparently the Chief had just arrived with Claude Briarley, and they were in the process of booking him. The Judge was now eager to get there, so they quickly finished their food and walked out. Jim assured that the door was locked. Clara politely said, "Thanks for the food. It really did help. I feel much better."

When they entered the jail, they could hear Claude Briarley cursing and screaming. "I got my rights, you know! You can't do this to me. Where's my wife? What have you done to her? You sons of bitches. Who do you think you are?"

The Judge's Story

The Judge put Clara in a room by herself to keep her away from the ruckus, then he and Jim went into the room where the deputies were struggling with Briarley. When the Judge and Jim entered, they found him still cursing and arguing. They also smelled him—he obviously had not bathed for several days of living in a barn. When he saw the Judge, he snarled. "What have you done with my wife?"

The Judge glared at him with no sign of pity. He responded firmly, in his best sentencing voice, "You killed her. She died at the hospital."

"'Twas your fault. If'n you ain't come out to our place, she'd still be alive."

He pulled against the chains holding him and tried to reach the Judge, who said firmly and without raising his voice, "I didn't pull the trigger. You did."

The Chief stepped into the room and told the Judge, "This man refuses to tell us anything and denies that he had something to do with the Brant robbery or murder."

The Judge responded, "Well, we know better, don't we? Oscar told us all about you. So did your wife."

"You're lyin'. Oscar wouldn't say nothin'. He's girly-like but my boy ain't no snitch!"

The Chief walked up to him, and face to face said, still without raising his voice, "You're going to jail for a long time for murder. Your only hope is to tell us what else is going on. What do you know about all that stuff in the Harper barn?"

The dirty and foul-smelling murderer actually spat on the Chief, causing both deputies to grab him. Only the Chief's loud "Leave him be!" stopped them from doing more.

The Chief said, "Fellas, I think we better just get this man washed up and taken to his cell. He's not going to help us, so we'll just prosecute him to the fullest extent of the law. No breaks for him. I'll see that the District Attorney asks for the death penalty. You know, it took seven minutes after being gassed in San Quentin for that murderer to die who raped and killed that little girl down in the L.A. area. I'm told it was a very painful death. He struggled and pulled to get away, but slowly and surely he died."

"You cain't do that. It was a accident. You'll see when I git me a lawyer."

The Chief said, "Take him away. We've got enough without his confession."

Two deputies held him, but not before he got off another verbal stab at the Judge, "I'm gonna have my lawyer arrest you for what you done to my Lila. If'n you hadn't—"

The door slammed, smothering his last words.

Jim looked at the Judge and said, "I see you've made another friend."

The Judge laughed at the tension breaker, and the Chief also smiled. Then the Judge and Jim motioned to the Chief that they needed to speak with him. They found an empty room.

The Judge saw that the Chief was exhausted. He'd been at the Harper place most of the day with his deputies trying to capture Briarley. But he was sure that the Chief—and the Sheriff as well—needed to hear what Clara had discovered as soon as possible.

"Chief, we have some new information that we couldn't tell you over the radio. The Briarley boy says there's a police officer involved with his father and whatever was going on in that barn."

The Chief sighed. He shook his head. He wasn't prepared for yet another surprise. "I don't believe it." He passed his hand over his forehead and tried to fit this latest piece of the puzzle. "You know, the barn was where they were storing stolen goods. Given the amount and variety of things there, it's obvious that this is a combined effort—some kind of group. I already let the Sheriff know. He's checking it out. But to hear that one of our own is involved?" He sighed again and looked down, shoulders drooping.

"We didn't want to broadcast it for fear of alerting the guilty person," Jim said quietly.

The Chief looked up. "Of course. What else did we hear from the Briarley boy? Do we really believe he knows what he's saying?"

Jim interrupted, "Was there a pickup truck in the barn?"

The Chief nodded. "Yes, there was."

"That was probably what the Winter boy used to get to and from L.A. We think it was how he delivered things from his stepfather's store."

The Chief again nodded. "That makes sense. Did the Briarley boy tell you anything else?"

The Judge responded, "We brought Clara Wilson with us. She's in the next room. You might want to speak to her yourself. She's the one who got him to talk."

Clara had been waiting for at least a half hour, where she'd been eagerly writing in her notebook all that had occurred that day, when the Chief, Jim, and the Judge entered the room together. The Chief sat down in front her. He looked exhausted. His eyes had dark circles under them, and his face was dark with a day's growth of beard. His usually immaculate uniform was dirty. He said to her, "Are you sure that Oscar Briarley really meant that a law enforcement officer might be involved in this group?"

She stared at him and simply said, "Yes. And it is most likely someone in a uniform. Oscar calls them 'sirs.'"

"Did he actually see this officer?"

She shook her head. "No. He said Frankie, his younger brother, told him."

The Chief looked annoyed. "But Frankie isn't even all together upstairs. He could mistake anyone in a uniform for a police officer."

She thought about that for a moment, but again shook her head. "Chief, Oscar thinks it was a police officer. He has only ever told us the truth. And everything he's said has turned out to be correct. He believes Frankie. They're brothers. Obviously, Oscar knows him better than anybody, so would probably know if he was making something up."

The Chief looked at Jim. "Any ideas?"

Jim nodded. "Maybe. But you're not going to like them."

"Tell me."

"First, we have to find Frankie. Then we need to talk to Oscar—and I suggest we ask Clara to do that—and get him to convince Frankie to identify the officer. You bring them all here in a sort of lineup. Fabricate some story about why."

Clara said, "But what if the officer is among those who finds Frankie and gets to him first—before we even have this lineup?"

Jim said, "I can't think of any other way. Given what I've heard about Frankie's mental capacity, my guess is that no one would be worried about what he might say. My concern is for Oscar here in the jail. You were very clever not to let anyone hear what Oscar told you."

Clara said, "What about Deputy Brown? Can we trust him? He seems to care about Oscar." That reminded her. "What about the search for Mr. Blakensfeld? Oscar drew a terrific map. Have they found him yet?"

"What map?" asked the Chief.

"When I asked Oscar about Mr. Blakensfeld, he said that he was a friend of his father's. He also said that they used to go together to a cabin in the hills near the Harper barn. He drew a great map and Deputy Brown handed it to one of the guards, who said he'd get it to the deputies so they could search for him."

The Chief shook his head. "First I've heard of it. Let me go check. I'll round up the Sheriff, also."

He left the room, and the Judge turned to her and asked, "Why do you say that the map Oscar drew was so terrific?"

She smiled. "Judge, he's an artist. It was incredible—the detail and perspective. He drew his place and the cabin like, well, for real." She added, "Isn't it incredible how this boy managed to grow up in such a horrible environment and still keep some type of artistic talent? I think he's got a wonderful future—if you can just keep him from spending it in jail."

The Chief and the Sheriff entered the room, walking fast, bearing down on Clara with a look that caused her to pull back. The Sheriff said, "What map are you talking about? No one told me about a map or that we had any idea where Blakensfeld was hiding."

Clara was panicked. She looked at Jim who also seemed concerned. If the Sheriff had not been alerted that meant that either Deputy Brown or the guard were criminals, accomplices, or, at best, incompetent. Clara explained again how Oscar had told them about how his father and Mr. Blakensfeld knew each other, that he'd followed his father to this cabin, and suggested that it might be a place where Mr. Blakensfeld could be hiding. She said, "Deputy Brown gave the map to the guard. He said they would send someone from the Sheriff's department to find him."

The Sheriff stood abruptly and left the room. The Chief explained. "No one here knows anything about a map or a cabin. The Sheriff is checking to make sure Oscar is safe and is sending two of his men to find Deputy Brown."

The Judge followed the Sheriff out of the room. He motioned to Jim to stay with Clara. However, he returned in a few minutes and said, "Clara, the Sheriff wants us to talk to Oscar now. Jim, can you go with the Chief in case either he or the Sheriff needs you?"

Jim nodded. He and the Chief left, and Clara followed the Judge to the visitor's room, where the Sheriff was waiting for them. Clara noticed that the Judge's watch said ten o'clock. She grew worried that her parents might be concerned and asked one of the deputies to call them.

A half-awake and frightened Oscar appeared, but when he saw Clara his demeanor changed. He looked relieved, happy, and almost jovial when he noticed her.

Oscar said, "Hi, Clara. Why are you here? Did they find Frankie?"

"No, but they're looking for him," she said.

The Sheriff interrupted, saying gently, "Oscar, thank you for your help. We captured your father, and he's in another part of the jail where he can't hurt either you or Frankie. We started to look for Frankie tonight, but it just got too dark. But there are several officers out there and as soon as it's light again, they'll start the search. They know what to tell him."

Oscar only said, "Yes, sir. Did the map help?"

The Sheriff answered, "Maybe we could all sit down. Clara, why don't you sit here across from Oscar? I'm sorry to bring you out here so late, son, but we wanted to let you know about your pa. We'll keep him away from you, and you won't even see him."

Oscar looked at Clara, who nodded and said, "That's right, Oscar. You won't have to see him. But we need to ask you about the 'sir' you whispered to me about earlier today. The Sheriff and the Chief are very concerned that there is a bad 'sir' in the group, and they want to know who he is so they can stop him from hurting other children like you and Frankie. Do you remember why you think it was a 'sir' that Frankie saw at the barn?"

Oscar looked uneasy. Clara said, "It's all right, Oscar. You can speak in front of the Sheriff and the Judge. They want to help you."

He said very slowly, "I'm sorry, Clara. I didn't tell you everything. I followed Frankie and Pa that day—and I saw the 'sir' myself." He bit his lip, and looked at her. "You ain't mad at me, are you?"

She frowned, then glared at him, and raised her eyebrows. He knew that look and corrected himself, saying, "I mean, you *aren't* mad at me, are you?"

"No, Oscar. You have helped us so much. But tell me, did you see the 'sir'? Did you see his face?"

Oscar shook his head. "No, I couldn't actually see his face, jest his clothes. I was hiding behind some stuff. He wore what they wear here. That's why I whispered about it to you."

"Could it have been Deputy Brown?"

"Oh, no, it was a big fella, more like that other deputy."

It suddenly occurred to her that Oscar might be able to draw him. "Could you draw a picture of him—the 'sir' you saw?"

"Sure—what I see'd of him."

The Sheriff pulled out his key and unlocked the door and returned almost immediately with paper and pencil. Oscar quickly produced a view of a stout man, from the perspective of the floor, but only up to his double chin with no face. The Sheriff, however, noticed something. He asked, "Are you sure those are his shoes?"

"Oh, yes, sir. I really like them shoes." Clara glared at him. "I mean, *those* shoes."

She looked closer. The shoes were indeed distinctive. They seemed to have some sort of letter carved in the side. The Sheriff turned to the Judge and said, "That's John Shapener. He was the officer on duty earlier today. He would have been the one responsible for dispatching the deputies to search for Blakensfeld."

The Judge said, "Is he a big guy?"

"Yes. And he has shoes just like this. He has bad feet and has to have them especially made."

"Does he have any close friends here who might be involved with him?"

There was a knock on the door, and Deputy Brown entered in his civilian clothes. He looked concerned and confused about why he was there, and even more so when he saw the Judge, Oscar, and Clara. Oscar smiled at him and said, "Hi, Deputy Brown. They caught Pa."

The Deputy smiled at Oscar, and the Judge was sure at that moment that he had absolutely nothing to do with the criminal ring. He was one of the good guys. The deputy said, "That's great, Oscar."

Then he asked the Sheriff, "What's happening, sir?"

The Sheriff responded, "Today, when Oscar drew a map where Blakensfeld might be hiding, who did you give it to?"

Brown said, "To Deputy Ogelthorpe, who took it to Shapener, I assume. He was the officer on duty. Why, sir? Have they caught Blakensfeld?"

"No, and no one here has heard about any map."

Deputy Brown at first looked confused, then pensive, and then his face cleared. He nodded and said, "That explains a lot of things, sir. Have you caught him?"

Then it was the Sheriff's turn to look confused. "What do you mean, it explains a lot of things?"

"Well, you know I've been studying to become a detective, and one of my lessons caused me to do some thinking. In the past few weeks, I've examined the types of robberies around here and the times they've occurred—

always when there were no police in the area. Then when we'd get close to picking up a juvenile, I'd hear from some of the other officers that the thief would disappear before they arrived. I can sit down and figure out each case and let you know more details, sir, if that would help."

The Sheriff nodded and told him, "Yes, it would. In the meantime, I need to go after Blakensfeld and Shapener. Oscar, son, do you think you could draw another map for us?"

Oscar smiled a big grin, and said, "Yes, sir. Here it is." He had been working on it while the others were talking with Deputy Brown. "Clara needs to put in the numbers." She completed the task and Oscar handed the map to the Sheriff. This version was just as spectacular as the previous one. The Judge whistled, and the Sheriff just shook his head in awe.

The Sheriff said, "Deputy Brown, you stay here with the Judge and the prisoner while I start the search for Blakensfeld. Make arrangements for you and at least one other guard to watch Oscar here. I don't know how far this might go. There could be other deputies involved."

Brown nodded. "What about Shapener, sir?"

The Sheriff's eyes narrowed and his face grew tight. He said, "I'll take care of him."

"Yes, sir."

The Judge said, "Would it make sense for me to take Oscar home with me? Deputy Brown could accompany us and guard him."

The Sheriff shook his head. "No, I think he's safer here. We'll keep him separate from the other inmates. Deputy, please choose someone you trust."

The Judge said, "You might want to involve the Chief in helping you with Shapener—for the sake of propriety, if nothing else."

The Sheriff turned and walked through the door, muttering, "Propriety be damned. He's mine."

While Deputy Brown called one of his fellow officers to come to the jail, the Judge and Clara talked with Oscar, who seemed to be having a great time drawing. The deputy got him more paper, and he was busy sketching while they talked.

The Judge asked, "Have you been drawing for a long time?"

Oscar grinned, his freckles very prominent in the electric light. "Oh, sure. Pa didn't like me to, but Ma did sometimes. I used to draw her flowers, but I never had no colored pencils to make 'em purdy." He looked up with wide eyes. "Can you get me colored pencils?"

The Judge laughed. "Yes, Oscar, we'll get you colored pencils."

Oscar continued to draw for a few more minutes, and then he looked up and asked, "Have they found Frankie yet?"

The Judge said, "Probably they won't find him until the morning, Oscar. It's too dark out there right now. But it's not too cold, so he should be all right."

"I just hope that Mr. Blakens— doesn't have him. It would be just like Pa to give him to that man."

The Judge looked concerned. "Would your pa do that, Oscar?"

"Oh, yes. Especially 'cuz Ma isn't around to stop him."

Deputy Brown entered the room again. The Judge said, "Get word to the Sheriff as soon as you can that Frankie might be in the cabin with Blakensfeld—and they should proceed with caution."

The deputy nodded. "Yes, I will. But now it's time for Oscar to return to his cell so he can get some sleep. Actually, we have a new bed for you, Oscar. You're going to sleep with me in my quarters."

The Judge nodded his approval. "That's a great idea. Clara, I need to get you home."

The last place Clara wanted to go at that time was home. She started to protest, but the Judge put up his hand and said, "You've done your job here. Oscar is safe, and he's told us what we need to know. Now it's time for you to go home to your parents."

Oscar said, "Clara? Can I meet your ma and pa? I bet they're nice."

She smiled at him and said, "Yes, Oscar, they are very nice. And you'll definitely meet them. I think they'd like that."

Chapter 32

The next day, the Judge asked Jim to go to Clara's school to give her the latest news. He believed she had earned the right to be kept appraised of what was happening and suspected that she would be anxious to know. Jim planned his arrival at the school to coincide with lunchtime, and was rewarded by her presence on the stairs outside the door. He smiled when he saw her and hurried over.

"What's happening?" she asked.

Jim smiled. "The Judge said you'd be dying to know, and he also said you deserved to be kept informed, but he wants you in school. So he sent me to track you down.

"First, they just found Frankie. I don't know any details, so don't ask. At the Judge's request, they're bringing him to the county jail to talk with Oscar. Apparently, he's incoherent and they're having difficulty getting him to co-operate. But there's still no word about Blakensfeld."

"What about Deputy Shapener, the one the Sheriff was going after?"

"I don't know the details, but so far, he hasn't found Shapener. His place is deserted, and most of his clothes are gone."

"Do you think he's with Blakensfeld?"

Jim nodded. "Yes. I think they're on their way out of the country. Look, I have to go. I'm part of a surveillance team watching for Blakensfeld and need to relieve a deputy."

"Thank you. I really appreciate you letting me know. It's been torture having to sit through my classes today," she said.

Jim waved and started back toward the Blakensfeld house. He was replacing a deputy who had been part of the group that captured Oscar's father. The deputy had only had a few hours sleep and was pleased to see Jim. He had found a spot across the street from the Blakensfeld house behind a clump of bushes. Jim noticed that passersby would have difficulty seeing anyone there.

The deputy said, "No activity so far. But his wife says he might come back to the house to get some money. He's probably running out. When the Chief questioned her about him, she said she didn't think he had enough to get very far. And he keeps all his money at the house in a strongbox."

Jim nodded. "I understood that there was a chance he might show up here. Thanks. Go get some sleep."

Jim settled into a chair the deputy provided. He had brought one of his books to study, but kept watching the house. After about an hour, he looked up and saw the two Franklin brothers knocking on the door, and then Mrs. Blakensfeld opening it. He stood, ready to move quickly if needed. A few minutes later, one of the brothers came back out carrying a box. He started to run down the street followed by the second brother a few moments later.

Jim made a quick decision. He realized he could have easily stopped them but then he wouldn't know where Blakensfeld was hiding. So he waited until they had passed him. Out of the corner of his eye, he saw Mrs. Blakensfeld open the front door, yelling, "Thief!"

Knowing that she was safe clinched his decision to follow the boys rather than capture them. The street where the Blakensfelds lived offered few places to hide, nor, given almost no traffic, could he disguise the sounds of his running. But neither could the boys. He could hear them plainly. They, on the other hand, he assumed, were watching for police in uniform who might be chasing them, so when they looked back he devised various methods to disguise himself, such as, dropping his book so that he'd have to lean over and pick it up, or leaning over to tie his shoe.

When they reached Main Street, he heard the sounds of car horns as they carelessly hurried across the street where they encountered shoppers on the sidewalks and had to slow down to appear less conspicuous. On Main Street, it was easier for him to conceal himself. He assumed the attitude of a shopper occasionally checking out shop windows to blend in. The boys continued to walk/run as fast as they could with the box. Then they stopped outside of the farm equipment store and entered.

Jim followed them into the store, which he knew was managed by the Franklin brothers' father. He looked around for a phone. He assumed Blakensfeld was somewhere inside, or it was possible that Blakensfeld was not there but that Franklin planned to take the money to him. Either way, Jim needed help, because he knew that Franklin would recognize him as the father of the boy his sons had beat up and he would lose the opportunity of surprising him and maybe catching Blakensfeld.

He found a telephone on one of the desks in the store. He did not ask for permission to use it, but quickly asked the operator to connect him to the Chief. He quietly told the deputy who answered where he was and why and asked for help, taking care to assure that none of the half dozen people in the store could hear him. Then he started to search for Blakensfeld and Franklin.

The store was larger than it appeared from the outside. Jim first went to one end of it and encountered only a tractor exhibit. Then he walked back to the front area and found a door leading toward the rear of the store. He came to several rooms with closed doors. He couldn't hear anyone talking, and there was no way to see into the rooms. He opted to check the back door to see if anyone was outside. He had not seen anyone leave the building, so figured that at a minimum, the Franklin brothers and the box they'd stolen had to be somewhere nearby.

One of the doors opened to reveal Mrs. Chissum. She recognized him from his clandestine approach of her at the restaurant. She looked frightened when she saw him, but she also pointed to one of the rooms and nodded, letting Jim know where her boss was. Jim put his index finger to his lips, cautioning her to be quiet and then motioned to her to get out of the building.

Just as he reached the room she had indicated, the door opened and Franklin stood there. He saw Jim and yelled, "Get out of here!"

But Jim did the opposite of what Franklin was expecting. Instead of running away, Jim ran toward him and pushed him back into the room, where he met up with the brothers, three other unidentified boys, and a strongbox full of cash sitting on a table. He stood blocking the door, planning to stall long enough for the Chief or his deputies to arrive. It was less than a ten-minute drive, but that could be a long ten minutes for Jim to hold them all in the room.

"So good to see you, Mr. Franklin. What have we here? A boxful of money stolen from the Blakensfeld house. Not good."

Franklin hissed. "Get out of my way, you—"

Jim interrupted without moving. "Now, now. Watch what you say. Let me see if I can figure this out. You and Mr. Blakensfeld—and Claude Briarley—work together to steal things from your neighbors, because you're so neighborly. And you use these boys to help you? What a great inspiration you must be. Which one of you is Fagin?"

Franklin took a step toward him and said, "There's no one named Fagin here. Now get out or I'll make you."

Jim laughed. "No Dickens fans, huh? Well let me enlighten you. Fagin was the adult leader of a band of young hooligans in old-time England. He led them to a life of crime."

"You're crazy," Franklin said. He grabbed the bills in the box on the table in front of him, yelled at the boys to run, and started for the open door, which was open but with Jim blocking it. Franklin moved toward him, with his fists ready to strike, but Jim was younger and in much better shape. He kicked Franklin's shins with a loud crunch, causing him to buckle over—and fall against the lined-up boys who fell over like a row of dominoes. Nonetheless, Franklin got up, believing Jim to be diverted and pushed him out of his way.

He stumbled out the door and into the drawn guns of the Chief and one of his deputies. "Mr. Franklin, you are under arrest for robbery—and I'll think of some more on the way to the station."

Jim managed to gasp, "Whew! I wasn't sure you'd get here in time."

Franklin protested. "Who the hell do you think you are? You can't come into my store and treat me like this!"

Jim motioned to the money on the table. Franklin yelled, "That's not my money! These boys just brought it here. I was just going to call you because I'm sure they stole it."

Jim stepped back and shook his head. "Chief, I saw the two Franklin boys take this strongbox from the Blakensfeld house, which Mrs. Blakensfeld can corroborate. I believe that Franklin and Blakensfeld have been running a gang of thieves using these boys to do their dirty work for them. And he doesn't even know who Fagin is!"

The Chief, an ardent Dickens fan, said, "That's the biggest crime of all. And we've already spoken with Mrs. Blakensfeld. She called us."

The deputy asked, "Should we take him to the city jail or to the Sheriff?"

The Chief responded. "Take him to the county jail. They can interrogate him to find out where Blakensfeld is. He obviously knows, because Mrs. Blakensfeld said the boys knew exactly where to find the strongbox and they also were able to open the combination lock. Also, if Jim's right and they are in charge of the countywide robberies, the Sheriff will be better able to put the pieces together. I'll take the boys to the city jail, and figure out what to do with them." He looked at the five boys in the room. He knew all of them. They had been attending his club for several months. He shook his head. "I'm really disappointed in you boys."

The youngest boy, age twelve, looked at the Chief and rubbing his hands together said, "We gotta eat. My folks ain't got nothing to eat exceptin' what I bring 'em." His two friends just lowered their heads and looked at the floor.

The Franklin boys appeared as belligerent as their father and held their hands out in fists, ready to take on anyone. The older one said, "You won't get nothin' from us. We ain't no snitches."

Jim nodded. "Good luck, Chief. I know it's disappointing, but these boys have been manipulated by these adults—and maybe others." He added quietly, "Have they caught Deputy Shapener yet?"

The Chief said, "I don't know. Thanks for this."

Jim shrugged. "Not me. You're the one that called for the surveillance of the Blakensfeld house. Oh, that reminds me, I assume Mrs. Blakensfeld is all right?"

The Chief smiled. "Yes, she called just before you. We have a deputy taking her statement."

"Mr. Alvarez, thank you." Jim looked up to see Mrs. Chissum standing next to the Chief.

"You're welcome, Mrs. Chissum. You might want to stay discreet for a few more days." He watched the Chief and his deputy leading the five boys away. "None of those is yours?"

She shook her head. "No, thank heavens." She looked around and pulled Jim away from the group. "Will you please tell the Judge 'thank you'? And that I plan to see Hiram next week down in L.A. at his school and will be sure to let him know? He only has one more month to serve, and then he'll come home to me. I just hope I can keep this job so I can support both boys."

Jim nodded. "I'll let the Judge know. Also, you be sure to contact him if you need him again or if there's anything he can do to help either of your sons."

The Chief interrupted, "I agree with Jim. Be careful for the next few days still. We don't know who else is involved, and I wouldn't want anything to happen to you or your son."

Nestor Morgan appeared and recognized Jim. He looked uneasy, but Jim said nothing to indicate he was the employee who had given him a tip during his interview at the farm equipment warehouse following the Judge's birthday celebration. Nor did he say anything to let on to Morgan that Mrs. Chissum was involved.

She looked at Morgan and asked, "Can you keep the place open?"

He looked doubtful. "I'll get in touch with the owners. I assume they'll not want Mr. Franklin to continue to manage the store. We'll probably have to close down the store temporarily while we figure this all out. I'll start an immediate audit. Perhaps you could help me, Mrs. Chissum."

"Certainly, Mr. Morgan."

Jim looked at the Chief and said, "So if you don't need me to catch any more criminals today, I think I'll go hug my wife and children."

The Chief waved at him, shaking his head. "Such modesty. If I hadn't shown up when I did, you'd have been the one being caught by the criminals."

Jim laughed and headed out. He rushed over to the county courthouse and up the stairs to the Judge's chambers, where he literally picked Irene up off her feet in a hug.

She complained, "Jim. That's unseemly. Put me down!"

He laughed, but he did put her back on her feet. "We got him, Irene. We got Franklin."

The Judge came out from behind his desk. "What happened?"

"I was watching the Blakensfeld house when the Franklin boys arrived and stole the box where he kept his money. I followed them back to their father's store, and found them all together in a room there—well, not Blakensfeld himself, but Franklin and his boys and the money. I managed to get a call into the Chief and he arrested them. And, you'll never guess what else!"

Irene said, "Jim! Get on with the story."

"Well, it looks like Blakensfeld and Franklin were running a gang of boys to rob stores. The Chief is bringing Franklin to the Sheriff next door to get him to tell where Blakensfeld is hiding, but he took the five boys in the room to his own jail. He's kind of disappointed—they were all in his club. But he's going to interrogate them. The one boy as good as confessed—said he needed food to eat and that's why he did it."

The Judge said, "Good work, Jim. But I'm disappointed about the boys, too. I never expected such a gang could exist here in Ventura, although I should. I certainly see enough crime. But to use boys." He shook his head.

Jim said, "Yes, I know. I hope we can get them all. Listen, I'm going to go see the Chief at the jail to check if he or the Sheriff needs me for anything. The Chief said he didn't but just in case."

When he left, Irene went back to her typing, shaking her head. She reminded the Judge that both the District Attorney and Clara were due to arrive within the next hour. A few minutes later the District Attorney sat down with the Judge. Then when Irene looked up next, Clara had walked in.

She said, "Hi, Clara. The Judge is expecting you. He's talking to the District Attorney right now. They're setting the final date and time for Oscar Briarley's verdict and sentencing hearing."

Clara was alarmed. "But surely they'll wait to find out what happens with his father and Mr. Blakensfeld."

Irene nodded. "I believe events are happening rapidly there. The Judge can fill you in. Besides, you can count on the Judge to figure out what is the most fair and just. Remember, Oscar did participate in a robbery that resulted in a murder, even if he didn't pull the trigger."

Clara was exasperated. She felt like she'd done so much to help Oscar, but that it wasn't doing much good. "But he was forced by his father into participating! And he's been helping us catch the people responsible."

Irene responded calmly, "Consider how Mrs. Brant and her children might feel. Do you think they believe that justice is served if Oscar is not punished? Those children have no father, and Mrs. Brant has to raise them and figure out how to support them."

"I know that, but—"

The Judge's door opened, and the District Attorney walked out. "Hello, Clara. How are you?"

"Hello, sir. I'm not sure. Things have certainly been happening lately!"

He nodded. "Yes, they have. It's very disturbing, but we certainly made progress today. Thanks for all your help." He started to leave and then turned back and said to her, "By the way, we'll do what we can to help Oscar Briarley. You've certainly given us something to think about. He's not at all the boy we first thought he was. We'll do what we can to see that justice is served for everyone involved."

She looked at the smiling District Attorney. All she could think to say was "Thank you."

He nodded and left. Just then the Judge came out and said to Irene, "Have we heard from anyone yet?"

She shook her head. "No, sir."

"What about Frankie? Is he here yet? Do we know if Oscar is ready for him? I thought they found him several hours ago."

Clara interrupted. "I could go over to the jail and find out. If nothing else, I could talk with Oscar."

The Judge looked at Irene. "How's my calendar? Do I have time to go to the jail?"

Irene looked at some papers on her desk and said, "Yes. You and I just had time scheduled today to review your budget and calendar. I'll work that into tomorrow's schedule."

"Let's go, Clara. I'll fill you in on the way."

She followed the Judge out of his chambers, walking briskly to keep up with him.

He told her, "Thanks to Jim, they arrested Franklin—and unfortunately five boys along with him. The Chief and Jim believe that Franklin and Blakensfeld were running a gang of boys who they used to rob various stores and other establishments." He smiled, "You know, like Fagin."

Although she was not a big Dickens fan, she certainly knew who Fagin was. She responded, "That's awful. Do they know which boys?'

"The Chief is talking to the five they arrested along with Franklin. In the meantime, the Sheriff and his men are interrogating Franklin to get him to tell them where Blakensfeld is."

As they entered the jail, they could hear screams and sounds of scraping furniture amid shouts of "Settle down!"

When they got to the source of the sounds, they saw several deputies trying to subdue a fighting Frankie—his contorted leg buckling under him as he tried to strike out at the deputies, his face full of slobber, and his chin red from having been struck.

Clara wondered how they had managed to get him this far. As hard as she tried she could not help but be repelled by his appearance. She could see no resemblance between him and Oscar or their mother. She wondered if he resembled the father. Certainly his panicked eyes did not show any of the awareness or flashes of intelligence she had seen in Oscar's eyes.

The Judge entered the commotion and tried to calm him. "Frankie, it's Judge Akers. We're not going to hurt you."

Clara looked around for someone who could help. She saw a deputy standing outside of the fracas and ran to him. "Go get his brother! Get Oscar Briarley."

The deputy nodded and buzzed himself into the cellblock. Frankie continued to yell and push and kick. His face became even more contorted, and he was slobbering profusely. He screamed repeatedly, "Leave me be! No sirs are gonna get me! Where's my ma?"

Clara smelled some new kind of foul odor other than the usual antiseptic scent of the jail. She assumed it was coming from Frankie, whose appearance—despite her best intentions—continued to repel her.

Deputy Brown and Oscar appeared in the room. At first Oscar looked confused by a chaotic scene of sweating, panting deputies. Then he saw Frankie in the middle of the room. He yelled, "Frankie, that's enough!"

The boy jerked straight up and stood still. His wide, wet eyes searched the room for the familiar voice. When he saw Oscar he screamed, "Oscarooti! Oscarooti!" and started to reach for him, which gave one of the deputies the chance to grab him. The Judge yelled, "Let him go!"

The deputy responded immediately, and Frankie went to Oscar and the brothers hugged each other. The Judge said, "This family has been through enough. Oscar, can you take your brother into the visitor's room?" He looked at Deputy Brown, who nodded and opened the door for them. "Deputy Brown, can you and Clara please come with us? And the rest of you, make sure someone is available in case we need help. Let the Sheriff know what's happening. Get a cell ready for him. On second thought, it would be best if you could put the two of them in the same cell with no one else temporarily."

Deputy Brown said, "I'll take care of that."

The Judge looked around but didn't see Jim or anyone else. "Where's Franklin? Have they finished with him?"

Deputy Brown said, "Yes. He wouldn't say anything. He's already been booked and is being processed into a cell now. We expect an attorney to appear any minute, but we're holding him for the theft of the strongbox at a minimum, which he claims was committed by his boys without his knowledge. Jim went to do something for the Chief who asked him to check out some of the other boys who might be involved."

Oscar gently put his arm around his brother and led him into the visitor's room where Clara and he had spent so much time together. Clara followed, uncertain of her role. She had always been sure that she could help Oscar, but as sure as she was of that, she was unsure about Frankie.

Oscar kept his arm around his brother and helped him sit down. He looked at Deputy Brown and said, "Mebbe you could get him somethin' to eat and some of these here clothes like I have." He pointed to his prison garb.

The deputy said, "Of course. And I'll see about getting a nurse to look at his wounds. All right? But we'll need to clean him up first."

Oscar nodded. He looked at Frankie. "Are you all right? Kin you tell me about it?"

Frankie was now crying, slobbering, and his nose was running. Clara tried hard to overlook his appearance, but he was definitely distasteful. She could not think what to say or do.

The Judge said to Oscar, quietly and with compassion, "Son, we need to know what happened to him, and what he knows about Mr. Blakensfeld and the 'sir.' Do you think you can get him to tell you?"

Oscar shrugged. "I'll try, sir." He returned his hand to Frankie's shoulder. The younger boy wiped his nose on the back of his own hand. "Frankie, we need to ask you some questions—about Pa and Mr., er, Blakiesfold."

Frankie shook his head freeing some slobber from his face onto the table. Clara backed up her chair away from it. Frankie said, "I don't like that Mr. Blakie, but Pa said I gotta do what he sez."

"Did he hurt you, Frankie?" the Judge asked gently.

"Naw. I got away from him. Oscarooti told me always to hide if'n there's someone I don't like, and that's what I done."

The Judge waited for Oscar to say something. When he didn't—or couldn't—the Judge said, "Frankie, your pa is going to go to jail, so he won't be able to hurt you either."

Frankie's eyes got big. "Where's Ma? I ain't seen her since Pa shot her."

Oscar swallowed hard, took a breath, and took hold of Frankie with a hand on each of Frankie's shoulders. "She died, Frankie. Do you understand? She's not with us no more. Pa kilt her."

The younger brother pulled away from Oscar and shook his head. His lips trembled, he moaned, his nose ran, and his slobber seemed to increase. He said, "But if'n Pa's in jail and Ma's gone who's gonna take care of us?"

The Judge said, "We'll make sure you have a place to stay—a good place with people who care about you."

Oscar looked at the Judge and shook his head. "Don't make no promises you cain't keep, Judge. I'm all Frankie's got."

The Judge stared back at Oscar and said, "No, Oscar. Look around this room. We'll work it out."

Clara smiled when Oscar looked at her, but she had no idea what they would do to take care of Frankie. Oscar tried to smile back, but his eyes were concerned. Then he looked at his brother. "We'll be all right, Frankie. Now I need you to tell me where Mr. Blakie is. Can you do that?"

"He was with me. He hid when the sirs came."

The Judge looked at Deputy Brown, who said, "I'll let them know." He knocked on the door, which opened quickly, and spoke to the deputy on the other side, who quickly turned to inform the Sheriff.

Deputy Brown said to Oscar, "Can you ask him what else he knows about Mr. Blakensfeld?"

Frankie said, "I heard you. I ain't deaf."

Oscar smiled, "No, you're not. And you're smart, too, Frankie. So I need you to think. When you used to go with Pa to see Mr. Blakie, what happened?"

"There was a bunch of us young'ns there. We was to have fun and play games." Frankie was smiling.

Oscar asked, "And what was you supposed to do—you and the other boys? Jest play?"

He nodded. "And there was girls, too. And they had boobies."

The Judge interrupted. "Do you know how many there were?"

Oscar said, "Were there as many as you have fingers, Frankie?"

Frankie responded eagerly and held up both hands to display ten fingers. "As many as this and mebbe more," he said.

The Judge continued, "Who else was there?"

"There was a sir there. He was mean to me. He said I couldn't play. He said I was too dumb." He sniffed loudly.

Oscar responded, "Aw, Frankie I know that ain't true. And you know it, too, right?"

Frankie smiled and said, "Yeah, we know." And he slapped Oscar on his back, almost knocking him off his chair. While Oscar recovered, the Judge asked, "Frankie, can you remember what kind of game the sir asked you to play?"

Frankie looked at the Judge, his tongue licking the snot coming out of his nose. Clara had to look away. Frankie responded, "Sorta. He says to go take stuff from a big place somewheres." He looked at Oscar and said, "Like we went to with Pa that time I gotta go so bad."

Oscar explained to the adults, "That was a place where they take stuff from the boats that come in. You know, before they take the things to the stores and sell 'em."

The Judge nodded. "The warehouses down by the docks. There was a robbery there about a week ago."

A knock on the door and the arrival of food disrupted the questioning. Frankie's eyes got big when he saw the tray of chicken, lima beans, potatoes, and an apple. He dug in while Oscar watched, nodding. He turned to Clara and the Judge and said, "That's probably more than he's 'et in the past week."

While Frankie was eating, a young woman arrived with clothes and a medical bag. Frankie was so busy eating that he didn't notice as she dabbed at his scrapes and cuts, and washed his face and arms.

The Judge looked at Clara and asked, "Are you planning to give Oscar a reading lesson tomorrow?"

She looked at Oscar, who responded, "Thanks, Judge. But I think I need to be with Frankie. I gotta help him. The food and medicine's good, but he needs me. I thank y'all." He looked at Deputy Brown. "Kin we be in the same cell?"

"Yes, Oscar. I'll arrange for you to be together. There are now four of us who'll watch over you. I'll introduce you to them so you know who they are. But your brother hasn't committed any crimes, so I'm not sure how long he can stay here." He looked at the Judge, who nodded.

The Judge said, "Keep him here as long as you can. Meanwhile, I'll see what we can arrange for Frankie."

Clara looked at Deputy Brown and said, "Any word on capturing Mr. Blakensfeld?"

Everyone, except Frankie who was concentrating on his food, looked at the deputy, relieved to focus on something other than the deformed boy. "I haven't heard anything. I passed along what Frankie told us. They found Frankie at that cabin where Oscar said Blakensfeld might be hiding. They searched for him there, I know. He must have another hiding place."

The Judge said, "Some of those old cabins have secret cellars, where people used to hide their booze during Prohibition. But I know the Sheriff and Chief would be aware of those places."

Oscar said, "Kin we go to our beds now? Frankie's purdy tired."

The Judge nodded to Deputy Brown, who turned and said, "Why don't you lead your brother to his bed? It's the one next to where you slept last night."

"Thanks. Come on, Frankie. You're gonna like it here. They got real beds, and they feed us every single day."

Although they were all drained, they watched the brothers leave the room to go willingly to a jail cell; it seemed they were happy because it might have been the best place they had ever lived.

Clara and the Judge returned to his chambers after they learned that there was no news from either the Sheriff's or the Chief's men who were still searching for Blakensfeld. The Chief was focusing on rounding up other boys suspected of being part of the juvenile ring according to the captured boys who seemed willing to offer names. Given what Frankie had just disclosed, the authorities were widening their search to also include teenage girls.

The Judge told Clara that the Sheriff and his men were concentrating on catching both Shapener and Blakensfeld. Deputies had spent several hours interrogating Claude Briarley and then Harold Franklin, but both had remained stubborn about revealing any information. The Judge had made sure that the two Briarley boys would not run across their intimidating father for fear that they would both stop co-operating.

Noticing that Irene was not at her desk, Clara asked the Judge, "They won't try to hurt Irene and Jim's children, will they?"

"Not if they know what's good for them. Jim wouldn't take kindly to someone going after his children. He's a fierce enemy to have."

"But if he's not there. What if—"

The Judge held up his hand. "First, Irene is an excellent marksman. Second, I sent one of our reserve deputies to watch their house. But don't tell Jim, all right?"

"All right. I guess I better head home."

Chapter 33

The next morning Clara again dressed for school while wishing she could instead spend her day at the courthouse. She worried about Oscar and Frankie, but had faith that Deputy Brown would look after them. However, she continued to ask herself who some of the other members of the juvenile crime ring might be, concerned that they might be classmates or boys from the club. And she really wanted them to capture Mr. Blakensfeld. Somehow, having him in jail would help heal the numbness she felt over Harry's gruesome and pointless death.

However, neither her father nor mother was willing to let her skip school. So she was sitting at the table eating breakfast when the phone rang. She jumped to answer it, but her father motioned she was to sit back down, and he proceeded to the parlor to pick up the handset.

"Oh, hello, Judge." He listened briefly and said, "I'll let her know. Yes, my wife is here. All right." He gave the handset to Clara's mother and said, "Irene Alvarez needs to talk with you."

He returned to the kitchen table and said to Clara, "The Judge said to tell you that they have not yet caught Blakensfeld. And he said that Oscar and Frankie are fine. Deputy Brown has them well guarded."

"What about the other deputy, Shapener, the one the Sheriff was chasing?"

"He didn't say."

Her mother returned to the table and said, "Irene wants me to check out the school for that boy you were talking about—Frankie Briarley. She said she'll go with you this afternoon when you stop by *after* school and talk to Oscar to tell him about it so that he can prepare Frankie."

Clara looked confused. "What do you and Irene know about a school for someone like Frankie?"

Her mother took a breath, looked at her husband, studied her daughter for a moment, and then said, "Actually I do volunteer work there, which gives me some privileges, such as requesting a place for a possible attendee."

"I didn't know you did that."

"I don't tell many people about it. The school is a little controversial. The students are, er, retarded or have some deficiency. I do my best to teach them."

Clara was disturbed that her mother had never confided in her. "But I'm not just anybody. I'm your daughter."

Her father looked at his wife and said, "I told you."

Her mother asked almost timidly, "How do you feel about that?"

Clara responded slowly, "Part of me is proud of you for doing it and part of me resents you for keeping it a secret."

"But you're proud of me, not ashamed."

"Oh, yes. I think it's wonderful!"

Her father looked relieved also and directed the conversation back to Frankie. "From what you've told us, almost any place would be an improvement over Frankie's home."

Clara smiled. "Yes, but he's not easy to handle. It will take someone who knows about people like him." She looked at her mother who was smiling. She then realized that her mother must be one of those people. "Oh, that reminds me that Oscar wants to meet both of you. Do you think we could arrange it? You wouldn't have to go at the same time nor stay very long. He's just never really met decent parents."

Both parents looked at each other and nodded. Her father asked, "How about this Saturday or Sunday?"

"Oh, yes. I'm sure of it. I just don't go on weekends to give Oscar a break from his lessons."

"All right. Why don't you check when would be a good time, and we'll stop by this weekend."

"I'll see if I can arrange it today." She turned to her mother. "Please promise that you won't keep other secrets from me. It makes me feel like you don't trust me." She stood up and grabbed her bag. "Gotta go or I'll be late for school."

The Judge's Story

The day dragged on through Clara's classes. She looked for Jim at lunchtime, but he didn't show. She was disappointed. She was poised to bolt from the end of her last class when she left school and walked/ran to the courthouse.

She arrived at the Judge's chambers out of breath. Irene was at her desk. The Judge's door was closed. Irene looked up and smiled. Clara barely let her say, "Hello, Clara," before she asked, "What's going on? Have they caught Mr. Blakensfeld?"

"Yes, they have."

"They did? How? When? What happened? What about the deputy who was helping him?"

Irene laughed. "Actually, they found Blakensfeld in a secret room in the cellar of the cabin where they'd located Frankie. And they're still interrogating him, but it sounds like he was helping Deputy Shapener, who, it turns out, was the real leader. He's also implicated Franklin. They both say they had nothing to do with the Brant killing. That apparently was an event Briarley cooked up to transform Oscar into a so-called man."

The Judge's door opened and the Chief appeared. He was smiling but looked as if he hadn't slept in a long time. The dark circles under his eyes had grown. He also looked dejected, like someone he trusted had punched him in the stomach. He still did not know exactly how many of the juvenile gang were members of his boys' club, but there were definitely more involved than he had originally suspected. He was disappointed that the club hadn't deterred them.

The Chief greeted Clara with a weak, "Hello, Clara" as he picked up his hat. He nodded to Irene and left.

Just then, the Judge appeared. "Irene, can you and Clara go see Oscar Briarley now to tell him about the school for Frankie? If so, let the Sheriff's office know that we'll be there—I'll go with you. Have you updated Clara about what's happened?"

Irene nodded. "I am available now, and, yes, I told Clara the latest." She picked up the phone to alert the Sheriff's office.

When she finished, the Judge said, "Let's go, Irene. Clara can brief you about Oscar on the way, but she'll be there, too, to help talk to him."

As they walked toward the jail, Clara asked, "I'm a little confused. Irene, why are you talking to Oscar about this school?"

Irene said, "Your mother didn't tell you?" Clara shook her head. Irene continued, "My brother is there, thanks to your mother. It was a tough decision for me to put him there. I tried for a long time to handle him myself, but I just couldn't. I have been very pleased with the outcome. So we figured I could explain that best to Oscar. So tell me about him."

Clara nodded. "I see. Well, first, Oscar is really smart. So don't talk down to him. If he doesn't understand something, he'll ask you to explain. Sometimes he says things that are not quite right or bad grammar. Let me correct him. He's used to that. I'll do it so it isn't disrespectful. And, above all, know that he cares for Frankie. He believes that he's the only one who can help him." She saw Irene nod like she understood. "It's important, I think, that he believes the decision is his. And if you can prepare him for the separation, that would be good. I don't know if it's possible to allow him to visit Frankie, but that might help." Clara was eager to contribute, so she was babbling.

The Judge remained quiet until they reached the visitor's room of the jail. They sat at the table waiting for Oscar. The Judge said, "Thank you, Irene, for doing this. I know it was difficult for you, but that's why maybe you can help Oscar understand."

The door opened and Oscar entered. He looked confused. He was expecting only Clara, but saw Irene and the Judge as well. Clara said, "Hi, Oscar. I brought some extra visitors today to talk to you. This is Irene Alvarez. She wants to tell you about a place that she and my mother found for Frankie. They want to know whether you think it would be a good place for him."

Oscar looked from Clara to Irene. He sat down at his usual place and said, "Hello, Irene Alvarez. Pleased to meet ya." He looked at Clara for approval. She nodded. She was pleased that the name "Alvarez" meant nothing to Oscar.

Irene said, "Hello, Oscar. I've heard so much about you."

The Judge interrupted. "Before we get started I wanted to let you know, Oscar, that the Sheriff captured Mr. Blakensfeld. You might want to let Frankie know that neither he nor your father will ever bother either of you again. And we thank Frankie for helping us."

Oscar smiled and then looked at Clara. "Thanks, Clara. You made this happen."

She started to shake her head but again the Judge interrupted. "Oscar, I can't say yet what your punishment will be for the robbery and death of Mr. Brant, but you will have to serve some time. You need to think about that when considering what should happen to Frankie."

Oscar looked at me. "Considering?" he asked.

Clara said, "Yes, that means when you think about how Frankie can live while you're in jail."

Oscar said, "I understand." He turned to Irene. "Tell me about this place."

Irene said, "My brother is there. I love him like you love Frankie. But he doesn't understand what goes on around him. It took me a long time to give up. I wanted to care for him myself, but I finally took him there. Now he can even read— simple books, but they give him such joy. And he can write his name. Most important, though, Oscar, is that they care for him. He has his own bed, clothes, and food every day."

"I cain't afford nothing like that. I ain't—" he looked at Clara and said, "I'm *not* rich like you."

Irene responded quickly, "Oh, Oscar, I'm not rich. The school is run by a group of dedicated teachers like Clara's mother, and they get donations, that is, people give them money to run the school. They can take only a few new boys a year, and only at the request of certain people. Clara's mother is one of those people. She volunteers there as a teacher. She's the one who got my brother accepted; and she can get Frankie in, too. We all help to raise money every year."

Oscar looked at Clara. "I really want to meet your ma and pa." Clara smiled, but was embarrassed because she had had no idea that her mother volunteered at this school, or that she was able to get students admitted there. She said, "I'm very proud of my mother."

Oscar said to Irene, "What kind of place is it? Do they got trees?"

Irene said, "Yes. Lots of trees. But there's a fence around the place to keep other people out so they can protect the boys. They have about twenty boys in all."

Oscar looked at Clara. "What do you think, Clara?"

"I think it sounds wonderful, Oscar. A chance for Frankie to be cared for in the best possible way—and so you won't have to be worried about him."

Oscar started to jiggle, stopped, and then he nodded. "All right. I'll talk to Frankie. When do you need him? It would be good if he could stay with me for another day or two. I just got him calmed down. I could talk to him a little at a time. Get him used to the idea."

The Judge and Deputy Brown looked at each other. Frankie had committed no crime, and there was no justification for keeping him in jail. They had already kept him at the taxpayers' expense for one night.

Clara had been thinking about this problem since the previous night. She had an idea and said, "Maybe Attorney Alberts could help with that. He could make some kind of motion that could take a day or two to resolve. It doesn't matter if it's successful. We just need to get some time." She looked at the Judge. He nodded. "I'll talk to him." Both Deputy Brown and the Judge were smiling.

Oscar said, "When kin we start our book-learnin' again, Clara? Mebbe after Frankie goes to his new place."

Clara smiled. "Yes, and I'll stop by again tomorrow to see you. My parents will visit this weekend, I think, but no promises."

Oscar actually clapped his hands. "Oh, that's good! I want to meet your ma especially. She sounds like a great lady."

Clara agreed. "Yes, she is."

Chapter 34

That Saturday, Irene and Jim arrived at the jail ten minutes early, after bicycling the children to a neighboring farm for a day of playing with their friends. The couple enjoyed the ride through bright sunshine and blue sky—and a comfortable temperature in the 70s.

Clara and her parents were due to show up to meet Oscar and Frankie, and then Jim planned to help Mr. and Mrs. Wilson drive Frankie to his new home. Attorney Alberts had been successful at preparing a motion to delay Frankie's removal from the County Jail for a few days by claiming he might have participated in one of the robberies. He was quickly cleared of that by interviewing those boys who did participate and by the testimony of Franklin and Blakensfeld. But it bought them the time they needed for Frankie to become accustomed to the idea of living somewhere new.

Jim approached the deputy at the jail and asked, "Have they found Shapener yet?"

"The Sheriff brought him in today."

"What did he have to say for himself?"

"He wasn't able to say too much with his swollen lips. Seems he tried to escape and the Sheriff had to restrain him. The Doc said he'd be fine."

Jim decided not to pursue Shapener's wounds, but he didn't envy the man's incarceration at a jail guarded by his peers. He suspected that his attorney would have him moved as quickly as possible. "Where did the Sheriff find him?"

"At the train station. We had his house and car under surveillance. I guess he didn't figure we'd be smart enough to think that he might try to get away on a train. He had thousands of dollars on him. Turns out he was the ringleader. He's the one that got it all organized." The deputy shook his head.

Jim was surprised. "Really? I figured Franklin was the head man."

The deputy nodded. "Me, too. But Franklin and Blakensfeld both fingered Shapener. Franklin knew both Shapener and Blakensfeld from the past somehow. We're working out those relationships."

They were interrupted by the arrival of the Wilson family. Clara was smiling as she introduced her parents to the deputy and everyone else in the office that morning. They all eagerly shook hands. Deputy Brown joined the group from inside the jail when he heard they'd arrived. He told Clara's parents, "You can sure be proud of your daughter. She's managed to help Oscar a lot. And thanks, Mrs. Wilson, for what you're arranging for Frankie. I don't think he'd make it in the real world."

Clara's mother smiled and beamed at mention of her daughter's contributions. "We're very proud of her. And it's my pleasure to provide for Frankie. That's why we organized this school."

Deputy Brown said, "How did it get organized? I never even heard of it. You've kept it quiet."

She nodded. "Yes, because no one wants a school with boys who lack mental capacities. It scares people. So a group of us teachers and educators, along with a few significant benefactors, organized to take over some private and isolated property with a large enough building to house and train twenty boys—a few are even able to hold down a job, although they almost all need someone watching after them. We've had help fixing up the place, mostly from parents of the boys we teach."

Deputy Brown nodded. "Add me to your list of donors. I can't give much, but I'd be pleased to donate whatever I can."

"Thank you."

Deputy Brown pushed the button into the visitor area and led the small group inside. He had arranged for them to have the room for an hour. Oscar and Frankie entered a few seconds later. Oscar was grinning and guided his brother to the table where they sat down. He explained to Frankie,

"Here we gotta sit at the table 'til the sir tells us we can stand."

Frankie nodded. Clara was pleased to see that his hair had been cut. He was dressed in a clean outfit, not prison garb, but slacks and a shirt. He was also carrying a handkerchief, which he used to wipe his nose and mouth whenever he slobbered. He would look at Oscar for approval whenever he did so, and Oscar smiled and nodded.

Clara first introduced her parents. "Oscar and Frankie Briarley, I want you to meet my mother and father, Mr. and Mrs. Wilson." Both Wilsons offered their hand to shake with the brothers. Oscar looked over to Deputy Brown and waited for his smile and approving nod; then he grabbed both hands and shook them vigorously. Frankie wasn't quite sure what to do, and decided to keep his hands to himself.

Jim interrupted, which surprised Clara. She assumed that the meeting was to be between her parents and the Briarleys. She had not noticed that he was carrying an envelope.

Jim said, "Oscar, the Judge asked me to give you this. He had requested that I search your place for anything that you might want to keep. We weren't sure if your pa owned it or what would happen. Anyway, after I found this," he tapped the envelope, "I did some more investigating. I found out that your ma was the daughter of a farming family down in Los Angeles County. Your grandparents raised oranges and avocados. She was one of seven children. I was able to determine that your grandparents had passed away, but I couldn't locate any of your aunts or uncles. But I'll keep trying.

"Anyway, they hired your pa to help out on the farm. At that time, he was apparently a hard worker and helped save a crop that was threatened by cold weather. Your ma fell in love, and they were married on the farm. And this is a picture of them when they got married."

Jim handed the envelope to Oscar. He didn't open it. He looked at Jim and said, "You say my ma loved my pa? And my pa was a hard worker? What happened?"

Jim shook his head. "I couldn't find out, Oscar. I'll keep searching. I'm hoping I can speak with your father to find out. However, until after his trial, his lawyer doesn't want me talking to him. But, go on, look at that photo. The Judge thinks you'll really like it."

Oscar opened the envelope and pulled out the black-and-white photo. His eyes grew wide and teary. Standing in front of a tree filled with blossoms was a young couple looking straight at the camera. The woman was smiling joyously. Her long brown hair was laced with flowers, and her slender body displayed a plain white dress pulled into the waist with gathers. She was holding a bouquet of daisies.

The young man, dressed in a suit that didn't quite fit, stood straight with his hands at his side. His hair was long but combed. He was clean-shaven. He, too, appeared happy, although his smile was not quite so broad as his bride.

Oscar said, "She's beautiful. And he's so—" he looked at Clara and asked, "is the word 'handsome'?"

Clara nodded, biting her lips so that she wouldn't cry.

Oscar looked at everyone, "They was happy once't. Mr. Alvarez, I cain't thank ye enough. Frankie, look, it's ma and pa."

Frankie looked at the photograph and shook his head. "No, that ain't them."

"Sure it is, Frankie. Look you can tell it's ma, when she was young." Oscar looked at Clara. "You know, Clara, I bet if'n my pa had an education, they woulda had a better life."

Clara managed to nod.

Oscar said, "Can I keep this?" He looked first at Jim then at Deputy Brown. They both nodded.

He started to put the photo back into the envelope, then looked at it again. He sniffed and said, "Thank you, and thank the Judge."

Irene nodded. "We owe much to the Judge, Oscar. He wanted you to know how sorry he is about your mother. That's why he asked Jim to find out more about her and your father. They weren't always like you know them. He wanted to know more about them—and about you." She hesitated for just a moment and then said, "But you need to know that he is still a judge, and he believes in justice for the victims of crime. He may show you compassion, but he will also assure that Mrs. Brant gets justice for the loss of her husband."

Oscar nodded. "I understand, ma'am. Thank you." He turned to Frankie and said, "These are the people who are going to take you to your new home."

Frankie, who had been sitting quietly and moving his eyes across all of the people in the room, said, "No, Oscerooti. I'm staying here with you."

Oscar shook his head and said firmly, "No, Frankie. You cain't stay here. We talked about this."

Mrs. Wilson, who had positioned herself to sit directly across from Frankie, said, "We have water at your new home. I heard that you like to squish in water."

Frankie looked at her. "Water? I 'kin walk in it?"

She nodded. "Yes, you can. And do you know what else we have?"

His eyes grew wide. "What?"

"Well, you'll have to come and see."

Frankie struggled with his desire to stay with his brother over the prospect of squishing in water and learning what else was there. He decided, "Well, mebbe just for a day or two. Then I'll come back to see Oscarooti here and Deputy Brown."

Mrs. Wilson said, "Maybe you won't want to come back here. Your new place has lots of fun things to do besides squishing. And we have rabbit stew tonight for dinner. And sometimes there's even cake."

Clara studied her mother as she soothed the troubled boy and talked him into his new place. She had only ever seen her as her mother. She had comprehended that women were judged all too frequently as second-class citizens after men, but she realized that was what she had done, too. She had only ever seen her mother at home. She glanced over at her father, who displayed pride and adoration for his wife. How fortunate she was to be the daughter of parents who loved and respected each other!

Her mother continued to win over Frankie. "So are you ready for your new adventure?"

Frankie jumped up, and Mr. Wilson and Jim got on either side of him as he shouted, "Oscarooti, I'm going to go squishing!"

Chapter 35

Although it was a Saturday, the Judge sat at his desk in his chambers waiting for Irene while reading through some reports she had prepared about current cases. He knew they were meeting Oscar and Frankie that morning with the Wilson family. Jim was going to accompany Mr. and Mrs. Wilson to drive Frankie to his new home. Irene was coming back to meet with the Judge to wait for the Wilsons to bring Jim back.

The Judge was pleased with the outcome for Frankie, as much for what it would mean to Oscar as for Frankie himself. He also was pleased at the wedding photograph of the Briarley parents that Jim had found. Both Jim and he wondered what had happened to the family. Both of them tended toward applying background information to understand the "whole truth." Jim hoped to get more information from Claude Briarley following his trial, but both he and the Judge doubted the veracity of anything Claude might say. Nonetheless, the photograph said much to them, and the Judge was sure Oscar would find it helpful in understanding himself.

Irene walked into the Judge's office. She hurried over to him, arms outstretched and hugged him, her emotions removing any care about decorum. "It was grand," she said, before the Judge could ask. "He cried when he saw the photograph. And Mrs. Wilson talked Frankie into going to the home. She's so good. It was a grand moment."

The Judge nodded.

Irene then burst out, "Judge Grover Roswell Akers, you need to stop and pat yourself on the back! You made this all happen—Clara teaching Oscar to read. Jim being able to find out who was responsible for the juvenile crime gang. Clara's mother leading Frankie to the home." She stopped as she saw the Judge's flabbergasted expression, but only for a brief moment. "Look at the lives you've helped—me, our children, Clara, Jim, Oscar, Frankie—and that's barely the tip of the iceberg." She picked up the pile of papers that held the notes from his cases. "Your judgments on all these cases included the most information you could factor into decisions that offered the fairest decision that justice could provide. You are, without a doubt, a hero. Do you hear me?"

The Judge, not accustomed to Irene shouting at him, simply said, "Yes, ma'am."

She turned and went to her desk, determined to alert the world to the contributions of one of her favorite persons. She sat down and started typing fiercely. She kept a folder with clippings and her own notes of all of the people the Judge had influenced. Maybe when Clara got older and became a real writer, she would ask her to write the Judge's story.

Chapter 36

The following week, the Judge sat in his usual place in the courtroom, in his black robe, looking down on those sitting in the gallery. Oscar and his attorney sat in the chairs behind the defense table; District Attorney Bilkins sat behind the desk for the prosecution. Clara and her parents sat behind Oscar, along with Jim and Irene. Mrs. Brant and her children, the Chief, and the Sheriff, and several of the Brant friends sat behind the District Attorney.

It was time for the Judge to deliver his verdict and sentence of Oscar.

Clara looked at the Judge, who was so different in his robe with the gavel in his hand. She had no doubt that he would deliver the fairest verdict and sentence humanly possible, despite all that had recently happened. Almost a week had passed since Oscar's father, Mr. Franklin, and Mr. Blakensfeld had been captured. All three had been arrested and held without bail.

Clara's mother visited Frankie daily at his new place to help transition him to his new environment. She also had started to teach him how to read a few simple words. Frankie loved the squishing more than he enjoyed learning to read. Oscar had encouraged his brother to listen to her. Mrs. Wilson told Clara that he was progressing but of course he wasn't as smart as Oscar, and it was unlikely that he would ever be able to read more than rudimentary books. She promised to take Clara there within the next few weeks so she could help. Following her success with Oscar, Clara convinced her mother that she was ready to contribute to the school.

That day in the courtroom, Clara's attention returned to the Judge, who was saying, "Before I deliver my sentence I need to update the court record on this case. I'd like the Chief to come to the stand."

The Chief, who looked more rested than when the Judge last saw him, was sworn in. The Judge asked, "Can you please fill us in on the most recent events pertaining to Mr. Oscar Briarley's situation? What has happened since the trial of this defendant?"

The Chief said, "The defendant has been helpful in tracking down and capturing the killer of Mr. Brant. It turned out that it was his father, who basically coerced him into participating in the crime. We may not have located him if not for the defendant's assistance. He also helped us to identify and capture the leaders of a juvenile crime ring. Again, without his information, which led to several other witnesses, we may not have caught them. We also believe that the defendant, Mr. Briarley, understands that what he did was wrong and is sincerely sorry."

The story had been in the newspaper, so no one was surprised by this testimony. The Judge thanked the Chief, and then asked that the defendant, Oscar Briarley, come to the stand.

Clara feared for Oscar. He had been jiggling in his seat, and he still appeared disheveled. His intelligence and new ethics only showed occasionally. She watched as he walked slowly to the witness chair, looking straight ahead, hands down at his sides, head high. She recalled how intimidated she had felt sitting there more than a month earlier—a level below the Judge who peered down at her.

The Judge looked down at Oscar the same way. He didn't smile at him, but he did speak with some empathy. He said, "Oscar Briarley, you've had time to think about this crime and your part in it. I want you to tell me your current perspective on your role."

Clara knew that Oscar would not understand the word "perspective." Fortunately, he said, "I don't know the word 'perspective,' sir. Could you tell it to me?" She had instructed Oscar to ask if he didn't understand something. She was relieved that he did so.

"Of course. I want you to tell us how you feel about what you did. Do you understand?"

"Yes, sir. Thank you, sir." He started to jiggle, then stopped and looked at Clara, his eyes showing concern. She had warned him about the jiggling. He licked his lips and said, "My pa didn't need to shoot Mr. Brant. It was wrong. I ain't, er, I'm not no squealer, but Pa shouldn't 'a kilt him. And I'm real sorry to you, Mrs. Brant, and to all your children."

He stopped talking. The Judge asked, "But what about your part, Oscar? What do you think about your part in this? You were there. You helped your father."

"Yes, I did. That was wrong, too. I wish't I didn't do it." He stopped and again looked at Clara. "But, sir, I don't understand, but I don't think I knew it was wrong then." He looked at the Judge. "Does that make sense, sir? Since I been in jail, I learnt a lot. Miss Clara Wilson learnt me how to read." Clara shuddered at the poor grammar, but felt proud at the sentiment. "And about, well, about what is right and wrong."

"And what do you feel is right and wrong?"

Oscar didn't hesitate. He must have been thinking about right and wrong. "Right is helping other people, like Clara and her ma and pa did for me and Frankie. And wrong is hurting other people like my pa and Mr. Blakensfeld did." He said the name slowly. Clara wondered if he had practiced it so he could pronounce it correctly when testifying.

"So, tell me, Oscar, do you think you should be punished for what you did?"

Oscar sat up as straight as he could and said, "Yes, sir, but more important" a new favorite word, "more important, I want to make up for it. I cain't bring back Mr. Brant, but I want to help others to know what's right and wrong. I don't know yet how to do that, but by book-learnin' and talkin' to people, I think I can even do somethin' from jail."

Mrs. Brant sniffed, and Clara saw that she was crying. She spread her arms around all of her children. Even the District Attorney looked sympathetic. Clara was amazed. She had no idea that Oscar had reached these conclusions. She saw that the Judge was impressed, also. He said, "Thank you, Oscar. I hope you're successful. You can return to your table now."

Before he stood, Oscar looked at Clara who smiled and nodded. He looked back proudly, and then quickly got up and returned to his place next to his attorney, who patted his hand when he sat down.

"I'd like to hear from Mrs. Brant now. Is that possible?"

The District Attorney turned to her. She nodded and stood up, letting go of her children. She walked slowly to the witness chair. Clara, Irene, Jim, and Attorney Alberts all knew that what she said was important to the Judge. Oscar's attorney had told Clara that the Judge always looked for a fair sentence, and it seemed to her that he probably had a range of punishment in mind depending on what this key victim of the crime might say.

After she was sworn in, she sat down, wiping her eyes and sitting straight, always watching her children.

The Judge said, "Thank you for agreeing to testify. I know that this has been a difficult time for you. I want to hear what you think about the defendant, and how much you hold him responsible for your husband's death."

Mrs. Brant swallowed. She tore her gaze away from her children and looked at Oscar. She licked her lips, studied her hands, and finally looked at the Judge. "Your Honor, sir, before I came here today I wanted this boy put in jail for the rest of his life. Why should he live a regular life when none of my family can? But I see that he's just a boy, just like my children. And I understand that he had a father who never taught him right from wrong. And I doubt that he could have stopped his father from pulling the trigger. I wish that had been different. I also appreciate that he helped capture the real person responsible, not just for my husband's death but also for other crimes. He has truly helped our community."

She looked at Oscar, who was jiggling again. She continued, with great emotion in her voice as if she would start to cry again. "And I truly do believe that he wants to give back something to all of us." She stopped talking, and the Judge did not prod her. He just sat and waited for her continue. "But, your Honor, he was there. He helped his father, and without him maybe there would not have been a

The Judge's Story

robbery. Maybe his father would not have done it alone, and my husband would still be here. I think he must be punished somehow. I guess I've changed my mind that it needs to be forever. That's all, sir."

She got up and started to walk back to her children. The Judge made no attempt to stop her. He looked at Oscar and said, "Oscar Briarley, please stand to receive your sentence."

Clara held her breath and noticed her mouth was dry and her hands were shaking. She had no idea what the Judge was going to say. She knew that Attorney Alberts had asked for two years at the Ventura County Jail until Oscar turned sixteen, but she didn't know whether the Judge would or could grant that.

Oscar and his attorney stood. The Judge said, "Oscar Briarley, for the participation in a robbery that resulted in the unwilling death caused by shooting, I find you guilty and sentence you to six years in jail. Because of your age and your assistance in capturing the true murderer, I accept your petition to serve the next two years here in the Ventura County Jail. When you turn sixteen, a new hearing should be conducted to assign where you should complete your remaining four years and to consider an appeal for probation based on your performance during the next two years."

The Judge looked out at the gallery, then, and his eyes rested on Mrs. Brant. She nodded at him. He stood and walked out as the bailiff said, "Court under Judge Grover Roswell Akers is dismissed."

Oscar looked at his attorney and asked, "Is that good?"

Attorney Alberts smiled and nodded. "Yes, Oscar. It means for the next two years, you can stay here in the Ventura County Jail. Then if all goes well, we'll check in with the Judge and see where you'll go for the next four years. We may be able to make it fewer than four years if you do well."

Oscar smiled, jiggling away, and turned to Clara as she walked up. "I'm gonna stay here for two years. You can keep giving me book-learnin'. And then I kin go somewhere's else."

Clara smiled and nodded, mindful of seeming too relieved with Mrs. Brant looking on. But she was pleased. Oscar was not his father. She felt that justice had been served fairly.

And she felt thankful that she was not a judge. She preferred just writing about one.

Chapter 37

The Judge walked onto Ventura Pier as far as he could over the water. He heard the relentless waves. He smelled the fish and seaweed mixed with the oil on the derrick barge. He heard the sea gulls screeching and watched them swooping for food. He felt the moisture in the breeze. And, given that the evening was clear, he could see the Channel Islands off to the West with the sun just above them getting ready to descend.

He leaned on the railing welcoming all of it. He wished his wife was there with him or that he could turn back the clock to when they were a family. He would cherish them and take them with him on his walks so they could share his feelings.

Laughter intruded on his thoughts. It sounded so much like his wife, but when he looked around he found its source to be a young woman on the pier with her young man. They were laughing at each other as they strolled together holding hands.

The Judge turned his reflecting to Oscar and his family. He considered Irene's claim that he was responsible for saving the boy and for bringing justice to so many in the town. The relentless surf made him feel insignificant, but Irene's words resonated. He wanted to believe that he made a difference.

He and the Chief both thought that the activities of the boys' club would help strengthen the positive actions of those participating. But instead it may have served as a meeting place for them. Certainly they had failed to help Harry—and almost a dozen more. What could they have done differently? More important, what should they change to yield more positive results? The Judge knew that the Chief would not give up. He would try to figure out ways to improve the club.

But the Judge questioned how effective they could be when adults such as Harry's stepfather, the Franklin brothers' father, and especially a law enforcement officer—when those adults maneuvered, controlled, and misled young minds? How helpful can a system be against those factors? Can they even protect the innocents?

He thought about Clara. How could he take credit for anything she'd done? Her spirit was inside her when he met her. He'd merely guided her energy. And Irene and Jim. What had he added? He gave Jim a break when no one else did, but it was Jim who was earning his way through school to become a lawyer. It was true that he stepped in and assisted Irene, but she became the strong woman she was probably in spite of him. He thought about his friend in L.A. who was heading up the boys school. He, too, claimed that the Judge had turned him into the contributor he'd become. And Mrs. Martinez who he'd hardly helped at all, although she thanked him for his support.

Then he recalled cases he had presided over. He had not accepted the appointment to Superior Court Judge when he was first asked. To him, it seemed just a little too much like playing god. Yet that day standing there on the pier he could say to himself that he had done his best to bring about just sentences for the victims and the perpetrators. Faces of juveniles and adults, men and women, passed through his mind. Some had become contributing citizens; others had not.

That's what happened when he came out on this pier with its pounding surf, sea breeze, and moist air. He saw a composite of who he was—a man willing to try to make a difference in a difficult world. And he planned to continue to be that someone.

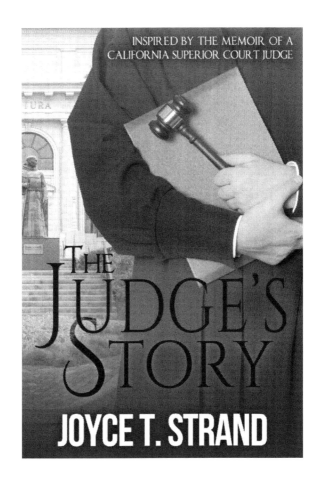

If you enjoyed *The Judge's Story*, watch for the second Brynn Bancroft mystery coming in late 2015 and the next historical mystery, scheduled for mid-2016. To keep current on Joyce T. Strand mysteries, you can sign up to receive her newsletter at her website http://joycestrand.com

The next Brynn Bancroft mystery: Having made the decision to stay at the Hilltop Sunset Winery rather than return to her life as a Chief Financial Officer, Brynn faces the issues of running a winery; raising a teenage boy; confronting her relationship with her ex-husband; and finally getting Jillian and Chad married. Will everything run smoothly as she transitions to her new lifestyle?

About the Author

Joyce T. Strand, much like her fictional character, Jillian Hillcrest, served as head of corporate communications at several biotech and high-tech companies in Silicon Valley for more than twenty-five years. Unlike her protagonist, however, she did not encounter any murders. Strand currently lives in Southern California where she and her protagonist, Brynn Bancroft, are exploring the benefits of hand-crafted wine in the Ramona/San Diego area.

For more information or to sign up to receive her newsletter, check out her website at http://joycestrand.com

Photo of author by Erin Kate Photography
http://www.erinkatephoto.com

More on 1939 Ventura County: Cases Used to Tell *The Judge's Story*

The following actual cases were mentioned in *The Judge's Story* with fictional names and circumstances to tell the story. The real judge (Judge Drapeau) was involved in many but not necessarily in all of them. The primary robbery-murder case involving Oscar Briarley is fiction and is not based on any actual case.

Cases reported in *Oxnard Daily Courier* newspaper from January to December 1939

- Three boys stole radios in Saticoy, CA. Held on $500 bail; bound over to Ventura County Superior Court.
- Unidentified body found. Sheriff sent dental request to LA; sent fingerprints to Washington, D.C. Sheriff speculated he was a Chinese man who refused to contribute to Sino-Japanese war in Asia.
- Prisoner in Ventura County jail: washing floors with others; went crazy; jumped out of third story window.
- Four juveniles and one adult (age 21) arrested for climbing Hueneme water tower and throwing fire crackers on cars.
- Four Ventura bookies appeared in Ventura County Superior Court; pleaded guilty; fined $200 and put on two years probation
- 1929 murder case solved in 1939 and tried in front of Judge Drapeau. Joe Meraz and Balentino Garcia of Santa Paula charged with murdering Joe Valencia. At first pleaded not guilty; then pleaded guilty. Valencia was found on a pile of rocks stabbed with 15 gashes. Took ten years to identify suspects. Note: in *The Judge's Story* the offended wife story is fiction.
- Hospital employee Thomas Anderson of Camarillo State Mental Hospital – sentenced for thirty days for drunkenness and disorderly conduct after a two-week

trial. Filed writ of habeas corpus with Judge Drapeau after new trial denied.
- Twenty-one-year old woman from San Diego arrested for reckless driving and having a car without permission. Sentenced to two days in Ventura county jail.

Cases described in Judge Louis Drapeau's *Autobiography of a Country Lawyer* in which he served as a defense attorney:
- Leo Rocco case – murder trial in which defendant eventually exonerated because so-called expert claimed blood removed with kerosene, not possible.
- Brown case – client paralyzed as result of accident but insurance company claimed it was his diabetes
- Man charged with burglary and was convicted although there were two other possible suspects; first assigned case Drapeau defended; defendant chose not to appeal.

More on The Storm

The Storm described in Chapters 28-29 was known as the 1939 California tropical storm, also called the 1939 Long Beach tropical storm, El Cordonazo, The Lash of St. Francis. Winds up to 75 mph; forty-five people killed on land and forty-eight on sea in Southern California and more than $26 million damage (2005 dollars) (or $2 million 1939 dollars) including crops, homes (such as those mentioned that were carried away by heavy waves in Belmont Shore), and other structures. In addition to the winds, heavy rains caused severe flooding: 5.6 inches in Los Angeles; 11 inches in Mount Wilson; almost 5 inches in Pasadena.

It was also known as the storm that ended a long-lasting heat wave.

It surprised people and caught some on the beach. As a result of the lack of being prepared, the Weather Bureau set up a forecast office for southern California.